# Under the Bones

A Lou Thorne Novel

# Kory M. Shrum

TIMBERLANE
PRESS

ISBN-13: 978-1721176335

ISBN-10: 1721176330

This one is for Josephine,
the best of writing companions.
Rest in peace, sweet girl.

under the bones

# 1

The blood loss was slowing him down. Darkness pooled in the corners of his eyes and he was certain at any moment, he would black out. The three bullets in his body shifted, burning in their punched-out sockets.

The toes of his leather boots scraped along the stone floor, but he kept moving. Crooked corridor after corridor, he tried to find his way out of this winding place. This palace of shadows.

It was sacrilege to die in Padre Leo's church. His old mentor had entrusted his empire to Konstantine to protect, to ensure his legacy. Not die at the hands of the first gunslinger to breach its walls.

Konstantine's knees weakened and he pitched forward. His right shoulder clipped an unforgiving wall. Pain shot through his side and stole the breath from his lungs. He crumpled to his hands and knees, the shock of impact ringing through his bones. Blood ran down his arm from the knife wound in his left shoulder. More dripped directly onto the stone from the puncture in his gut. It splattered against the corridor's floor in a soothing *pit-pat-pit-pat* that made him think of summer rain.

*Not here,* he thought. He wasn't sure if he was begging or praying. It didn't matter. *Not here.*

"Konstantine!" a cheerful voice called out. "Are you leaving us so soon?"

Cruel laughter echoed through darkness. It sounded as though it was everywhere at once. Behind him. Ahead. Above and below. The sound of a hungry beast in pursuit, nearly on top of him.

"Behold your fearless leader, Ravengers," the voice went on. That omniscient, all-encompassing orator. "This pathetic boy you worship, he is nothing. Nobody."

Konstantine spat blood onto the floor, and pulled himself up to standing. His desperate fingers scraped the wall. But he was moving again and the white-hot pain sharpened his mind.

Where was his gun? He needed his gun.

"Did you really think your man Enzo could hold us back? Or the others you sent after him? *Nothing* can hold me back, Konstantine. The Ravengers belong to me. Your life belongs to me."

"No," Konstantine replied. Then his chest tightened again and he could say no more.

"No?" A hard kick to his ribs made Konstantine gasp, the leg coming seemingly from nowhere.

Konstantine dropped onto his left side, his head connecting with the sharp corner of a wooden pew. Even as red sparks exploded in front of his eyes and his vision swam, he knew where he was now. He'd made it through the bowels of the church up to the nave. There was only the center aisle and then the door that would let him out of this place.

*Only a few feet more…*

Yet the world was shaking. No, it was the blood loss and the coursing pain. His body would go into complete shock at any moment.

"No?" Nico teased again. His voice hissed directly into Konstantine's ear now. "Surely you knew this was how you would die. Surely you knew I would be the one."

Konstantine supposed he did know he would die like this. On his back, his guts pumped full of gunmetal. His flesh singed with ash.

But he had always hoped it would be *her* on the other end. *Her* hands that drew his soul from his body.

*My life belongs to you—if anybody. Louie Thorne. My goddess of death.*

He began to laugh then, hysteria washing over him. The men beat him harder for it until all that remained was the darkness, the pain, and one clear invitation.

*If you still want to kill me, Louie, mio amore, you'd better hurry*, he thought. *Before it's too late.*

# 2

Lou lifted the orange pill bottle from the windowsill and turned it in light. She set it down, selected another, her thumb picking at the edge of a peeling label. The entire ledge was covered with these white-capped bottles like little plastic soldiers in formation.

Waiting for orders. Waiting to die.

Her hand shot out and slapped them from their sill in one furious swipe. Some bounced off the counter and spun on the kitchen floor. Others clanked into the sink.

When her petty strike wasn't enough to release the rage bubbling inside her, she curled her left hand into a fist and put it through the window.

For a moment, nothing. Then pain bloomed across her knuckles. Her whole face grew hot and she could feel her pulse spread through her chest down into her fingertips. A six-inch shard of glass protruded between her third and middle fingers. She gripped the shard and pulled. Blood spurted into the kitchen sink, splashing onto the demolished windowpane and a couple of pill bottles. Her heart rate returned to a slow, steady calm as she watched her blood coalesce into red pearls.

When she felt in control of herself again, she thought, *better clean this up before Lucy comes home.*

Her second thought, *Lucy is never coming home.*

Aunt Lucy couldn't care less about a broken window or a lost security deposit. The blood in the sink or the glass shards in the garbage disposal. Nor the pills on the floor.

She would leave NOLA Cancer Center in an urn. And that would be the end of it.

Without her aunt, she'd have no reason to pretend anymore. No one to convince that she was still human with a human heart.

Lou turned on the tap and rinsed her bloody hand until the pierced flesh looked as pale as a corpse's. Bloodless.

*Why am I even here?*

She wrapped her hand in a dish towel and stood in the kitchen entryway. She surveyed the apartment. There sat the sofa with its afghan, where Lou had done most of her homework until graduating eight years ago. There sat the wooden rocker holding her aunt's meditation pillow, where Lucy herself liked to sit in the evenings with a glass of iced tea in her hand, no matter the temperature outside.

True, she'd replaced the rug recently. But the pictures were all the same, and the coffee table with its scuffed legs was the same. And the sparse second bedroom at the end of the hallway still looked the way it did the last night Lou slept in it. The last night she called this place home.

The only thing that had changed was the damn pill bottles. So many damned pills bottles.

Lou didn't need to pack any of this up. She could make King do it. She could hire someone. There were whole companies that specialized in bubble wrap and cardboard boxes.

She had no reason to be here. Yet here she was.

*This was your home. The only home you had after I died.*

It was Jack's voice. Her father's steady tone unmistakable.

*And she's the only family you have left.*

Jack's ghost was never far these days. She knew her aunt's would join him soon enough. A menagerie of spirits to keep her company through the long days and nights stretching before her.

Lou pulled open a kitchen drawer and grabbed a second blue hand towel from the top of the pile. She rewrapped her bleeding hand and cast one more look at the busted window and scattered bottles before stepping into the pantry and closing the door.

For a moment, she only stood in the dark. Breathing. Her eyes slid unseeing over boxes of macaroni and cheese and instant rice that would never be eaten.

Lucy hadn't been able to use the pantry for slipping. The cold, thin light wedging itself through the cracks was enough to keep her pinned to this side of the world. Her aunt had needed complete pitch to slip through the thin places.

It wasn't the same for Lou. The light seeping between the trim and door didn't hold her back. Nor the light spilling across the floor. As Lou stared at a bag of potato chips, sealed closed with its red clip, the world thinned anyway.

It shifted beneath her. Softened. Already the slot machine handle had been pulled, and a new time and place was lining up in the dark for her.

She thought of the mess of broken glass, blood, and destroyed hand towels she was leaving behind.

Later. She would deal with that later.

*You can't run from this,* her father's ghost chided.

Not running. Hunting. Two hours and it would be full dark.

This one promise of violence loosened a growing knot in her back. Some women dream of slipping out of their heels and having a nice glass of wine at the end of the day. Lou dreamed of the smell of gunsmoke and the itching feel of blood drying on her hands.

She knew peace only when staring into the wide whites of a man's unseeing eyes. When she knew their heart beat out its last rhythm to the sound of her gunfire.

She slipped.

The pantry and Aunt Lucy's Chicago apartment fell away. An ambulance siren was replaced midwail by whooshing water in pipes. A steam engine honked in the distance. An announcer from Busch stadium called out a play.

Her towel wrapped hand pushed open the closet. The orange rays of a late afternoon stretched across her studio's bare floor. In the enormous picture window, an unobstructed view of the Mississippi river. Lou watched the water shimmer, the great red wheel churning on the back of a steamboat, a tourist vessel that seemed to float up and down the river 365 days a year. Ant-sized people wandered the boardwalk. Dogs chased the pigeons. Children splashed in a fountain. A couple paused to share a kiss.

Where were they going? Home? To their families? To warm dinners waiting or their nightly television shows?

Could she have been one of those people—if her life had started out differently? If her parents hadn't been murdered when she was a twelve. If she hadn't been born with such a terrifying and extraordinary gift…

Did it even matter?

Every body she dropped took her farther away from the life her parents and aunt had imagined for her—even if she never had the chance to imagine such a life for herself.

Lou unwrapped her bloody hand and inspected the puncture between her knuckles. The bleeding had stopped, a clump of dried blood crusted there. She tossed the towel onto her bed.

Sunlight from the adjacent buildings sparked in her eyes. While cabs honked down wide boulevards below, she crossed the room and removed a painting that hung on the brick wall. A replica of Picasso's "Girl with a Mandolin."

She remembered the first time she'd seen the painting in the MOMA, with her aunt standing beside
her.

*I love this painting*, her aunt had said, a floral dress swaying softly along her thighs as she came up onto her toes for a closer look. *Isn't she intriguing?*

Lou hadn't been intrigued. She'd known only clear comprehension, convinced the painting was the closest thing to herself she'd ever see represented. Not because of the mandolin. In no world would Lou pick up an instrument—her only melody was gunfire—but the fragmentation, *that* was something she understood.

*This is what happens to me when I slip through the darkness.* Lou was split into pieces, fed through the cracks and reassembled on the other side. She kept the painting to remind her of who she *really* was—not the woman Jack or Lucy wanted her to be. They saw nothing more than pieces, assembled in the shape of a woman. A familiar image the mind constructed when confronted by the unknown.

Not the truth.

Lou knew the truth.

That if someone opened her up, they would find only darkness inside. That it was the emptiness—all the space between—that made her what she was. Lou lifted the painting from the wall and propped it against her leg. She pressed three bricks and the façade clicked. Her thumb worked under the edge, prying it free to expose a steel safe set into the wall. Lou entered her six-number combination until the safe opened itself. She took the two Browning pistols from the top of the cash and the extra magazines.

She considered tonight's possible targets. Henry deVanti—a pimp in Atlanta who specialized in sex trafficking young girls from South Africa. Ricky Flint— a heroin dealer in New York who beat his wife and kids. Or maybe Freddie Calzone, a coyote in So-Cal who took the money from poor Mexican women dreaming of a better life, before raping them and leaving them to die in the desert, either killed by militia or captured by ICE.

So many men in the world that she wanted to see at the other end of her gun.

Once the safe was resealed and the painting back in place, she stood in her apartment with a pistol in each hand.

Her eyes roved over her counters, the bare island, and the unused stove. The mattress shoved under the large windows, the place in the apartment offering the most sunlight, and a safeguard against slipping in her sleep.

Every item she saw. The plum throw pillows. The slate gray sleeper sofa. The glass coffee table. The art deco lamp—every piece of it was Lucy's doing. It was Lucy who had begged her to get an address. To stop roving from vacant home to vacant home. Lucy who kept trying to tie her to this time, this place. Lucy…her last tether to this world. And when it's cut—

Lou looked at the pistol in each hand. The extra ammo clipped to the belt around her hips.

The compass inside her whirled to life. That internal intuition that dictated where she slipped and when. More instinctive animal than logic.

*Go, go, go*, it howled. *Before it's too late.*

She resisted. Her aunt may want her to visit, to hash out their last argument again, but Lou wanted none of it. Not the arguing. Not the disagreement. Not the relentless bright light of the hospital, the least safe place in the world as far she was concerned.

Lucy wanted peace. No more violence. Lou couldn't give her that.

But it wasn't her aunt on the other end of this tug. No sense of that benevolent, Buddhist essence.

There was darkness on the other end of the wire. The promise of violence.

Lou didn't like to think about her compass as having an intelligence of its own. Doing so forced her to consider an uncomfortable truth: she wasn't as in

control of her ability as she wanted to be.

As a child, this was apparent. Every slip was accidental and seemingly unprovoked.

As an adult, she'd convinced herself she'd grown into it. *She* chose her locations and moved where she wanted. But she knew a lie when she heard it. And she'd been forced to confront this uncomfortable truth in June, when Konstantine, the bastard son of her sworn enemy, came crashing back into her life.

*Konstantine.* She recognized the dark energy now. Konstantine was in trouble.

*Go, go, go*, the pull begged again. *No more time.*

Hadn't she warned him the last time they spoke that he'd better hope he never saw her face again?

He must be very desperate then.
And ready to pay the price.

# 3

ore guns, the better. Lou removed Monet's "Waterlilies" which hung to the right of the Picasso, and opened the much larger safe behind it. She grabbed a shoulder holster from its metal shelf. She put it on and holstered her twin Glocks, one on each side. Then twin Berettas on each hip. And she kept one Browning at the small of her back and more ammo at the belt.

Safe closed, picture in place, she stepped into the closet. It was midnight in Florence, if that was where she would find him. The cover of darkness would be on her side.

Even with the three walls bare, her converted linen closet wasn't large. Her back pressed against the wall as she pictured Konstantine in her mind. Those infuriating brown eyes. The perpetual pout of his lips.

The world shifted. The steamboat's horn was cut short as the world thinned. Lou felt herself falling through the darkness, the wall at her back disappearing.

A stone floor rushed up to meet her, unyielding as it pressed the guns into her palms.

She stared at her pale hands on the stone, reorienting herself. The gash between her knuckles began to bleed again. No matter. She felt nothing. She turned her attention to the laughter. Cruel and deep. The rolling purr of Italian echoed off the walls.

She was in a church. Some ancient construction that smelled of crushed bone dust and the souls it was built on.

Flesh struck flesh. A foot or fist connected with the meat of another man.

Someone groaned.

She inched forward slowly, between the pews toward the center aisle and the sound of violence, until the clear outline of leather clad feet could be seen in the swimming candlelight.

Konstantine was on his back in the center aisle. At least three circles of blood had bloomed through his shirt, small bullet holes torn in the fabric. And when he rolled away from the kicking feet, a dangerously deep cut spread on the side of his neck, revealing far too much corded muscle beneath.

They were going to kill him, whoever these men were.

Probably crime lords like Konstantine himself. Rivals perhaps? Old enemies?

A man pulled a gun from his waist and pointed it into Konstantine's face.

Konstantine said something in Italian that she didn't understand. *Ci vediamo presto, mio amico.*

Lou was in a crouch, a Beretta in her hand, before she'd fully decided she wanted Konstantine to live. She pulled the trigger. One shot and the side of a man's head ruptured. The skull cap lifted like a divot from a golf swing, up into the air while the body itself hit the ground. Brains spilled into the center aisle, cereal sloshing from the rim of a dropped bowl.

The man closest to her turned immediately. Their eyes met over the church pews between them.

He fired, but she'd already rolled beneath the pew and slipped, falling through the stone floor and reemerging behind a pillar on the opposite side of the church, with all four backs to her.

Konstantine's enemy found her again, easily and his second bullet bit into the stone column three inches from her head. Dirt and grit sprayed across her face, coating her lips with salty earth.

A third shot hit her square in the chest, knocking
her back. Even with the vest, it stung. A fourth bullet
grazed her upper arm. It burned.

The bastard was a fast shot.

But she was faster, already falling through the shadows and rising up between two pews behind the man's right shoulder.

Her re-entry wasn't clean and he must've heard it, the pew shifting under her sudden weight. He was halfway to turning toward her when she fired. The bullet slid along the side of his face, grazing the cheek and cutting through the flesh beneath the eye. A curtain of blood now cloaked that half of his face.

He rolled out of sight, seeking shelter in the opposite pews. She emptied the Beretta into the wood, splinters flying into the air like confetti on New Year's Eve.

The Beretta clicked, empty.

She pulled the Browning without stopping to reload. Two of the hiding men popped up from between the pews.

A round was already chambered and she dropped the second man with a bullet between the eyes. He hadn't even hit the floor when she put a bullet in the third's throat. Blood spurted between his fingers as he tried to compress the wound.

It didn't save him. He sank to his knees and bled
out in seconds. His own puddle meeting Konstantine's halfway.

Only two men were left of the original five. Konstantine's *mio amico* and the man closely watching his back.

Three more rapid fire shots hit her chest with three hard punches. She fell, but her back never hit the ground. The shadows swallowed her up, spitting her out on the right side of the large wooden doors. There was Konstantine, still lying in a heap in the center aisle, breath labored. If she didn't move this along, he wouldn't make it.

At least the men had forgotten about Konstantine. She proved to be very distracting.

*Mio amico* scanned each dark corner, eyes wide. One hand pressed a torn purple cloth to his face, soaking up the blood she'd drawn.

A purple cloth. The mark of a Ravenger.

Was he in Konstantine's own gang? Or had he simply taken the cloth from someone?

Questions she didn't have time to think about. *Mio amico* was on to her. He wasn't inching toward the row where she'd fallen. His eyes were searching the room, ready for her to appear anywhere.

His comrade bent down to examine the space between the pews. When he rose, she blew out his brains with a double tap from the Browning.

*Mio amico* was already turning toward her when she stepped from the darkness.

Their eyes locked as both guns raised. She emptied the clip into his chest. He got off two more rounds into her vest. He fell backwards over the pew behind him, Italian leather boots pointing skyward before his head cracked against the stone floor on the other side.

She waited for him to rise. To pop up and seek revenge like the villain in a horror story. But the church was quiet. The scent of blood and sweat bloomed bright in the cool air.

She holstered the guns and knelt beside Konstantine.

His eyes fluttered, seeming to see her for the first time. He murmured, "*La mia dea. La mia regina oscura.*"

"You're welcome." She grabbed the bloody lapel of his shredded clothes and pulled him through the night.

# 4

Robert maneuvered his enormous body down the crowded corridor of NOLA's Cancer Center, a white paper bag of beignets clutched in his right hand. He flashed polite smiles at every nurse he passed, most recognizing him and returning the smile. They were a perpetual carousel of movement, in and out of rooms like drones in the hive.

Georgette, a blonde beauty queen of a nurse, stepped out of Room 716, carefully closing the door behind her. She brightened when she saw him. "Good morning, Mr. King."

"How's she doing?" Robert asked, reaching up to smooth his hair out of his face. It didn't matter that he saw Lucy every day, that there were a million things on her ailing mind besides his misplaced hair. He stood as nervous outside her hospital room as he had on their first date. Back when he was still a seasoned DEA agent and she the head-turning sister of his brightest mentee.

Something flashed in Georgette's eyes before she could mask it. She tried to hide it by picking at a clump of mascara tangled in her lashes. The black smearing across her thumb.

But the damage was done.

It wasn't Georgette's fault. King had decades of interrogation experience. It was all about the microexpressions, those hints of real emotion laid bare before a formal façade could conceal them. He didn't need her to tell him this was a bad day and it would be best to lower his expectations before stepping into the room. The flash of sadness that pinched her face told him so.

But Georgette's painted red lips projected only kindness. "She'll be happy to see you."

Robert thanked her and stepped inside the room.

The woman confined to the bed was rail thin. It was as if the breast cancer that had started in her chest before moving into her bones was liquefying her from the inside out. Only a husk remained, like the cicada husks he'd found as a child. The shape of the insect remained intact, but paper thin, and vulnerable to disintegration under the slightest touch.

"Hey baby," he said, quietly closing the door behind him.

For a terrible moment, only silence filled the room.

She was dead.

She'd left this world while he'd stood in the hall with the nurse. She'd slipped right out from under him, the way a few dealers had slipped right out the back door of their haunts as he'd kicked down the front.

Then Lucy turned toward him, repositioning her head on the white pillow.

"Why hello, Robert." Her voice was as dry as sandpaper.

The fist crushing his heart relented. He drew a breath.

He came to her bedside and eased himself into the plastic chair. Not an easy task given his size. He'd lost weight in the last three months since their reunion, but his nights in the gym had bulked him up.

Exercise. Hospital visits. Paperwork. And end-less cups of black coffee filled his days now.

It wasn't the retirement he'd envisioned. He wasn't complaining. Only marveling at how even the most well planned, diligently laid tracks were rendered useless in the course of a life. Life, like water, cut its own path.

He sat the oil-soaked paper bag on the attached hospital tray. Then tore the white paper to reveal the beignets.

"I had Millie make these fresh for you," he said, sucking the powdered sugar from his thumb.

He reached into his duster and pulled out the card. Everyone at the café had signed it. Red, blue and black inks competed for each available inch of the cardstock. A watercolor tree painted on the outside, and a corny message—*Get well soon. We're all "rooting" for you*—was scrawled in calligraphy within.

He propped the cardstock tent on the table beside the beignets. "They miss you."

"I miss them too," Lucy said, her voice weak and dry. She didn't try to pick up the card. The first bad sign. She only turned her head slightly to regard it.

"It's a good thing that this room isn't darker. Or else I might fall right into the donut fryer." She tried to laugh and fell into coughing instead.

Robert had wondered. When the illness got bad enough that Lucy couldn't stay away from machines and medical supervision, he had worried how this

could work. Lucy had tried to explain that her gift—
what Lou called *slipping*—wasn't the same. She had
never slipped by water for example. And unlike Lou
who seemed to step through the thinnest shadows,
even this dimly lit room was enough to hold Lucy
and her failing body in place—no matter how
desperate her desire to leave it may be.

Face red and chest rattling, Lucy tried to prop
herself up. The plastic tubing running to her arms
and nostrils trembled as her body shook with the
effort. A vein stood out on the woman's face.

"Easy there," he said. He put a hand under each
arm—god, when had she become so light—and
lifted, easing her onto the pillows.

Then she reached for the large plastic cup and
red bendy straw. He beat her to it, angling it
between her cracked lips. She'd aged twenty years
overnight. He was sure part of it was the hair loss,
which made her face look older. And the black
circles beneath her eyes amplified their sunken look.

Lucy stopped drinking, following his gaze to
the inside of her arms, to the bruises he couldn't
help but scowl at.

"It's fine," she said.

"It doesn't look fine. What did they do? Let the
new kids practice on you?"

He scowled at the new IV.

She rolled her eyes up to meet his. "The nurses say I'm dehydrated. When you're dehydrated, the veins constrict."

Her iron was already low. Surely, that didn't help.

"It's all right," she assured him again in that quiet voice. The ice shifted in the cup.

He settled back into his seat.

"How's Lou?" she asked, those blue eyes searching his.

King didn't know. He hadn't had a proper conversation with Louie Thorne for months. He could see her plainly in his mind. He'd climbed the stairs to his loft and had found her on his red sofa. He remembered how he had sat beside her with an empty cushion between them, saying nothing for a long time. The way her scarred shoulder had looked in the moonlight, not unlike a burn scar except for the ring of deep punctures forming, what could be mistaken for a shark bite. But it hadn't been a shark that had gotten ahold of her. King knew that much, though he hadn't dared to ask more.

King tried to keep his voice level despite the anger rising. "She still hasn't come to see you?"

"Don't be mad at her," Lucy chided, flashing those big blue eyes. "She's probably the only reason I'm still alive."

He frowned. "You mean you aren't living for the beignets?"

He got the grin he was fishing for. True enough it had been Lou who'd saved her, not him. When Lucy collapsed four weeks ago, Lou had been there in a heartbeat. Emerging from the darkness as if from thin air. She'd scooped the woman up and taken her straight to the hospital without hesitation, even though King knew Lou would rather bleed to death—had almost bled to death—than step foot inside a hospital. It was something about all the harsh, unforgiving light. A perpetual daytime.

Yet when the moment of reckoning came, she'd done it without the slightest pause. It seemed that before Lucy's body had fully rest on the floor, Louie had been there, scooping her up into her arms and disappearing through the dark with her.

Lucy seemed eternally grateful for this salvation. King's gratitude had limits.

The straw slurped at the bottom of the cup. Lucy shook it gently to shift the ice around. "She can't fight her way out of this."

King twisted off the white cap from the plastic water bottle and refilled her cup.

Lucy went on. "There is no killer to hunt. No one to point her gun at. She knows death, but not like this. This is different. Do you understand?"

King wasn't sure he did, but he didn't interrupt. Strength was coming back to Lucy's voice and he liked to hear it. He wanted her to keep talking. And he wanted her to drink more water.

"When I die, Jack, she won't have anyone to blame. Then what will she do?"

*Jack.*

All the medication they had her on at times made her fuzzy around the edges. As long as she kept breathing, he didn't care what they pumped her with—or what she called him.

It was more than that. The drugs kept her from the worst of the pain, which he knew despite all her calm reassurances, was bad.

"I'll look after her," he said, angling the straw toward her cracked lips again. He would bring Chapstick next time. And maybe some sunflowers to brighten the room. "I promise I'll keep her out of trouble."

They were supposed to have six months at least. That's what the doctors said in the beginning. But it was all moving so quickly now.

Lucy's eyes fluttered and King took the cup from her hand before she could drop it. He pulled a small pad of paper from his front pocket and a ballpoint pen. In black ink he wrote:

*Chapstick*

*Gatorade*

*Maybe Ensure*

*Flowers*

He listened to her steady breath, certain she'd dropped off to sleep.

But then she spoke. "You'll have your work cut out for you, Jack. She's as smart as you are, and twice as stubborn."

Her mouth dropped open a few minutes later, and the real snoring began.

King didn't mind.

He had his paperback and enough cash in his pocket to wander down to the cafeteria if he got hungry. Change for vending machine coffee or a Coke if he got thirsty.

There was nowhere else in the world he'd rather be.

It was enough to be with her.

He only regretted not searching for her sooner. He should have tracked her down long before she'd turned up in his apartment three months ago, begging for the favor that had sent his life careening off the tracks.

He should have forgiven her sooner, too.

Forgiven her for disappearing. Forgiven her for dropping him like a summer fling so she could assume the mantle of guardian to a pre-teen Lou.

He'd been angry, sure. But it'd taken him a long time to realize he was only angry at himself. Angry mostly for not going after her.

How many years they would've had together if he'd only gone after her.

More time with Lucy. With Lou. He could've steered the girl toward a better life. Gotten her into legal work or the DEA. Done right by her like Jack would have wanted.

*Coulda, woulda, shoulda.* Useless.

All that wasted time—and he would never get it back.

They'd had only two good months together before her illness had taken this turn. Two months of picnics in Jackson Square. Long nights in his bed with the French doors open and jazz music filtering in from the streets below. The sweat drying on their bare skin. Two months of pralines and red bean jambalaya and coffee on the balcony in the early morning light, her cool hand in his.

Then the collapse. Lou's rescue. A two-day coma to stabilize her.

He leaned across the hospital bed and brushed the damp bangs off her forehead. He listened to the machines click on and off, measuring her heartrate, her breathing and whatever else it deemed necessary.

He plucked a beignet off the white paper and ate it. He sucked the sugar from his fingers but it was already souring in his mouth.

In the beginning, when the weight had begun to drop off and her bones became as light as a bird's, he'd managed to get her to eat as many as six beignets in a single go. Then only four. Three. A bite. And this week—none at all.

They were running out of time.

Lucy. King. And Lou.

They were *all* running out of time.

# 5

Lou dropped Konstantine on the floor of her apartment. She left him there, crossing to her back bathroom where she opened the cabinet and removed her kit. A tin box the size of a laundry basket. It had plastic shelves within, army green. The top row held tweezers and twine, needles and iodine in its square compartments. The second row, rubbing alcohol and gauze of every conceivable shape and size. Wraps and cotton. Surgical scissors and clamps. Fire for cauterizing. A small bottle of whiskey. A mouthguard and bit of leather for biting down. A belt for slowing circulation.

She carried the box into the living room with a handful of old, faded and stained towels, their edges frayed. She rolled the man onto his side and put two towels beneath him to protect her floors. Then she pulled him up long enough to get the shirt over his head. With his cheek to hers, she could smell him.

Blood and gunsmoke and beneath that…something that belonged only to Konstantine.

She let go and his head hit the hardwood floor too hard. He didn't complain.

She inspected the wounds. The deep cut in the neck. Four bullet holes—not three—in the torso. Two knife wounds in the back. He'd lost a lot of blood, but she could help with that. She, like Aunt Lucy, was O negative. If it came to it, she had the tubing for a transfusion in the bottom of the kit.

But she would begin with sanitizing the cuts, then digging the bullets out. She dragged the lamp over and angled it, giving her a bright, unobstructed view of the work ahead of her. Then she filled a plastic white bucket with warm water.

She settled down beside him to begin, her knees pressed against his ribs.

With alcohol and iodine, she disinfected the wounds. She pried open the scorched flesh, checking for debris. She inserted the locking tweezers into the first bullet hole, feeling it scrape against metal. A sensation she felt in her teeth. She opened the tweezers wider, spreading the wound until the metal slid around either side and clamped down.

With a sucking sound, she plucked the bullet free and dropped it into the pan beside her utensils.

Konstantine's eyes flew open, followed by a stream of Italian curses. "Abbi pietà di me!"

His eyes fluttered and she hoped he would drop back into sleep. But as she grabbed the second bullet. He was awake and cursing again. She moved fast, dropping the second bullet into the pan beside the first.

His hand seized her wrist when she inserted the tweezers into the third hole. He rolled those brown eyes up to meet hers. He was fully awake now, panting. He clutched her wrist hard enough to bruise it, but her face remained placid.

She slowly arched a brow. "Do you want me to leave it in?"

His nostrils flared, eyes dilated. A sheen of sweat stood out on his brow. "Be quick."

She plucked the third bullet out as he opened and closed his other fist. The bloodied knuckles went white, filled with color, only to go white again with each clenching motion.

She moved onto the fourth hole without pause. This bullet must have been blocking an artery rather than sitting squarely in muscle. Once plucked, blood ran like rivulets across his abdomen, following the lines of his muscles. He groaned, releasing her wrist as the tweezers hit the pan.

Too much blood. She grabbed the metal rod no wider than the face of a dime. She plugged it into the wall socket beside her bed and the heating element immediately began to glow.

"What are you—?" Konstantine began.

"You'll bleed to death if I don't."

"If you don't *what*?"

She stuck the white-hot rod into the oozing bullet hole and straight out again. The blood smoked and hissed.

Konstantine howled and kicked the floor with his boots. Lucky for him she'd already moved the rod away or he'd have cauterized more than the bullet wound.

She wet a towel in the bucket of warm water and raked it over his skin, trying to see what was left to be done. She let her left hand rest on his stomach, the towel pressed beneath it as she inspected each wound in turn. That gash where his neck and shoulder met would certainly need stitches.

He came up onto his elbows, trying to inspect it for himself. "I'm fine."

"Lie down."

"No more. I'm *fine*."

"Lie down or I'll put you down."

He didn't. He placed a hand over hers. The sweat on his face shone.

Lou met his gaze, weighing it with her own.

"Please," he said, squeezing her hand.

She threw a right hook across the man's jaw. He dropped, the elbows folding out from underneath him.

She shook out her fist before breaking open one of the nylon suture packets.

"I don't have a way to anesthetize you and I don't want to listen to you cry anymore."

*You don't have to explain. He can't even hear you.*

She took a breath and pushed the needle through his flesh, deep enough to close the wound in his neck without popping through the skin. When metal peeked through the other side, she tugged the black string through in small jerky movements until there was enough blood to make the string glide slick.

She stitched the bullet holes and the ugly cut in the side of his neck. Then she added the rough gauze pinning it into place with masking tape. The water in the bucket was pink by the time she finished. Stained, bloody rags bobbed on its surface.

Confident she'd repaired the worst of it, she pressed her fingers to his pulse and found it rapid. His breath wasn't shallow. No blue tint to the lips or fingernails. His skin was warm to the touch. He might need that transfusion yet.

The urge to bend forward and lick the blood and salt from his skin swirled in her mind. She ran a finger across his jaw where she'd struck him. The line of it already darkening with the promise of a bruise.

*You need fucking therapy,* her exasperated aunt had cried once. Lou snorted at the memory.

She sat back on her heels and stared at the unconscious man. She rolled him onto his side to check his back.

If she had wanted to kill him, why stitch him up? Why stare at his body, searching for signs of hypovolemic shock? Why give him blood from her own veins if only to kill him later?

*You know why,* her father said.

If she was being honest with herself, she did know.

It was what had happened one night a month after her fourteenth birthday. She'd slipped in her sleep, unbidden, to the bedroom of an Italian boy.

*Why him?*

Of all the boys and all the bedrooms in the whole wide world, why had she appeared in his?

She had theories.

Their shared hatred for Martinelli had been enough. The man responsible for killing Lou's father was the same man who ruined and betrayed Konstantine's mother.

But was that really all of it?

Two dark-hearted children drawn to each other because they hated the same man? But Lou hadn't known Martinelli was behind the kill yet. So this theory was shit.

As well as a second theory that he could slip too. That perhaps they were drawn together out of that commonality. But if he could slip, he would have saved his own life tonight. Used it to cement his power with the Ravengers. So that wasn't it either.

And why should she care about the *why* anyhow? Konstantine was a street rat, like any other piece of gang trash that she wiped from the world.

Worse, he was a *leader* of the trash heap. He was the puppeteer and she wanted to cut his strings.

And she could. Right now. While he was laying on her apartment floor with the Martinelli crest on his ring finger. A gold ring bearing an ornate capital M and two dragons chasing one another head-to-tail around the letter.

*He's an enemy. I should be putting a bullet in his head, not draining my veins for him.*

She pulled her reloaded Beretta and pressed it against the temple of the sleeping man. The cool trigger thrummed beneath her finger. The slightest pressure would be all it took to spray his brains across the floor.

He didn't stir. He didn't open his eyes, his soft breath fogging the wooden floor beneath his mouth.

*I'm not your enemy,* he'd said to her once.

Was that true? Or the sort of lie that a man like Konstantine relied on?

It felt as though they'd reached some agreement in their last encounter. He'd delivered the information needed to clear her father's name, and restore him to hero status. And she'd helped him find his mother's unmarked grave. Helped him unbury her and carry her back home.

But he was still the son of the man who had her father killed. He was still one of the crime lords she was trying to wipe from the face of the earth.

It didn't matter how he'd looked the night they dug up his mother. The glow of his relaxed and pensive face as they'd stepped from his dark apartment into the Italian countryside to find the night alive around them with insect song, summer in full swing, and the heat so thick it was like trying to breathe with a blanket over her face.

Yet she remembered how the sweat on his neck and back had shown in the moonlight, every muscle shifting as they dug their spades again and again into the dirt. The look in his eyes when the spade hit bone—when he knelt and uncovered what remained of her with gentle hands.

Lou lowered the gun from his head.

Nothing needed to be decided now. Others waited. Henry deVanti. Ricky Flint. Freddie Calzone.

She would start there. And if those three men weren't enough to slake her bloodthirst tonight, Konstantine would still be here.

He wasn't going anywhere. There was nowhere in this world he could go that she couldn't find him.

Her own wounds cleaned, and guns and ammo replenished, Lou stepped into the emptied linen closet once more. She planned to start on the East Coast, where the sun was below the horizon, and work her way West. Henry deVanti in Atlanta or Ricky Flint in New York—either would do. And hopefully by the time she was done with them, sunset would have made its way to San Diego.

*Surprise me*, she told that inner compass. Henry or Ricky, it made no difference to her.

The thin veil between this side of the world and the other began to give, sliding out from under her. Her hand shot out and touched the grainy wood of the closet's opposite wall. She held this space.

The sounds materialized first. A taxi laying on its horn. Someone shouting in a harsh New York accent. Voices speaking Chinese excitedly. Tourists arguing over prices while a tired child cried.

She stepped out of the closet into the streets of New York's Chinatown. The scent of fried noodles and fish hit her nose. The red gates at the end of the avenue were spotlighted, twin dragons ready for a fight. The street itself illuminated with paper lanterns suspended on string.

So where was Ricky?

She scanned the crowd, checking each face in turn. She spotted him on a metal stool outside Mr. Wang's Noodle Shop, a walkup window where any passerby could stop for a quick bite. Ricky with his black baseball cap turned backwards slurped fat noodles into his mouth. His motorcycle boots with bright brass buckles kicked out arrogantly into the walkway, so that pedestrians had to maneuver around his extended legs in order to continue down the street. A mother scowled, angling her large stroller around Ricky's legs first, and then a grate spewing foul air.

A subway train screeched somewhere out of sight.

Lou leaned against the wall, her guns hidden beneath her leather jacket. She pretended to look at her phone, no doubt resembling any number of women her age all up and down New York's streets. Few would've noticed her occasional glance over the top of her screen at the man slapping cash onto Mr. Wang's counter before entering the wave of nighttime bodies.

He worked a toothpick in his mouth as he walked past Lou up the sidewalk.

She fell into step behind him, noting how he moved, which side he favored. If his gait was short or long. His pants loose or tight. Buckles or straps that could be pulled or wrapped around a throat. Bulges where a gun might sit, or the hint of a sheathed knife.

She enjoyed this part of it almost as much as the kill itself. Measuring her prey. Sizing them up. She always knew a great deal about her targets *long* before she put her hands on them.

When he started down the steps of the subway tunnel, she followed. She kept the same pace and distance. When he slapped his commuter card to the turnstile's sensor, she paused to glance at a magazine stand, pretending to give a damn about a European prince and his impending marriage, a celebrity's new baby. Someone's bout in rehab.

When he moved toward the northbound platform, she put the magazine down and stepped between two ticket-dispensing machines, and out onto the platform. She hovered there, at the very edge where the darkness met the stairwell.

This put her in front of Ricky.

No matter. She calmly walked forward, spacing herself evenly away from everyone else as the others had done. The train came. Everyone got on. Ricky worked his way to another car while she stood near the door between a pregnant woman reading a romance novel and a black man with a purple mohawk and gauged earrings wide enough to hook a finger through.

She hovered, not daring to raise her hand to the handles overhead, lest someone see how much heat she was packing under her leather.

When Ricky exited four stops later, she let him go. Making her way to the back of the car as a new throng of passengers wedged themselves aboard. A gaggle of drunk girls cackled loudly, everyone a similar shade of blonde, eyes painted black. They were her age and yet she couldn't have felt more different from these candy-coated creatures than if she'd been born with a second head.

Lou slipped through the shadows connecting the two cars and found herself in Central Park.

A small stream babbled off to her right. A dog and its master trotted by, white reflectors bouncing in the darkness.

She spotted Ricky a few feet away, smoking a cigarette and talking to a Latina woman with hair as red as the dress stretched tight over her comically large breasts. When she turned away from him, he grabbed her wrist and brought his open palm across her face.

Lou's hand was on her gun before she thought about it. She was going to put a hole through that hand. She caught herself, reigning in her thirst.

She would have him, but there was a process. A foolproof procedure and she wouldn't throw that away just because he'd pissed her off.

*Be careful*, Jack said. And he'd said as much when he was alive. *When you're angry, that's when you have to be careful.*

They'd been doing dishes together. He was wet up to his elbows and she was drying plates. She'd been complaining about her mother, no doubt. And Jack told her the story of Bernie Jensen, a young agent who got himself shot twice in the face because
he couldn't control his temper.

*Anger is powerful*, he'd told her. *That's why you have to be very careful when it's on you.*

When it's *on* you.

He'd made it sound like a beast that could seize you in the dark if you were caught unaware. She'd had quite the education in anger before his death, and much more after. And she had to agree with him. It *was* a beast in the dark and sometimes you didn't know it was on you until the teeth were quite deep.

Her eyes scanned the park. Most had vacated this area in the coming nightfall. Just as well.

When Ricky's hand connected with the side of the woman's face a second time, Lou slipped up right beside him.

She grabbed the back of his neck and pulled, yanking him clean off his boots, away from New York and what remained of his life.

Central Park was replaced with an isolated lake thick with midnight fog.

Once the fresh air hit her, she let him tumble to the sandy bank. One of his hands, the one that had slapped the woman, hit the water's edge. The place didn't smell like pine as her Alaskan retreat did, but of dense forest all the same. Trees she'd never smelled in the U.S. mingled with the evergreens. Linden perhaps. Maybe scotch broom.

Lucy would know.

Her chest clenched.

The frogs fell silent, the croaking chorus stalling at Ricky's splashing. But the rest of the night remained alive with sound. Something screeched in the darkness overhead. Nighthawks or an owl searching for a meal. Crickets continued to sing. She breathed deep. The only shame was the cloudy sky blocking out the stars.

This wasn't her favorite lake. But this little plot of remote Nova Scotia wilderness was priceless in its own way. It was harder to find water like this far from human eyes and the industrialized world. The perfect entry point to her alien dumping ground.

Ricky's boots slid in the dirt as he regained his balance. He reached behind his back for the .357 he kept there. Then his face pinched with predictable confusion. They always reached for their guns like this, only to find she'd already relieved them of it.

Lou pointed the pistol at his face.

This was her process. A clear-cut, no error approach to killing. Take them to the water's edge. Somewhere dark. Somewhere remote. Slip through the waters to La Loon, that otherworldly destination unknowable to any but herself and her victims. Kill them and leave their bodies for the beast who prowled its shores.

No bullets. No casings. No gunpowder or evidence. No bodies. No blood. No witnesses, except maybe those from the point of abduction—like the prostitute turned drug mule who no doubt stood in Central Park right now, trying to wrap her head around Ricky's disappearance.

"Get in the water," she said.

He didn't. Instead, he lunged toward her, hands out to grab the gun.

No sense of self-preservation then. She shot his hand. The one he'd used to slap the woman in Central Park. It stopped him in his tracks. He turned, howling, crushing his wounded hand protectively against his body. This did nothing to staunch the blood. It ran down his front, soaking his shirt.

"Get in the water."

"Fuck you!" His whole arm shook as he cradled his bleeding hand against his chest.

She shot him in the shoulder, four inches above his heart. He cried out, collapsing to one knee.

"If I have to ask you again, Ricky. I'm going to shoot you in the face."

And she would. She didn't like talking and if she had to, she wouldn't waste the energy on a man like this.

The furious man stumbled to his feet. He considered diving for the gun again. She saw the desire written all over his face. One smile from her lips, a silent *I dare you* convinced him otherwise.

Instead he dove for the water. His leather jacket slapped at the surface. The image of it reminded her of Angelo Martinelli, the night she killed him. He'd swam away from her too, his jacket also floating on the water's surface.

She stooped to pick up the two bullet casings before tucking his gun into her waistband and diving into the water after him.

When he saw her coming, he turned to face her, probably believing he had the upper hand now. This only excited her. Her pulse jumped in her throat. She caught up to him in a few, long strokes, her hands seizing wet fabric of his jeans beneath the water.

He grabbed a handful of her hair. Pain bloomed through her skull. No matter. She had her arms and legs around him. A python's grip as she pulled him down.

And down.

Until the nighttime waters turned red, became a different lake in a different place. Then she pushed off his body and launched herself up.

She broke the surface first. The red patina stretched out endlessly before her. The white mountains in the distance. The strange yellow sky overhead holding not one, but two swollen moons. A black forest with short trees and heart-shaped leaves. Incongruous colors that were so different than those of her home world.

La Loon.

No matter what waterway she entered in her world—be it a river, an ocean, a bathtub—La Loon with its eternal dusk was the only destination.

Ricky surfaced behind her, screaming. He kicked and flailed in the water, no doubt drawing every predator within a mile to its shore.

She swam toward the beach in slow, controlled movements. Not panicked. Not like prey. Each easy stroke was an act of self-control. And should she find herself jerked under by some creature, that was what her knife was for.

But she wasn't attacked. The silty bottom rose beneath her like a partially submerged boat ramp. Each step elevated her out of the water until she reached the shore. She stood there dripping wet, watching Ricky flail in the water.

"What the fuck? What the fuck?" He paddled tight circles. He seemed unwilling to swim toward the shore. Instead he gaped at the moons, at the water, at the mountains.

Had she looked so bewildered the first time she'd fallen through and broke the surface of Blood Lake? No doubt. But she'd been a child.

"Keep screaming and you'll be eaten," she called to him, enjoying his wide panicked eyes. She could put a bullet in him here, spray his brains across the water's surface. Watch the little creatures bob up to gobble the bits the way fish often did in their tanks. And even if she did nothing, he would exhaust himself soon enough. He couldn't tread water for long in that leather coat and boots.

Something flashed in her periphery and she pulled her bowie knife without pause.

A monstrous black face broke through the trees and screeched. A mouth opened wide showing no less than four or five rows of long teeth the color of puss. A large white tongue lolled in its mouth, and the interior cheeks puffed, which always made Lou think of the cottonmouth snakes she'd seen as a child, hiking the woods with her father.

The first time she'd seen this creature it had tried to eat her. Bit clean through her shoulder and tore the muscles there. She'd survived only because she'd fallen backward into the water, the creature still
astride her.

Since then, they'd reached an understanding. This beast might have the same black-scaled, white-mouthed coloring of a cottonmouth, but she was no snake.

She had six legs with talons, curved nails that dug into the earth as she walked. Between the toes was webbing, no doubt useful in the lake spreading out before her.

"You could eat him," Lou told the creature. "But I don't think he's going to come out."

She lowered the knife.

"Come up here, Ricky. Someone wants to meet you. Don't be an asshole."

Ricky, who'd been gaping at the mountains, pivoted toward shore and saw the beast. Nothing short of abject terror seized him. Screaming as if he were being boiled alive, he paddled with all his might away from the shore, toward those white mountains in the distance.

As if he'd ever reach it.

With an excited purr, the scaly creature slid off the bank into the water after him. Her long, graceful body skimmed the surface, the contracting muscles propelling her forward in a smooth glide.

*I guess she does look like a snake,* Lou thought, grinning.

"Come back, Ricky," she called out. "You'll only excite her."

# 6

Nico stood bare-chested in front of the bathroom mirror. Splattered blood had dried into his chest hair, matting the coarse strands together. He met his eyes, a dark amber and took a deep breath. For good measure, he wrapped his hand around the sink basin. With his other, he slipped a thin blade into the puckered wound below his left collarbone.

Metal scraped metal.

Gritting his teeth, he dug deep then flicked upward, dislodging the bullet from its hole. It hit the basin with a fresh splatter of bright blood. It rolled toward the drain, resting on top of the silver grate.

Her eyes burned in his mind. That slender neck he wanted to wrap his hand around.

So she was real.

He'd heard the stories.

Before he'd moved against Konstantine, he'd learned all he could about his "brother." He'd heard of the woman. But he hadn't believed she was real. That Konstantine was stupid enough to devote himself to a woman—of course. He was soft the way his father had been soft.

But it had been the way the Ravengers spoke of her, as if she wasn't really a woman at all.

*She's a ghost. A strega. A demon.*

*Konstantine sold his soul to her and she made him invincible.*

Cacca di cavallo. Nico didn't believe a word of it. Men could be superstitious fools.

They made her immortal. Untouchable. A creature who couldn't be reasoned with or bought. Coerced or demurred.

*She comes for your soul and she eats it.*

*That* he believed.

He'd seen her with his own eyes. Her stare had been cold and unforgiving. There was no woman on the planet who had that look about her. Like she would have blown out his brains and licked the skull cap clean.

But he saw the truth tonight—along with the horror.

Not only was she a monster, but the beautiful beast did, for whatever reason, serve Konstantine.

He had a monster—but she wasn't immortal.

She hadn't used teeth and claws to tear his men apart. She'd used guns. And he'd seen the way she fell back when he put a bullet in her chest. The vest saved her life. And how lucky he'd been wearing one himself.

No, she wasn't immortal. She was only a very dangerous woman with a very powerful gift.

A knock came at the door.

"Sì?" Nico said.

"The men are restless, sir."

They would be. Their master has disappeared and while he was certain he held most of the dissenters at bay with his own small army, he had to bring order. He needed to calm them, push them into line.

"Gather them in the nave. I'll be out in a moment."

The footsteps trailed away.

He thought of the bright bathroom with its blessed light, and the twisting, dim corridors that stood between him and the nave.

He met the wide dark eyes of the man in the mirror. He laughed. One firefight, and he'd become terrified of shadows.

That wouldn't do.

This empire was his birthright. And his chance to seize it was at hand. He wouldn't let a *thousand* bloodthirsty she-demons keep him from it.

He ran a hand over his shaved head, fingering the new cut she'd given him.

He straightened, running a wet cloth over his bloodied chest. He stuffed the bullet wound with a wad of cotton, no time for suturing now, and pulled on his bloodied shirt.

Let them see the damage.

The blood crusted under his fingernails and the cut across his face, where her bullet had kissed the bone. The oozing sockets.

Let them see that he was ready to pay any price.

Reloading his guns, he slipped them into their holsters. Every movement made his lungs constrict with pain. No matter. He could lick his wounds when he was alone. Now was not the time for it.

He stepped out of the bathroom into the darkness. His heart sped up, his eyes darting to the corners, ready for any movement beside his father's old bookshelves, the fireplace where the hearth burned. Flame flickered across the desk and chairs, the stone floors. The shadows danced, seemingly alive.

He didn't linger.

He stepped through the great wooden doors and found his personal guard waiting at attention.

They fell into step behind him as he took the

lead, up the stairwell to the church above.

Voices murmured through the open space.

The pews had been righted, but wooden splinters sat clinging to the red carpet of the center aisle.

When they saw him, all their eyes fixed on him. The conversation died.

"Where is Konstantine?" someone called.

Nico's right guard put a bullet between that man's eyes. Brains splattered onto the men closest to him as the body hit the floor like a sack of flour. A mist of blood hung in air where his head had been.

Nico waited for the commotion to settle, for the men to stop cowering in the pews like scared children. Then he spoke.

"You've heard the stories about his *strega*," Nico said. "She came to claim him. Spirited him away earlier tonight. I don't think he will be back."

He saw the hate in their eyes. There was a great deal of loyalty to that traitorous bastard. This didn't matter. He would win them over in time. For now, he would settle for obedience. And if they wouldn't obey, well, he had a plan for that too.

Uneasiness shifted through the masses. The soft murmuring began again.

"And why would you want him?" Nico asked.

"She preys on you. She's plucked so many of our

own men from the streets and he has done nothing to protect you. He *lets* her take your lives, sacrifices you like little children to a hungry demon."

Every eye was fixed upon him.

"Is that what you want? To fear the darkness? To live each day, dreading the coming night?"

Murmurs of dissent rose.

"I can offer you more. And why shouldn't I be the one?" he said. "*My* father, our beloved Padre wanted to name me his successor, but he feared Konstantine and the strega."

Some outrage burst from the pews. The guard on his left raised their guns but Nico waved them down.

"You don't believe me? You think Padre preferred that traitor to his own flesh and blood? Does that sound like the Padre you knew?"

Confusion rippled through the crowd.

"Konstantine is not who you think he is. He uses you only as a means to an end and will betray you, if you give him the chance. He is a Martinelli. Old World power. And we do not need him."

Someone cheered. A few clapped.

Most sat silent.

Maybe he hadn't sold the idea, but he had sowed the seeds of doubt. That was well enough. The rest would come in time. When he dumped the bodies of Konstantine and his strega at their feet, they would have no choice but to bow to their new king.

# 7

Lou stared down at the man in her bed. A man. In her bed. The idea itself made her itch for her gun. She supposed it was only fair. Hadn't she slipped into his bed all those nights ago?

She had tried leaving Konstantine on the floor but the pressure from the hardwood made his wounds seep. She considered dumping him on the couch, but if he bled on it, she would be forced to scrub at the purple suede, more effort than she was willing to invest.

The bed at least was soft enough to cradle his wounds without pulling them open, and also easier to clean. Sheets could be washed—or burned—much easier than couch cushions.

And she'd be lying to herself if she said she wasn't curious.

Is this what it had been like for him?

When he woke one night twelve years ago to find a girl in his bed?

She tried to imagine herself as that girl. Her hair had been long, nearly to her waist. His room had been full of moonlight, as her apartment was now.

How long had he stood there, thighs pressed to the side of the mattress staring down at her? That's what she remembered seeing when she woke up.

A looming boy, his hand reaching toward her cheek. When his fingers had brushed her, she'd shot up, realizing she wasn't dreaming.

Despite the extra lights, all their precautions, she'd slipped in her sleep anyway.

She remembered how he'd stepped back when she'd gasped. Held up his hands in apologetic reassurance. The soft Italian rolling like a song between his lips. Such an innocent boyish face. And he was a boy then. None of the sharp angles and battered flesh he was now. He'd grown just as hard over the years as she had.

And what had she thought the first time she'd seen Konstantine the man?

She thought her compass was only bringing her to another target. Another hit. She expected another quick, efficient kill.

But when the bathroom door had finally opened, there he was. His hair in his eyes. Green eyes widened at the sight of her pointed gun. She'd recognized those eyes immediately. Even before she registered the scruffy jaw. His bare chest and a tattoo snaking up one bicep. A crow and crossbones tattoo that now shone in the moonlight from her open window. As he lay turned away from her, his back swelling with each rhythmic breath.

Why *him*? Why did her compass keep throwing them together?

"I can't stay here," she said. As if he were awake and needed her excuse.

She grabbed the Browning off the coverlet and stepped into the closet before he could wake to the sound of her voice.

At first she only stood in the dark, slapping the gun against her thigh. *Anywhere*, she told the darkness. *Take me anywhere.*

Instead of directing the compass as she often did, following some predetermined pull, she let go.

She let go and fell backwards through the dark.

Cold tile pressed into her back. A metal bar running the length of one wall appeared under her sweaty palm.

A strip of light spilled from the space between door and jamb, cutting across a porcelain toilet.

A bathroom then. Another bathroom. So often Lou's world felt as if were made up of bathrooms and closets. Like stop signs on every corner. A common thoroughfare.

"Louie?" a voice called.

Her heart faltered in her chest, her empty hand tightening on the metal bar. And she knew in that instant where she'd gone.

More betrayal. Could her compass even be trusted at all anymore? This is what she got for loosening her grip on its reins. For being stupid enough to trust the wild horse galloping within her.

"Lou?"

She stepped into the doorway and stopped breathing.

Lucy lay in the hospital bed. Her blue eyes shone wide in her gaunt face. The clear breathing tube in her nose matched the tubes running from her bruised left arm. Machines clicked on and off. That smell…that *horrible* smell. Acrid and sour.

Not coming from her aunt exactly, but the hospital itself. As if it were a living, breathing creature and they were huddled in its bowels, soaking in its stench.

It took her a moment to recognize it as the scent of death. It was so unlike the death she knew.

Violent death that bloomed like night jasmine, opening its petals to the full moon. This scent was fruit dashed

against the kitchen floor. Fragrant decay burst open.

This was a death she didn't know. Seeing the different side of someone you thought you knew well. Shocking and in its own way, more terrifying than anything she'd faced on the other side of her gun.

"Please don't go," Lucy said. Her voice cracking with the effort.

She tried to sit up.

"Stop. Just stop," Lou begged her. "Let me help you."

This seemed to settle the woman. Lou lifted her gently, flinching at her aunt's hiss of pain. This close she could smell the scalp. The medicine oozing from the pores in her skin.

Lucy's hand clamped onto hers. It was so cold. As cold as any number of the corpses she'd heaped onto the shores of La Loon.

"It's so good to see you," Lucy said, her breath labored.

Lou couldn't return the compliment. Not because she didn't have tremendous bittersweet love for the woman dying before her, but because her aunt looked horrible. There was nothing nice about what she was seeing. She was death personified. A mummy that someone had dressed up as her aunt.

"Has King been keeping you company?" Lou asked.

The idea that her aunt could've been alone in this bed, trapped in this place…

"He comes every day." Her blue eyes searched Lou's face. "You have blood on you."

"It's not mine."

Her aunt gurgled. Choking. Then Lou realized it was laughter.

"What a relief," her aunt said with a wry smile.

Lou wanted to sit down. Her shaking legs threatening to buckle under her.

Her aunt's hand tightened on her own, probably mistaking the movement for an early departure. "I'm sorry I got sick."

"Don't say that. It isn't like you could help it."

Lucy's soft smile vanished. "I want you to promise me something."

*Here it is,* Lou thought. *The command to stop killing. The final bargain between us.*

She missed their old arguments. When her aunt began with gentle encouragement, before devolving to guilt-tripping and outright demands. At least then they'd been on equal ground. This was like fighting a child. Like pointing her gun at a dog in the street.

"Don't blame yourself for this."

Her words stole the breath from Lou's lungs.

"I know it will be hard, but there is no one to blame for this."

Lou's throat tightened in on itself. She hoped her face didn't betray her.

Lucy raised a shaking hand and touched Lou's cheek.

"You have so much strength, Lou-blue. You need to turn it *out* instead of turning it on yourself. Promise me you'll try."

"I don't know what you're asking for." She was fairly certain she'd turned all her abilities against the world. Every time she plucked a man from the streets, soaked her hands with his blood—wasn't that what she was doing?

Lucy's hand seized her own. "Use your gift to *protect*, not punish. You could help so many. All I ask is that you try. *Promise me* you'll try."

"I—" Lou began, but she didn't finish.

The door to Lucy's hospital room began to slide open and Lou only caught sight of the barest hint of blue scrub pants. She tore herself from her aunt's grip and bolted. She dove into the bathroom's darkness and through to the other side.

# 8

Konstantine's eyes fluttered open. Sunlight cut into his vision, whitewashing the world. When he turned his head to escape it, all the air left him. There she sat, on a sofa the color of a king's cloak. Eight or nine guns were spread on the table before her, their shapes flashed prismatic onto the floor beneath. He watched her clean and inspect their chambers, the sunlight radiant on her skin.

So it hadn't been a fever dream. She had truly pulled him from Nico's merciless grip.

But the idea was as strange as seeing her here in full daylight, his creature of shadow.

He rolled onto his side and groaned. Pain flashed red behind his eyelids. Sharp pricks all the way to his toes.

"Bust another stitch and I'll let you bleed to death," she said, looking into the barrel of a .357. His gun, he realized. "I'm tired of stitching you up."

"Are you cleaning my gun for me?"

"My gun, you mean?" It sounded like a joke, but

she wasn't smiling.

He sat up, inspecting the gauze taped to his chest and neck. What he could see was pink, soaked through with blood. She'd left the blood crusted across his knuckles, the few good hits he'd gotten in.

Nico.

Konstantine had known there would be opposition to his rule. When Padre Leo had taken him into his study beneath the church and made his wishes clear, the old man had said as much himself.

He hadn't expected it to come from his own men, those who'd known and loved Padre as long as he had, who'd known his wishes. But they'd known Nico too. All of them boys, having the run of the church and the Florentine streets—Konstantine should have guessed what would happen if they were forced to choose sides.

"Problems with the wife?" Lou asked. Her voice pulled him from his memories.

Her face was placid and unreadable.

"I don't have a wife." If he wanted anyone in the world to know he was available for such a union, it would be this creature. Though he couldn't imagine marrying Louie Thorne any more than he could imagine transforming into a crow and flying into the sunset. This woman, with an arsenal laid before her,

that cold and unwavering glare—his *wife*?

He began laughing and instantly regretted it. His ribs throbbed as if a knife was wedged between each one.

"A boyfriend then," Lou said, inserting the magazine into the clean gun and picking up another.

"Nico Agostino would sooner drown me in the Arno river than kiss me," he said, daring to look at her again. Had he been permitted to simply gaze at her like this before?

He supposed he hadn't had the luxury since the night she appeared in his bed, a mantle of black hair flowing around her. But her hair wasn't black, was it? It looked so in the moonlight, as rich as crow feathers. But in the sun, he realized it was actually a radiant brown, warm hues of red underneath. And her face wasn't alabaster. A Michelangelo come to life. Pale, yes. But a hint of freckles across her cheeks.

"I'm just trying to understand how one of the most powerful crime lords in the world was able to get jumped. In his own house."

"We grew up together, Nico and I," he said. It was hard to speak with his chest as bruised as it was. The wounds made it tight. "As boys we had the same friends. We all entered Padre's gang around the same time." *Francesco. Matteo. Vincenzo. Calzone.* And

how many more? "They helped him."

"No honor amongst thieves," she said.

Thinking of the betrayal hurt more than he expected. He tried to think of anything else.

Anything.

Fortunately, here was the most beautiful distraction.

So different was his goddess by day, that if he'd seen her on the streets, would he have recognized her?

"Did you kill him?"

"Your boyfriend?" she asked. "I emptied my clip into his chest, but I'm pretty sure he had a vest on."

"You didn't check?"

Her cold stare met his. Ah, there was his death goddess. His Kali come to dance on his stone cold corpse. "If I'd wasted time checking on him, you'd be dead."

She had let a kill slide in order to scrape him off the church floor? Abandoned a thrill to save his life? A fortnight ago he would have sworn it impossible. *I wonder if she herself understands the significance.*

She was still watching him, eyes narrowed. "Would you rather be dead? Because I can fix that."

She chambered a bullet.

"No. I'm…surprised."

She put the gun on the table and twisted the cloth between her fists. "That makes two of us. Who knew the great Konstantine would call for help."

"I didn't."

"You *did*. I—" Her teeth clenched. She swallowed whatever she'd meant to say next.

"Is that how it works?" he asked, unable to hide his curiosity. "You can feel people call to you and you simply go to them?"

It was clear the question unnerved her.

"I don't come like a dog."

"I didn't call you," he said, sitting up on his elbows.

This admission only seemed to trouble her more.

"I didn't call you the first night you fell into my bed either," he added, his voice tight. Pain ricocheted through his body. Every movement hurt. It felt as if he'd been lifted and slammed against the church's stone floor a hundred times.

She stood from the sofa suddenly and stepped into the adjacent hall. A cabinet opened. A tin lid clattered to the floor. A tap ran, splashing water into a basin.

She reappeared with a wet rag and a bundle of gauze.

Instead of kneeling before him, tenderly wiping at his wounds as he desperately hoped she might, she threw the rag into his face. Its wet body hit home, blotting out the world. A heartbeat later, the plastic wrapped gauze hit his chest.

"You're bleeding again," she said. "Better wipe it up or you'll be sleeping in it."

She was right. The white gauze covering one of the bullet holes, one about six inches below his left nipple had blossomed red. A geranium in the afternoon sun. He carefully worked a nail under the curling tape and wiped the cloth across his bare skin.

She scowled. "Don't wipe it. *Press*."

He rolled his eyes up to meet hers. "I have done this before."

"And you've got ugly scars to prove it."

"They aren't ugly."

She cocked another gun. "They're *hideous*."

He caught a hint of a smile before she stood and walked away from him toward the kitchen. Then he seemed to see the apartment for the first time. The regal sofa the color of bruised fruit, yes. But also the large windows and mattress on the floor. Four pieces of art on the brick wall running the length of the apartment. The wood floors and an island with a gray marble top. A kitchen that looked as though it belonged in a museum—untouched. Her apartment

was only a little larger than his own.

"Is this where you live?" he asked. He didn't say *you brought me back to your place?* But he was certain the astonishment was clear enough.

"I don't usually perform minor surgeries in dark alleys. Even for ungrateful men who *call* for my help."

"I didn't call you," he insisted. Then his mind betrayed him with a pristine memory.

*If you still want to kill me, Louie, my love, you'd better come now.*

"Not exactly," he amended.

She stood there with a glass of water. Eyebrow raised.

"I only thought, 'if you want to kill me, you'll miss your chance if you didn't come.'"

Her long ponytail rested over her shoulder, her face the same unreadable mask it always was. But he thought he saw something in the eyes.

"How considerate," she said finally, putting the glass on the table out of reach.

"May I have a drink of water?" he asked.

She pushed the glass toward him. He tried not to flinch at the sound of it scraping across the surface. He was fairly certain she did it to rouse him. To provoke him to anger.

He only said, "Grazie."

When he opened his mouth to sip, his jaw clicked. Fresh pain welling up with another memory.

"You hit me," he marveled.

"You wouldn't stop crying."

"I was *not* crying."

"Maybe not with Nico. But with me, you wouldn't shut up." She picked up another gun from the coffee table, meeting his eyes over its barrel.

Was this affectionate teasing? *Mio Dio,* how he had dreamed of this. When he laid in his bedroom, surveying the starlight on his ceiling, he'd imagined what it would be like to hear her voice. To speak with her. To feel her smooth skin under his hands, her legs and body wrapped around him.

Yet the moment was tainted by Nico's snarling face. His promise to undo all that Padre had built. A legacy he had trusted to Konstantine with his last breath.

He couldn't let that happen.

"I will need your help to bring him down," Konstantine said, setting the water glass on table.

"Again—not a dog."

"And I would never treat you as such."

Her face pinched, her gaze sliding up and away at a memory. Was he asking for too much?

"I'm only asking you to do what you would do anyway," he said. "Take down a dangerous man who would hurt so many. Restore order."

"Is that what you do, Konstantine? Keep order in the criminal world? How is Nico any different than you?" She removed the magazine from a gun, pressing her thumb against the top bullet. His body softened at the sound of his name.

He wanted her to say it again. And again. He wanted her to moan it.

"Why should I care about your petty turf wars? If you kill each other, it's less work for me."

"Do you really think we are all the same?" he asked her. He didn't hide his offense. "Is there a line in the sand for you? With all the narcos and crime lords and bastard sons of thieves on one side and who then is on the other? You?"

She leveled him with an unmoving glare.

It occurred to him that she might be nervous. All the guns between them, the incessant unloading, cleaning, reloading—did he make her nervous? He was wounded, vulnerable. But so was she in full daylight. And he was here.

Where was *here*? He sat up on his elbow and gazed out the large windows. There lay an unadulterated view of the shining river. A steamboat like something out of a Mark Twain novel, floated on the water. Tourists ambled up and down the cobbled river walk and to the right, a tall, sweeping arch, shining like a fish in the sunlight. He'd seen this structure in movies and on postcards. The Arch.

St. Louis.

But the part that stuck in his mind was the apartment facing a river—like his own. Were they really so similar? Or was he a romantic fool?

For all he knew she brought men here all the time. Any man she wanted.

Fire surged up his neck into his face. He would sever the fingers of any man who'd touched her. He'd draw his knife right across those knuckle bones, feel the blade scrape the joints, then *crack*.

He released his anger with a laugh, falling back onto the pillow and covered his face with his hands.

Forget Nico. This creature would drive him mad long before that fight came.

"What's so funny?"

He groaned. "Me."

The bed smelled of her. God help him. He was swimming in her scent. He put the pillow over his face and breathed.

Something poked through the pillowcase, catching the corner of his eye. His finger traced its outline. A tag? No. This was thicker, and larger. He slid his hand into the cotton casing and plucked the object free.

A photograph came away in his hand. The edges were curling in on themselves. Perhaps for being so poorly preserved inside a pillowcase instead of in a frame where it should be.

In the picture, a large man smiled up at him. His eyes were haloed by dark hair, the same color as Lou's, wet and falling into his eyes. But the eyes themselves were different. She must have her mother's eyes.

When Konstantine registered the massive arm around Louie, a girl then even younger than when they first met, he realized who he was looking at.

It was her father, Jack Thorne. He saw the resemblance now. But his gaze kept sliding to the girl tucked into the crook of her father's big arm, one ear pressed to his chest, a front tooth missing.

A child. To imagine such a creature was once a child.

And as if by premonition, Konstantine imagined another girl this age in ten or fifteen years, looking like Louie, but with Konstantine's green eyes.

The photo disappeared from his hand as if by magic. And Konstantine turned in time to see Lou slip the plucked photograph into the back pocket of her cargo pants.

"Touch my things again and I'll dump you on Nico's step, hog-tied with a ribbon pinned to your ass."

"I'm sorry," he said. Because for all his jokes and banter, her father was no laughing matter. He knew this was one untouchable part of her. A bone that had been broken long ago and reset poorly. If he prodded this carelessly, she would end him. This he understood. It was like the wound he carried for his mother.

*Go watch your movie, amore di mamma.* A cool hand brushing through his hair.

This was a day for memories it seemed. A day for ghosts.

Silence stretched between them. The light from the large windows turned orange with afternoon.

"At least we understand each other," she said, finally, settling onto the sofa across from him again.

"We do?" Konstantine turned toward her. Every inch of him ached, but for now, it was enough just to look at her, watch her body move as her scent

cocooned him.

"If anyone is going to kill you, Konstantine," she said with a delicious grin. "It's going to be me."

# 9

Nico crossed the plaza enshrining the Duomo and headed south, toward Konstantine's apartment. The crisp September air slid along his shaved scalp, prickling his skin. The scent of food wafting through restaurant windows and petrol burning from engines surrounded him.

Florence.

He'd been born and raised in this ancient city, before his traitorous father exiled him. But it had changed in the ten years since he'd left.

He loved Florence. With its cobblestoned town center and statues as old as civilization itself. Loved the stone walls, bridges, and ancient churches. Loved the river cutting through it as pigeons the color of sheet rock perched on buildings. Loved how one could turn a corner and suddenly be staring at a fountain built centuries before.

It was an old city built on the corpses of men. Bones fertilized the earth beneath his feet. Kingdoms rose, flourished, and fell here. Some of those kings had even been banished, like himself, only to return and dance on the corpses of their enemies.

And Nico would dance.

He thought of his father. Of his last night in this city before he'd been shackled and thrown into the back of a truck.

He'd been seized in his own bed. Gagged, shackled, and dragged through the street. He rode in the back of a squat car, bouncing on the cobblestones in the early morning mist. When the brakes squealed at the water's edge, for a terrified moment, he thought they were hefting him into the river. Surely the shackles would have pulled him down, pinning him to the bottom of the Arno's dark floor.

He was certain it was a rival gang. Enemies that had found his home in the night and had moved against him.

But when the tailgate dropped, and he saw his own father—he knew the truth.

He was to be the sacrificial lamb.

And why? Because his father's friend Giovanni lost a daughter. Bella had been caught in the crossfire of a petty bust, taking a bullet from Nico's own gun, and now he would be thrown to the dogs for it. As if it was meant as a personal offense.

What story did his father tell himself? An exiled child in exchange for a dead one? That he was saving Nico's life from Giovanni's retribution? He probably painted the betrayal as mercy.

Lies.

The truth was Nico had always been ambitious. He wanted the Ravengers for himself. He thought he'd hidden this desire to usurp his father well enough. But looking into those pale eyes in the morning mist, that unforgiving face in the light—he knew he'd done a poor job of it.

His father, the great *Padre,* or *Father Leo* to every street rat in the city, had the power to placate Giovanni.

A thousand men in the city would've answered his every beck and call. If only he'd raised his hand or voice to rally them. Instead, he'd used the first transgression brought against Nico as an excuse to be rid of him. If it had been Konstantine who'd slain the girl, there would've been no hesitation. Padre would've moved Heaven and Earth for his *Tesoro.*

But Nico was not Konstantine.

*I know why you're really doing this!* He'd shouted through the gag as three men dragged him from the truck bed and tossed him into the back of the waiting truck, the coarse straw pushing through his night shirt. *I know why!*

Nico was the only real threat to Padre's empire and his *Tesoro.* For if given much more time, Nico would've risen up and seized his father's throne. He was what the Ravengers needed. To be the most feared crime family not only in Italy, but the world.

His father had grown weak and indulgent in his old age. It wasn't only that he'd sheltered all the brats in the city. Or his soft ways with women. It was that he viewed his work as something other than what it was. *This is an opportunity to shelter the forgotten. To offer discarded souls a way out of the gutter. Out of the dark.*

Bullshit!

They sold drugs! They governed the underworld. The cities they built were meant for those like themselves. Souls without a future. Souls with no way out but down. His father spoke of revolution, of freeing the people. And Konstantine was infected by the same blindness.

Nico was the only one who could see the world clearly. Some were meant to live beneath the boots of others. There was no shame in that. The notion of equality and freedom for all—*grow up, brother.* There was no place for idealism in their world.

Nico had thought all of this as the truck shifted and swayed. There was only one salvation on that terrible night. The truck and pre-dawn exile meant his father hadn't had it in him to kill him outright.

That was his mistake.

Because if he'd lived long enough, Nico would have put a bullet between his eyes.

After the exile. After the ten long years in a work yard where he toiled and sweat and endured endless humiliations until news of his father's death reached him.

And he knew he couldn't wait any longer. The time had come.

At the edge of the Ponte Vecchio, Nico paused to look out over the water. The camp felt like a lifetime ago. His father, a mere dream.

And maybe this was not even the same city. For now the sun shimmered on the surface, like pebbles tumbling in a stream. Tourists clustered around the shops and gelaterias. A beggar woman lay prostrated, face down with her open palms cupped in offering.

Nico put a euro note into her outstretched hands. He knew what it was to be hungry and to have nothing but your own will to sustain you. It had been his hate for his father that had kept him breathing all those years in the labor camp. Konstantine was *nothing* in the face of that hatred. The will.

He'd survived hell. He'd rallied the others in the

camp and overthrew their guards. They killed every single one of them, stole every gun, every ounce of supplies. They'd traveled the treacherous miles between the camp and Florence, hard weeks of living hand to mouth, stealing for food, sleeping where they could.

What obstacle did Konstantine pose compared to what he'd already overcome?

How would it have hurt him to know that for months his old friends had sent word to Nico, letting him know Padre was dead, that he should come home. That they would help him reclaim what was rightfully his?

He remembered the look on Konstantine's face when Calzone and Vincent pulled their guns on him, and Nico stepped victorious from the shadows.

He would replay that memory for years to come, wringing every ounce of joy from it.

Nico crossed through a portico into the apartment's atrium and courtyard. He passed beneath the rounded archway and ascended the old stone steps, noting each number beside the apartment door. The attic then. Overlooking a lush courtyard and fountain on one side and the Arno itself on the other. He paused to admire the carved cherub, his delicate mouth spitting water while his fingers poised above
the strings of a lyre.

He turned the key in the large metal lock and heard it release.

He could've sent anyone for this mission, but he'd wanted to see for himself. How better to know his enemy than to see where he slept, where he dreamed?

Nico stepped into the cool apartment and hit the light. He pulled the curtain, revealing the courtyard below, giving the room even more light by which to see. A large chair in one corner and a desk with a computer in the other. A red and brown rug covered the length of the room.

He went up the stairs to find the loft. A rumpled bed. The compressed pillows. He opened the double doors on a balcony and the glory of the shining Arno river. Someone was cooking in an adjacent apartment, rich spices and sweet cream wafted through the open window, carried on the cool river breeze.

He opened drawers, looked in closets. The closet lights were already on. And strangely, when he tried to turn them off, it seemed the bulbs had been screwed into a socket in such a way that the lights couldn't be turned off. A quirk of an old apartment perhaps?

He found a collection of shoes. Some Italian leather. Some American. Two leather jackets and an abundance of black shirts and several pairs of sunglasses. A toothbrush on the sink. A single bottle of soap in the shower stall. Cologne on the bedside table.

Downstairs he searched again. Pencils and pens and paper in the desk. The laptop itself which was password protected. Some novels in both English and Italian.

He unplugged the laptop from the wall and wrapped the cord around it. This was likely his only find.

A giant oil painting of a man with a sword raised high hung on the wall. Is this how he saw himself? Konstantine The Great? A warrior astride his horse? More like a joke of a man. A stolen horse.

He'd stood sneering at the painting until he heard a small sound behind him. A shoe scuffing on stone.

"Konstantine!" A boy called out. "I'm back. We've—"

The boy's voice froze in his throat, his Adam's apple bobbing as he swallowed the rest of his sentence down. He took one look at Nico standing the middle of the apartment and bolted.

He didn't get far. Nico seized the back of his jacket and hauled him into the apartment, kicking the door closed. He slammed the boy against it, eliciting a cry.

Nico's hand pressed over the kid's mouth, the same moment he tossed the laptop toward the chair. It landed squarely on top of the rose-colored cushion and bounced. Good enough. Nico needed his free hand to pull his blade and press it to the kid's throat.

The boy's body went perfectly still.

"Where did you come from?" Nico asked. Because he'd laid siege to this city in the last 48 hours. Surely this boy had learned of the change of power.

"Prato," the boy said, without hesitation. Good. Perhaps Nico wouldn't have to kill him.

"And what were you doing in Prato?"

"Where's Konstantine?"

"Dead." *Or he soon will be.*

The boy's shoulders softened against the door.

"*What* were you were doing in Prato?"

The boy swallowed. The knife pricked the skin.

"He wanted me to check on something."

"Check what?" Nico pressed the blade against his throat. Blood trickled down, soaking the collar of
his t-shirt.

This terrified the boy into silence. His eyes going as wide as cow's before the steel bolt penetrated its head. He released the pressure only enough to encourage speech.

"He's having a room built there."

"Go on."

The boy looked horrified for a moment, as if he wasn't sure exactly how he would go on.

"It's—it's just a room, signore," he said, sweat beading along his hairline, matting his bangs to his forehead. "In an old winery outside of town. It's in the basement."

He believed him. After all, if Konstantine was smart, he would've chosen the boy for his ignorance. If he himself were commissioning a room for some dark purpose, would he tell anyone what it was for? As a safe for his fortune or a bunker against one's enemies? No. He suspected that secret would stay quite close to his chest. As close as this terrified boy with his panting breath stood now.

He released the kid. "What purpose do you *think* the room is intended for?"

Visible relief washed over his face as he stood and tugged his shirt and jacket back into place. "I can't imagine. It's a strange room."

"Describe it to me."

"It's padded. Floor to ceiling. Not even a ceiling really. It's only lights up there. Every inch. Too high to reach. The lights do not turn off and it makes the room so bright. It hurts my eyes."

The lights do not turn off.

Like the closet in the apartment.

*What a mad man you were, Konstantine*, Nico thought.

"He sent you to check on this project of his?"

"Yes." He used the collar of his shirt to mop up the blood from his throat, crushing the cotton against his slender throat.

"And what was the message you came to deliver today?" Nico asked, wiping the boy's blood on his pants.

"It's ready."

# 10

When King stepped into the hospital room with a cup of coffee and a wrapped po'boy sandwich, he knew something had changed. Lucy was sitting up in bed. Nurse Naomi, King's favorite of all the caregivers at the center, was beside her. Naomi was a lovely woman with dreads tied at the base of her neck. The woman spoon-fed Lucy a steaming bowl of soup, in slow, patient offerings.

"Good morning, ladies," he said, sliding the door shut behind them. "Looks like I'm in time for lunch."

The nurse spared him a small smile. "Good morning, Mr. King. Miss Lucy and I were talking about my niece Cassandra. She's getting married at St. Thomas parish this weekend."

"Congratulations," King said, pulling up the chair on the opposite bedside. "I hope the weather holds for you."

Lucy turned her face away, her features pinching closed. Naomi and King exchanged a look.

Naomi set the bowl down on the side table. "You

tired? We can pick this up later."

"Leave the bowl and we can try in a little while," King said.

Lucy didn't speak until Naomi had excused herself, slipping unobtrusively from the room. Then seemingly to the wall she said, "Weddings are lovely."

King unwrapped his sandwich. The smell of fried shrimp, vinegar, and BBQ sauce wafted up to greet him.

Her face pinched again.

"Is this smell bothering you?" he asked, wondering if he'd made a mistake in bringing it. He'd given up on the beignets. If he was sick, dying from the cancer eating away at his bones, would he want someone trying to force feed him donuts every other day? Probably not.

She didn't seem to hear him. "I'm so nauseous today."

"Is it the smell?" he asked again. No food at all then. That's where they were now. His heart sank even as she shook her head no.

He was torn between his own hunger and trying to read unspoken cues.

"I'd always hoped that I'd see Lou get married."

King snorted. "Imagine the domestic disputes over drawers left open or socks on the floor."

It was either eat the sandwich quickly or throw it away. King dared to take a bite.

Lucy turned and smiled at him then. "We could get married."

King coughed, choking on the po'boy. It wasn't what she'd said. It was the clear eyes and sweet smile. Perfect lucidity. This wasn't the drugs talking.

"What's wrong, Robert?" she asked with a broad grin. "Not the marrying kind?"

If there was a woman in the world that he would dare to love again, to give himself completely to, it was Lucy Thorne. But he'd already done that. Not on paper. But what did that matter?

"I didn't think you'd have me," he said, cracking open a water bottle and washing down the shrimp stuck in this throat.

"Don't I already have you?"

"Yes." He wiped at his fingers with a flimsy paper napkin.

She turned away then. "I'm a fool to expect more than I've already received."

He snatched her hand. "Not a fool."

She laughed, a tired, dried out sound. He offered
her the water but she turned her face away.

Her blue eyes measured him. She wanted a real answer.

And what could he say to her? As she lay in this hospital bed, her body turned against her. And so young. She would never see her fiftieth birthday. He had already seen ten years that she wouldn't. And why should he get the extra time? What in the world was he doing with his life that was so damn grand? She was a thousand times worthier of a long life than most of the bastards who got one.

She had every right to feel like the world had jilted her. He couldn't count on one hand all that it had taken from her.

Her brother. Her health and sometimes her mind. Twenty or more years of life that she could've spent seeing Lou become the amazing woman she dreamed she would be. Her chance to guard and guide the young woman. Any hope of fulfilling her promise to Jack.

And what about his own selfish wants? He would've given his testicles for twenty more years with her. Hell, for ten.

"Can you imagine the wedding? In my condition?" she said, more to herself than to him. "I should be grateful I had one more good summer with

you. It was a great summer, wasn't it?"

"The best."

He was certain she was drawing deep on some Buddhist bullshit. Non-attachment. Gratitude. Some-thing to lessen the fact that she was too young to be dying, yet still had the audacity to dream. And why shouldn't she, damnit?

He squeezed her hand. "If you're serious, and if you'll have me, I will marry you. Big wedding and all."

Lucy smiled. "Lou might even come."

"I'd make sure of it. Say the word and I'll make it happen."

"The word," she whispered, and her eyes fluttered closed, a smile tucked sweetly into the corner of her lips.

With his car parked in the alley behind him, King stood on the curb outside Melandra's Fortune and Fixes and watched the world go by. On the worst days, like this one, when Lucy was as ill as he'd ever seen her, the world felt like a dream. It floated past him like clumped debris in a river.

When the nurses had tried to get Lucy up and walking, the screaming had frightened him so badly they'd asked him to leave.

*How long do I have?* he'd asked the doctor before getting into his car and coming home.

*It's so hard to tell. She's still having good days. The best we can do is keep her comfortable.*

Good days, but not as many King knew. How long could she last now that the pain made it impossible for her own bones to support her?

And what happened when they couldn't make her comfortable anymore? How could he watch her suffer, knowing he could do nothing for her?

The world came into focus again. A breeze from Lake Pontchartrain cutting across St. Peter.

The first thing his eyes registered was a group of Asian tourists across the street, talking rapidly as they read a map. Filipino maybe.

"What are you looking for?" he called out to them, switching the briefcase from his left fist to his right, feeling the weight of the world again.

A short man with thick black hair said, "St. Louis Cathedral."

King pointed them toward Royal Street, with instructions to follow the long and winding road until it opened up on the square and grand white cathedral they were looking for.

They thanked him, and disappeared down the adjacent street, leaving King on the sidewalk.

A small brass band a block up played bluegrass music.

He breathed deep, caught the scent of fried pralines. Could the world really go on without her?

It had to. It had no choice.

He would never say this to Lucy, knowing it would hurt her feelings more than help her. But when he returned home after long mornings in the NOLA Cancer Center, sometimes he stood on the street corner, or on his balcony above and breathed. Cajun spice, fresh air. Hell, even the scent of booze or vomit was more pleasant than the hospital stench.

The French Quarter smelled like life. No matter how boozy, or marijuana-ridden that scent became in the hours between midnight and dawn, he welcomed it as he welcomed the ruthless heart beating in his chest.

And it was more than that.

He could no sooner stop pulling air into his lungs than the world could stop spinning.

His heart, like the world, was slave to its own momentum.

When he spent three days in the rubble of a collapsed building, King had been sure he would die then and there, his organs crushed beneath tons of poured concrete and metal beams. For a long time, that moment was his Big Bang. The cataclysmic remains that he carried with him through the gravity of the day.

Now the low-ceilings of the cancer center were what he dreamed of. His fear of Lucy's impending death and his own claustrophobia had entered his psyche and mixed somehow. Lucy's death would unmoor him again.

Already his nightmares stretched the cancer center corridors to funhouse lengths. Pressed the ceilings down on him from above and Lucy's screaming filtering through the space that remained. On most nights, he had to transverse the darkness to find her. To claw his way through the rubble to rescue her trapped body.

None of this would stop him from visiting her of course.

Not the claustrophobia. Not the anxiety.

No number of sleepless nights or nightmares. But he would be lying to himself if he didn't admit that standing here on the open bustling street, so full of life and vibrancy, was better than the center. He was freer here. The air came easier.

And he didn't think she would hold that against him.

"You drunk or something?"

King pried his eyes open and followed the voice up. Piper stood poised on a metal ladder, hanging cobwebs from the Melandra's Fortunes and Fixes sign. She wore baggy jeans and a black Star Wars t-shirt with its iconic yellow script. Chucks on her feet. Her bleached hair was braided into a side ponytail, revealing the silver cuffs on her ears. Her hemp necklace with its glass beads caught and reflected the sunlight across the metal sign.

"No," he said, with a smile. "Do I look drunk?"

"You're standing there sniffing the air. It's freaking weird. You high?"

"Maybe I'm happy to be alive."

"You almost get hit by a car? Someone clipped me on my bike the other day. Monsters."

"What are you doing up there?" He gestured toward the cobweb and lights in her hands.

"Mel wants this Halloween shit up today."

"It's September."

Piper rolled her eyes. "I'm thinking she's hoping to draw the Halloween crowd early."

The central streets of the French Quarter were enough like a perpetual Halloween party as it was. It didn't have to be Mardi Gras or any other holiday to see masked revelers crawling the streets.

"Have you ever planned a wedding?" King asked her.

Piper wobbled on the ladder. "Do I look like I've planned a wedding?"

"Maybe you have a sister—"

"Only child—"

"Or your mother—"

"My mother has been married four times, but she's more the weekend-in-Vegas kind of bride. Why? Who's getting married?" Genuine concerned scrunched her features. Her eyes were painted to resemble an Egyptian cat's. Strangely, he thought it suited her, her features striking him as kittenish, even on makeup-free days.

"I think I am," he said. He placed one hand on the metal post, cane height and topped with a horse's head. This was his ritual, of checking his feet before stepping into Melandra's shop. If the city decided to remove these historical markers of old tie-up posts, used for horses in the last century, he wasn't sure his old body would know how to proceed. The pointed ears pressed into his palm as he struggled to balance himself, scrapping the bottom of his shoes against the curb.

"You *think* you are? You going to propose to Lucy?" Piper teased, the tension leaving her face as she wrapped a fresh coil of eerie purple lights along the sign's post before pivoting toward the black iron railings of his balcony.

"Hey, hang those from inside. You'll fall leaning over like that." His heart ratcheted at her precarious position. "Who did you think I meant?"

Piper hesitated, pretending to fiddle with a knot. "I don't know. Maybe Lou was engaged or somet-hing."

King grinned and Piper saw it. She burst out laughing. "Right. Okay. Glad to know I have a chance."

He didn't think she had a chance with Lou at all—and wondered if he was cruel for thinking so. Was he fool enough to think he knew anything about Louie Thorne's interests? Apart from slaughtering drug lords, of course.

King watched Piper work against the backdrop of the building, fire engine red with hunter green shutters. The oversized windows overlooked both

Royal and St. Peter streets. Ferns lined the balcony. Something about the ladder made him uneasy. *A goose on my grave*, he thought.

"You know if you had a case for me to work on, I wouldn't be up here fooling with these damn lights," Piper grumbled.

"I'm waiting on my license to arrive." It was a lie. King had already completed the forty-hour training course and sat for the licensing exam. He'd paid the agency fees and submitted all the paperwork with his fingerprint cards. He'd been certified weeks ago, updated his concealed carry permit, and even informed many of his old colleagues across America that he was in the business again.

Most congratulated him on finding something worth his skill and time in his retirement and promised to send work his way soon. A few affectionately teased him, calling him *Uncle Robbie,* a jab against cops who didn't know how to exit the force.

What had stopped his burgeoning new career in its track had been Lucy. When Lucy turned the corner and her move to the cancer center became permanent, King had stopped answering emails. He respectfully turned down offers from the local precinct and pulled his ad from the *Times-Picayune*. He even turned down his side gig of adjuncting for LSU—teaching Intro to Criminology courses as needed. He told them this fall semester was impossible and likely the spring too.

Lucy was his concern now. And Lou.

"It's fine," Piper said with a huff. "I'm making great progress in my apprenticeship. I've only got ten hours left before I'm a certified tarot reader."

"That's great." Though King had no idea who certified fortune tellers.

"But hunting criminals is more fun and tarot is more of a side gig. So…you know." Piper wagged her eyebrows at him.

"I'll let you know if anything changes," he assured her, before stepping around the ladder and into the shop.

The skeleton by the door shrieked, vibrating the hairs inside his ears. He took a breath, slowly unclenched his fist and stared around the shop.

The store was smoky with incense. Patchouli and jasmine today. Despite the open door and late breeze, a visible cloud hung in the air, haloing the bookshelves and trinket displays full of sugar skulls, candles, statues of saints, and porcelain figurines. Beside the wall of talismans hung the purple curtain. He could hear Mel's soft voice muffled by the thick curtain, the tone dramatic and grave. Whoever was having their fortune read in that candlelit nook wasn't receiving good news.

No one else was in the shop.

He took the stairs up to the landing above, veering left to his apartment. If he kept walking around to the other side, he'd be met with an identical door leading into Mel's own apartment, a mirror image of his own.

But he worked his key into the deadbolt first, then the lower knob.

His red leather sofa against the left wall and his beast of a coffee table that looked like a floating door salvaged from a shipwreck, bolted onto wooden feet. His collection of mismatched cardboard rounds were stacked nicely in one corner of the table, each he had stolen from local bars.

He remembered how worried he'd been about Lucy seeing those. That she'd think him a drunk. Or a pothead for the 8th of weed he kept inside his Bob Dylan vinyl with a pack of rolling papers. He hadn't smoked in months. Or drank more than a beer or two for that matter. Part of it was the drug test required for the P.I. license. The other part was simply time. He couldn't show up at Lucy's bedside smelling like weed or a distillery and there wasn't a day he didn't visit her.

He supposed that even without the illness, he would've cleaned up for her, if for anyone. He only wished the twilight of her life hadn't been the reason.

King plopped onto the sofa and opened the briefcase.

Document after printed document lay sandwich-ed on top of each other. He pulled them out, exam-ined each one. Beneath the stack, he fished out the yellow legal pad and began a new list. It was the sixth or seventh such list on this page. But each that had come before it had been crossed out, with little side notes marked.

All the print-outs had a single thing in common. Lou Thorne. They either bore an image of her face or description of her person. He'd been scouring every public and private database he could for news of her. Files or suspicious reports. He was doing this for Lucy, he told himself. Or sometimes he told himself that he was doing it for Jack. Rarely was he able to convince himself that all the hunting, the searching, was for Lou herself.

Because while she may be the direct beneficiary of his efforts, he couldn't seem to believe that she really *needed* him. They could send a hundred men, maybe a thousand. And King suspected that she might very well kill them all.

Scouring reports for her name, silently deleting files and photos, all of it was for someone's benefit. He just wasn't sure whose.

He canvassed the disappearances until an incident caught his eye.

A man was reported missing in New York three days ago. His girlfriend, who looked like a clown with magenta eyeshadow and fuchsia Lycra pants in the photo, said that a woman fitting Lou's description had come around looking for him the day before.

Two known drug mules, brothers in Dallas were reported missing by their mother. She said they'd gone to the park across the street to meet up with their friends, but never came home. The last thing she saw was her boys talking to a young woman in a leather jacket and sunglasses—despite the late hour. In the report, the mother openly admitted to wondering if the woman was a prostitute, saying quote *knowing my boys, I wouldn't of been surprised.*

Senator Thompson of New York never reached his benefit gala in the city. The last person to see him alive was the limo driver. Russel Postma swore that Senator Thompson had gotten into the limo alone. He'd asked Postma for silence while he reviewed his notes for the speech he was to give somewhere between dessert and coffee. Postma obliged, rolling up the partition and turning off the radio. They were two miles from the banquet hall when he heard Thompson shout. By the time he pulled the limo over and rolled down the partition, he found the senator gone. The notecards strewn across the leather seat. He was certain that the senator hadn't exited the vehicle, he simply disappeared.

After reading the new reports and interviews, King had a list of five new sources to investigate. Nothing that mentioned Lou by name, no. But each disappearance had an unmistakable *Lou*-ness about it.

King's hand paused in scribbling a name when the sudden urge to look up overtook him.

There she was.

"Fuck!" King threw the notebook and sheets of computer paper briskly into the case, slamming down the lid once, twice, before managing to get the gold clips settled into place.

"Am I interrupting something?" she asked. He couldn't see her eyes behind the mirrored sunglasses, but her voice was flat, uninterested. Only the arched eyebrow gave away her amusement.

"I have *two* doors." He wiped his hands down his face. "You could knock. On *either* one of them."

"I'll come back." She slid her hands into her leather jacket and turned away.

"No," he barked, perhaps too earnestly because she shifted her weight. He sucked in a breath and tried to relax. "No, I need to talk to you."

A deep crease settled between her eyes.

"How's Lucy?" she asked.

King was about to launch into his lecture. The prepared speech that began with *you would know if you'd visit her your damn self!*

"She looked like shit when I saw her," Lou added.

King's prepared defense fell out of his head. Everything he'd meant to say, about her hunting, about Lucy's dying wish for a wedding, even a half-hearted plea to say hello to Piper or Mel—all of it vanished.

"You saw Lucy?" he said, staring at her. He wished she'd take off the sunglasses. "When?"

As if reading his mind, she pushed them up onto her head. "Last night."

A million responses danced on the tip of his tongue.

*Would it kill you to spend more time with her? She raised you! And as hard as you might be trying to kill yourself, she's* actually *dying.*

*This is your last chance, kid. Don't fuck up like I did.*

He exhaled all his unspoken grievances and fell back against the couch. He put his large hands on his knees because he didn't know what else to do with them.

This wasn't really about what Lou did or didn't do.

This was about figuring out where the two of them stood—Louie and him. And where they'd go from here, once Lucy was gone.

Once Lucy was gone.

His heart clenched. "How've you been?"

He was surprised by the gentleness in his tone. And he wasn't the only one. First her eyebrow arched higher, then she said, "No complaints."

*No complaints? Your last remaining family member has one foot in the grave and you have no complaints?*

He opened and closed his fist compulsively. Looking for something else benign to say. Something. Anything. He wanted to keep her here, keep her talking.

This had to work. For Lucy's sake, he *had* to make this work.

But *god*, did he want a reaction out of her. He wanted Lou to scream. To cry. Hell, he'd settle for having her pull a gun on him.

But she gave him nothing. Every muscle in her body was the calm patina of a lake in the early evening. Not a ripple in sight. And no matter how many rocks he threw into it, he couldn't change her any more than the stars in the sky.

*God, Lucy, how did you do it?*

King was suddenly grateful he'd never had kids of his own.

Lou said, "How was Lucy when you saw her?"

He said finally, squeezing his knees. "In a lot of pain. There was a bit of an emergency this morning and they sent me away. She was stable when I left, but…"

Lou wasn't stupid. With her life, absolutely. But in her head—not at all. There was nothing King could tell her that she likely didn't already understand herself. Not about Lucy's health or her time left in this world.

He wanted to ask *why did you finally visit?* He considered how to frame this. "It's good to see you, kid."

There. Concern. He'd nailed it.

"Did you drop in to say hi?" he asked. "You could've called."

"I needed to get out of my apartment."

Irritation bit at the back of his neck. Was that really all? She finally gracing them with her presence because she was a little stir crazy. No, wait. That didn't compute. King knew for a fact that she left her apartment all the time.

"What are you saying?" he asked.

"My apartment is crowded."

"Why? Who's in it?"

"Paolo Konstantine." She gave him one of her measuring sideways glances. "Martinelli's bastard son. He runs the Ravengers. Or he did."

The name spun King's mind in a different direction. "Martinelli? The man who had your old man killed?"

Paolo Konstantine. He remembered hearing the name for the first time from Lou herself. What had she called him? *He's the new Martinelli.*

That's right. She'd been bleeding to death on Ryanson's boat deck.

He remembered Konstantine now. Remembered his hands going up in surrender when Lou turned her gun on him. A good-looking guy. Dark hair. Green eyes. He looked as tough as Lou, with that crow and crossbones tattoo on his bicep, the hungry look in his eye.

*What the hell are you going to kill him for?* King had asked.

*He's the new Martinelli.*

That was when King had told her the truth. That Ryanson had ordered the hit on her father. But surely that wasn't enough to change her opinion of the crime lord's son. This bit of truth was enough to befriend him rather than put a bullet in his brain? No way. She hunted those bastards. She didn't play sleepover with them.

There was quite the distance between revenge and taking a man home…wasn't there?

He gave Lou a good hard look.

She had new wounds. The first two knuckles on her left hand were faded purple. Repeated blunt trauma. She had a cut on her chin. Hard to tell if it had been a bullet or a blade. And her upper arm had been grazed. But none of this told him why Paolo Konstantine was in her apartment.

"Are you bringing the strays home now?" he asked, trying to find his footing again in the conversation.

"He was bleeding to death. I thought about dumping him on the ER floor," she said with a shrug. "But I didn't know if he had a record and if that would've been like throwing him to the sharks. And he'd blacked out, so I couldn't ask."

"What happened?"

She smiled. "Someone kicked his ass."

"Who?"

"From what he's said, it sounds like there's been a hostile takeover of his little gang. Nico Agostino is in charge of the Ravengers now."

"Who the hell is that?"

"Nico is Padre Leo's biological son. Leo built the Ravengers, then left it to Konstantine when he died."

King felt like he was watching an Italian soap opera. A drama surrounding infamous crime families. Only he'd missed six or seven episodes and now couldn't remember who was who and all the Italian stallions looked alike.

"So Padre chose Konstantine over the son, Nick—"

"Nico."

"—Nico. And he's butthurt about it."

"It doesn't sound like Nico was ever an option. He killed someone's daughter and was banished to a labor camp in Russia. He broke out as soon as he heard his father died and came back to reclaim the Ravengers."

"Konstantine told you all this?"

"Parts of it. I did some digging. Asked around."

Asking around meant breaking fingers and slitting throats.

"Why are you telling me all of this?" King asked, draping one arm across the back of the sofa.

"I want to kill him," she said.

"Nico or Konstantine."

She smiled again. "Maybe both."

King snorted. "I don't think you're asking my permission."

As if she needed it.

"I'm looking for the right time. And I want you to let me know when that is." She shifted and King saw the butt of the Beretta tucked against her ribs.

She bent and snapped up his briefcase.

Before he could process what was happening, she had it open, a collection of papers in one fist, the yellow legal pad with his lists on the other.

He opened his mouth to defend himself, but she was already speaking.

"Yeah, like this," she said, meeting his eyes over the legal pad.

He hesitated. "Like what?"

"Listen to the wires," she told him. "If Nico makes any moves, over reaches, or if you get the sense that he's planning to strike, let me know."

King's pulse leapt in this throat. "Strike against who? You?"

"I shot him a couple of times," she said. "I don't think he's dead. When you shoot people and don't kill them, they tend to be pissy about it."

"Did you spare him on purpose?" he asked, unable to imagine her missing any target.

She tossed the papers back into the briefcase's gaping mouth. "I was distracted."

*Distracted.* What in God's name could distract her?

"Is Nico a superhuman mutant or something?"

"It doesn't matter." She slid her shades down over her face again. "It won't happen again."

He sensed the shift, her imminent departure and shot up from the sofa. His knees popped from the effort and his back groaned.

There was still so much to tell her. About Lucy. About their plans for Lou once Lucy was gone. Things that he and Lucy had discussed about her future.

But she didn't wait for him. She'd already disappeared through the shadow of his large armoire, leaving him alone in his apartment with his pile of paperwork.

"Next time then," he said to the darkness.

If they had a next time.

# 11

Konstantine woke to full darkness, heart hammering. He sat up, looking around the unfamiliar apartment. Then he saw the purple sofa, two feminine throw pillows tucked into each corner. Lights from the river dancing across the brick walls. No. That was the pool. Steam rose into the chilled night. Lights shimmered beneath its surface, casting a glow against the *No Lifeguard on Duty* sign fixed to the surrounding gate.

A luxurious studio with a heated pool. Wasn't she living the life?

But the apartment itself sat dark.

He rolled out of the bed. Or he tried. Every muscle in his body groaned. His stitched up bullet wounds, yes. But also the muscles that had been tenderized by Italian leather boots.

He placed his feet on the cold wooden floor and hissed.

He ran a hand over his chest, as if to reassure himself that it was intact. Then with much effort, he pulled himself to standing. Bones creaked. Tendons popped. He was that man from the children's story, who'd fallen asleep beneath a tree and woke a hundred years later. Or at least he felt as if he'd aged a hundred years in one night.

He turned on a lamp, pulling the metal cord hanging from the bulb beneath the shade. He stood there, listening to the night bustle around him. One of the windows was open, and a light breeze blew through, rattling the horizontal slats.

The air licked the feverish sweat from his skin. The moonlit sheets fluttered. Outside, a train whistled and huge iron wheels screeched against their rails. Horns blared even at this hour.

It was as loud as his Florentine apartment. Even the river seemed the same, the water's surface shimmering with collected moonbeams.

His .357 sat on the glass coffee table.

He lifted it from the glass top, inspected it, and found it to be loaded.

Beside it, another present. A brown bag held a burger and fries, the paper so soaked with grease that it sagged from the weight of the burger. Cheap American food. Back home, under no circumstances would he ever eat such garbage. But he was far from home and his stomach grumbled the moment he peeled back the plastic wrapping and the scent of cooked meat struck him.

Yet he ate it with relish, sucking the salt off his fingers the way a marooned man sucks water from the stream. He would've eaten two more burgers and another five fistfuls of fries had they been in the bag.

His hunger sated for now, only his curiosity remained. He opened the closet closest to the couch but found it empty. Three bare walls no wider than the door itself, and a carefully swept square of wooden floor serving as its bottom. He scraped at the notches in the wall with his bloody nails, noting the places where shelves had once been.

No light above, only smooth plaster.

He closed the door, releasing its brassy handle.

He found the two safes behind the paintings and could guess at their contents. All manner of destruction no doubt. Perhaps cash. He didn't think passports or documentation would be in there. After all, hadn't he searched for such items himself and come up short?

She was a ghost in the modern world, no license. No credit history.

Not counting the brief blip in the news which had surfaced when her father's story surged to the surface again in June, there'd been no mention of her. The news hadn't even had a recent picture. They'd

relied on one over a decade old.

Reporters no doubt wanted to interview the daughter of a man who'd been exonerated of treason fourteen years after his death. Her interview would have been prime time. Her account of surviving the murder, only to have her father slandered after—living with that cruelty all those years. The American public loved emotional drama. They would have sopped hers up like a biscuit through gravy on a dinner plate.

If Lou had been an emotional woman.

And if her privacy had been threatened by the reemerging interest in an old story, he supposed he'd have himself to blame. Hadn't he fed the evidence himself to the public? He'd provided the clips and conversations between Jack's partner Brasso and Senator Ryanson. Proof of the money that had changed hands. Photos of their conversations. Counter bait that had perhaps deterred the press from looking too hard at a fallen hero's daughter.

For now.

The manhunt for both Ryanson and Brasso went national. And of course, the press only

amplified when neither could be found. That had been Lou's doing—no doubt she disposed of the bodies in that untraceable way of hers. A secret she kept close to
her Kevlar vest.

He'd almost seen that dumping ground himself.

He touched the notch under his chin, the place where she'd pressed her gun.

*I'm not your enemy*, he'd said. *I believe we are drawn together for a reason. You came to me when you were dreaming. Did you dream of killing me?*

He'd been trying to reason with her as her gun had remained perfectly steady against his chin. She'd only regarded him with those placid, unreadable eyes.

But she hadn't killed him. She'd done as he wished and taken him to his mother's grave.

When he closed his eyes, Konstantine could still hear his mother begging for his life as his father stared down at her in a shadowed Italian field.

*He's your son! Prego. Prego, Fernando!*

Konstantine would never forget the *POP* of the gun. Her mouth opening in a surprised *O*. The sight of her pitching forward, nightgown billowing, into the dark hole. Her gown seemed to glow in the bottom of the dark cradle, but her body had disappeared, swallowed by grave dirt.

Grief swallowed him whole in that moment and when he came to his senses again, seemingly months later, he hadn't known where they'd been. A field,

yes. But there were a thousand fields near Florence.

His mother could've been in any one of them.

He would've never found her without Lou's help. He owed her everything. Would give her anything.

*You lie to yourself,* he thought, chiding himself inwardly.

*I want to give her everything. I also want to take everything from her.*

His fingers caught on a something. His memories broke through the surface of his mind.

Konstantine ran his hand over the kitchen island again, his fingers tracing its cool surface until he found it. Beneath the counter was a small metal latch that could be undone with the flick of his finger. He looked nervously at the closed closet door behind him, wondering how much time he had to investigate with impudence before the lioness returned.

He flicked the latch and the side of the island popped away from its frame. Not the side of a counter, but a secret door.

He opened it wider and discovered stairs descending into the dark.

Heart hammering, he took them one at a time, his bare feet gripping the wooden steps cautiously. The hem of his jeans scrapped over their surface.

Cold air licked up his bare chest. Something brushed his face. He mistook it for a cobweb, but quickly realized it was much too thick. Pawing the space above his head he found the string. He pulled it and light spilled across the room.

Konstantine's breath stuck in his throat.

*Cristo!*

Shelves lined three of the four walls. The one accommodating the stairs was the only bare space. Every other inch was given over to her arsenal. For there was no other word for it. Guns, large and small were crammed into every available inch. But not only firearms. Switch blades—a whole shoe box full of them—and throwing knives. Then a machete the size of Konstantine's arm, shoulder to wrist. Grenades. Tear gas. A flame thrower with four exchangeable tanks fit into a backpack. Full body armor that would have fit her form like a glove.

She could lay siege to a fortress. To a kingdom.

He loved her.

His desire for her rose so suddenly that its crushing throb pulsed between his legs.

He ran his finger over a throwing blade, so sharp it pricked his fingertip at the slightest touch. He sucked the blood from it until the finger went numb.

He wanted to fuck her down here. Right against this wall, her back shoved into the concrete cinder blocks. Or maybe on the floor, her astride him, his back ground into the dusty floor until her knees were rubbed raw.

He turned off the light and dragged himself up the stairs.

He half expected to find her standing at the top. Perhaps she'd slit his throat and kick him down the stairs, retrieving his desiccated corpse in a week or two, whenever the rot began to bother her.

But the apartment was quiet. Nothing moved.

He stood there, watching the moonlight on the river until the heat drained from his head and the only throbbing that remained was in his pricked finger.

There was nothing else to search. He noted the lack of personalization. No photos of family, apart from the one he'd found in her pillow. There wasn't a television or a bookcase—though he did see a small stack of paperbacks under the end table, wedged between the sofa, bed, and wall.

Apart from the central area including kitchen, living room, and bedroom, there were two doors. One on the right side of the hallway had shelves above for towels and a four-drawer dresser below.

A second door sat at the end of the short hallway.

It was a large bathroom.

A small-tiled mosaic in blues and golds stretched beneath a sink, clawfoot tub and shower stall. The tub itself looked most inviting. And Konstantine's jaunt up and down those hidden steps had left him light-headed.

A bath would help the ache in his muscles.

He bent over the porcelain rim and turned the silver faucets. Warm, but not too hot, he filled the tub. He tore the worn gauze from his body and tossed it into the trash bin in the corner, right of the sink. He noted the only piece of furniture in the room. A white cabinet sat against the far wall beneath a window only large enough for a cat to squeeze through. He opened the cabinet and found a tin box the size of a laundry basket.

It looked like a medic's kit. Something a soldier would use on the battlefield, a moving surgical unit. He suspected he was looking at the reason he was alive.

He'd clean himself up again after the bath, suspecting that now he was awake, Lou would no longer play nursemaid.

With the water close to the brim, he closed the faucets. Removing his bloodied jeans and black briefs, he eased himself into the tub, careful to hold the edge should a muscle choose this moment to give
beneath him.

The heat bit deep, working its way into his muscles with its ruthless fingers.

He grabbed a wash cloth from the shelf above the tub and soaked it in the water. He used the bar of soap, with an emblem of a bird punched into its soft skin, to lather the rag. It smelled like her. The scent was enough to send his mind careening toward desire.

A door creaked open. Konstantine didn't think it was the front door. He leaned forward in the tub in time to see the closet door shutting and a holster full of weapons, and two knives clatter to the wooden floor, where the hallway and central living area met.

Then she was standing naked before him, wet from head to toe. Her nipples were hard and goosebumps stood out along her arms and legs. Her dark hair stuck to her cheeks. Droplets dripping onto the mosaic tile at her feet.

He began to harden.

He leaned over the tub's edge to hide it. He would think of anything, *anything* to soften it. His own mother's soft brunette hair. Padre Leo coughing

blood into a white napkin.

As long as he didn't look directly at her nipples, and the gooseflesh on her thighs, he thought he'd be all right.

Her eyes. He would only look at her eyes.

But her eyes were on his crotch.

*This is it,* his mind said, ever hopeful. *She will climb into the tub, slide those beautiful milk white thighs on either side of my body and pull me inside her.*

The erection throbbed painfully.

"Do you know how many dead bodies have been in that tub?" she asked.

Then her gaze flicked away, the perfect mask of disinterest.

He burst into laughter so hard his stomach ached. "Signora. That one look could have destroyed me."

"I'll try harder next time." She shut herself into the shower, and turned on the faucet.

With her body hidden away by the frosted glass, reason returned. His mind turned to more practical concerns. He glanced at the weapons, wet, lying outside the closet door again. "Did you just emerge from your closet, naked?"

No answer.

"Is that something you do often?"

Still no reply. Instead he was forced to watch her through the frosted glass as he half-heartedly soaped his arms and legs.

*You do this to yourself.* He could get out of the tub, and go into the other room. He could…wait.

"Would you happen to have a man's clothes?" he asked her. He would put on his filthy rags again if he had to, but it didn't hurt to ask.

If she said *yes, I have a whole drawer of man's clothes* that would cure him of his erection. He was certain jealousy and blind rage would likely replace it.

The water turned off. He braced himself for her reappearance, another confrontation with her nipples and the slender tuck of dark hair between her legs.

But only a hand emerged between the glass to seize the towel from its hook. When she did emerge, her body was blessedly concealed beneath the gray cotton. Only the suggestive curves of her hips and the bare outline of breast poked through.

"You used all the hot water."

"I'm sorry."

But she didn't seem to hear him. She'd stepped out of the bathroom and reentered the closet, it's handle clicking closed behind her.

She appeared a moment later clutching a fistful of clothing in her hand. She dropped it on the floor just inside the bathroom doorway. "I don't know men's sizes."

"Thank you," he called. But she'd already closed the bathroom door, separating them the only way she could in her small studio.

A drawer opened and closed. The sounds of her dressing herself.

He stood from the bath, toweling the water from his body using a towel of the same soft gray cotton.

He pulled on the clothes. The shirt fit well, snug across his shoulders and stomach. It was the color of crushed violets. The black jeans were loose with a wad of black wool stuffed in the pocket, which Konstantine recognized as socks. The underwear, black briefs. He paused then, uncomfortable with the idea of wearing another man's underwear.

While he was certain she'd stolen these clothes from some drawer in some bedroom, and the clothes did smell like detergent…well, he supposed beggars couldn't be choosers.

The pants were a hint too long and too wide. He rolled up the bottoms once, and cinched the waist with the leather belt she'd provided. Good enough.

By the time he'd dressed himself, he'd found she'd done the same.

She stood in the living room in tight jeans that looked poured onto her thick legs, hanging low on the curve of her hips. Her shirt was white, a black tank top or sports bra showing underneath. Her wet hair had been brushed back away from her face.

"You need to leave," she said.

"If it's about the hot water—"

One glance silenced him.

"I hoped you would help me," he said, hoping that if he made his intentions clear, the thrill of the chase and kill would be enough to pique her interest.

"Of course you did," she said, rolling her eyes up to meet his. "You want your gang back."

He didn't like the word, but nodded. "I do."

She ejected a clip, checked it, reinserted it into the gun. "You have people you trust."

"Yes."

"Then you need to ask for their help."

"We could speak to them together."

Her glare could have boiled the flesh from his bones. "You're confusing me with someone else. I pulled you out of a bad situation. I let you heal up here so you wouldn't be arrested or assassinated in a hospital. That's it. We aren't friends. We aren't business partners. And we don't *talk* to people.

*Together*."

He looked away. He grabbed at the threads unravelling before him. He thought sleeping in her bed, staying in her home had changed something. But now this sudden pushback.

The watch on her wrist buzzed, its black face lighting green. She rotated the face toward her and his gaze slid down the curve of her neck, tracing its collarbones.

The visual feast was lost when she grabbed a leather jacket off the sofa arm and slipped her arms through.

"I'll drop you off wherever you want when I get back. There's food in the fridge."

Drop him. Like a body in the Arno river.

She stepped into the closet and was gone.

# 12

She lingered in the closet, heart hammering. Her face and chest were unbearably warm. What the fuck was wrong with her? Konstantine swore in Italian and then her bed groaned as a heavy body collapsed onto it. No doubt he thought he was alone.

She should've put a bullet between his eyes instead of picking him off the church floor. Why had she done it? She didn't save crime lords. She rid the world of them. *But he's different. He salvaged your father's name.*

It was true that Konstantine had supplied the evidence to clear her father's name. In exchange, Lou had carried him to his mother's unmarked grave. Waited for him to uncover her remains as the moonlight beat down on their backs and the insects sang their nightly choir.

She wondered what he'd done with her bones— as that was all that was left of her after so many years in the bare earth.

He'd given her what was left of her father. And she'd given him what remained of his mother.

They were even. She owed him nothing. So why was she fetching him clothes and food and letting him sleep in her bed?

Forget about it, she warned herself. She was about to work a job. She didn't need her mind wandering on its own. She needed to be absolutely focused or she'd get herself killed. Just like her father. But she saw Konstantine's black hair, wet and curling around his hard face, the hungry look in his green eyes.

*Fuck this.* She gave herself over to the darkness, feeling the wall at her back go soft, and the warm air replaced by a fresh breeze.

Lou's hand found purchase on the rough bark of an oak tree. A mourning dove on an electric wire cooed at her entrance. A light breeze ruffled the grass in the park, which had been recently mowed. She could see it, saw it sticking to her black boots as she settled all her weight in this time and place.

A woman sat alone on a swing twenty feet away. Her back was to Lou, dyed auburn hair falling down her back, stark against a black wool coat. The swing creaked as the woman swayed back and forth, her boots trailing through the wood chips and sand beneath her.

Plastic tubing coiled and unfurled like caterpillars, yellow and green between the swings and adjacent fence. Lou scoped the area. The chain-link fence on all sides. The quiet houses settling beyond. The cars parked on the street with empty windows. Dogs barked somewhere on her left. Maybe a block over. Then understood why when the mail truck rumbled past.

Now certain they were alone, Lou crossed the play yard. When the woman didn't look up at her approach, Lou intentionally stepped on a twig. Her black boot snapping it in half where it lay, no doubt blown down by the last storm.

The woman named Benji turned and fixed her wide brown eyes on Lou. "Shit. You scared me. You got my page?"

*Obviously*, Lou thought. But she didn't say it. She'd come to accept that people repeat the obvious all the time. In fact, it made up the majority of her conversations. And the quickest way to glean the information she wanted, was to let the babble run its course. If she pointed out what was useless, people became defensive. Or they stalled and stammered, weighing every word before uttering it until the conversation twisted in on itself like an ouroboros eating its own tail, stretching the conversation painfully toward infinity.

"You told me to page you if Jason got out of jail," she said.

*I know what I told you.* "So he's out?"

"Yeah." She worked the cell phone back and forth between her palms nervously. Its bejeweled case sparkled, casting diamond shapes across her skinny jeans. "He came to my house last night, with flowers. Said he'd changed."

Lou was struck by her long nails. Ridiculously long, at least a full inch beyond its fingertip pads, and the color of maraschino cherries. How could she do anything with those? "Do you know if he's talking to Camry again?"

"He's with him now. I saw his mom's car in the driveway on my way here. His girlfriend Teena says they went down to the beach."

Lou didn't need to know where Jason was. She only needed him out of jail. If she could put the two of them together—Jason and Camry—it would confirm Camry as the supplier. And if she plucked Miami's major supplier off the streets, well that would be a great day.

Lou glanced at the darkening horizon and realized she'd lost an hour jumping from St. Louis to Miami.

A white Cadillac rolled by blasting a Spanish pop song through its open windows. It hit the speed bump beside the park too fast and popped up comically.

"The restraining order is shit. Ain't no body gonna enforce it," Benji said. Her black makeup looked a day old, smudged around her eyes. You promised you'd get rid of him."

"I will," Lou said, feeling the Beretta shift against her ribs.

The woman loosened a breath from her chest. "I need him out of our lives."

*Our lives.* Lou had forgotten about the kid. A little girl, four or five years old. She'd seen her sleeping beneath a My Little Pony coverlet one night, as Lou had stood in the dark of her bedroom, listening to Benji and Jason scream at each other in the other room.

The girl had woken to the sound of Jason's fist connecting with her mother's stomach. Her eyes were as wide-set and brown as her mother's. But she'd gotten a thick head of curly hair from someone else. Not Jason. Maybe Benji didn't even know who the father was herself.

"Are you—" the girl began, but Lou had put a finger to her lips. The girl sat up in bed, but said nothing.

Then they'd both hovered in the dark, listening to her mother cry against the backdrop of Family Feud.

"I hate it when they fight," the little girl had said.

"They'll stop," Lou assured her, tucking her into the pony sheets.

"When?" Her eyes were black marbles in the thin light through the curtains.

"Soon," Lou had promised.

But she couldn't take credit for Jason's disappearance one week later. It was the cops that had pulled him from the little girl's life.

"He's being good now," Benji said, brushing her auburn hair back from her face. "But in a week or two, he'll be back to his old shit again."

"He'll be gone soon," Lou said, her eyes scanning the street again.

She imagined it was something her father would say. She pictured Jack Thorne, six feet of solid muscle in his full DEA SWAT gear, storming into Benji's home and arresting Jason. Slamming the scrawny man to the kitchen floor, twisting his arms up behind his back and cuffing them.

If he'd seen the little girl what would he say? *He can't hurt you now.*

Something meant to reassure her.

And there was something about her own path—how even though Jack had been removed from her world twelve years ago—somehow she ended up here. Chasing men like Camry Sanderson. Following the leads up the chain of command. Was her work so very different than her father's? He hunted with the full force of the law at his back, true. But Lou didn't need any of that.

But if he'd lived, would she be on the other side? In a vest? Part of a team?

Or was she always meant to do this her way?

She thought so. And how would Jack have felt about that? Sometimes she wondered if his death might have been a gift, a way to preserve his perfection for all of her days. If he had lived, there was the chance they would've grown apart as he'd grown apart from Lucy.

She can't imagine he would've approved of her methods.

He cleared the streets of drugs by arresting the men, obeying due process, only taking their lives if necessary. She plucked them from the earth. Judge, jury and executioner. Her father had only fired his gun a dozen time during his time on the force. She'd lost count before she was 20.

Not executioner, not always, she thought. Sometimes, Lou gave that job to Jabbers.

Is that why Konstantine wanted her? Because she was ruthless and unforgiving as he was?

She hadn't needed to see his erection to know he'd wanted her.

She'd known from the moment she'd seen his face on the deck of Ryanson's boat. The blind desire that had consumed him even as she shot down man after man around them.

It didn't matter what he wanted. It mattered what she thought of him.

And there was the rub.

Her mind couldn't reconcile Konstantine the crime boss with Konstantine the Italian boy. Or Konstantine the man who so lovingly dusted soil from his mother's moonlit bones.

Or even the Konstantine she'd stood over with a gun in her hand, weeks after killing her father's murderer. Konstantine had been bare-chested and laying on top of his sheets. Italy asleep outside the window behind her. She'd stood there and watched him, unsure for the first time in her life of what she wanted to do.

All she knew that she wanted was to hit him in his pretty mouth with her pistol.

But she hadn't.

*I understand drive. I know how hard it is to stop before a thing is done. If you need this, take it.*

But she hadn't needed to kill him. The rage that usually filled her, rolled her like a wave never came as she'd held the gun to his head. For the men walking the streets, polluting the lives of those around them. *Yes*. Without effort.

She held no hate for Konstantine.

*You came to me when you were dreaming. Did you dream of killing me?*

No. She'd dreamed of having someone who understood her like her father did. Someone as steady and immovable. Someone to replace what had been taken from her.

What sappy pathetic bullshit was that? *What the hell is wrong with me?*

Konstantine was probably asking himself the same thing. She saw his mortification when he'd bent over the side of the tub to hide his erection.

Another car rolled by the park slowly. Men hung through the open window shouting obscenities. She realized the men from the stopped car were shouting at her.

Movement in the corner of her eye drew her attention. One hung from the driver's window, his other hand on the wheel.

"Hi Mami!" he called, dragging a thick tongue over his golden grill. His voice was distorted by the bass rattling the car. "You wanna show me what's under that leather coat, baby?"

"Sure." Lou pulled the Beretta in one fluid extension of her arm and shot the car. Three clean bullet holes punched through the back fender and the red Camaro dashed forward, hitting the first speed bump so hard it popped up. A chorus of male voices howled inside, mixing with the excessive bass rattling its tinted windows. A loose hubcap spun off the back wheel. Its tires squealed as it disappeared around a corner.

"Jesus Christ!" Benji screamed, clutching her red hair in each fist. "You could've killed someone."

"Hardly." She'd clipped the very back of the car. If someone had been in the trunk, she supposed, then yes. They were dead.

But people didn't usually ride around with living people in their trunk. So she hoped the odds were with her.

Lou had the decency to reholster the gun and flash an expression that could've been mistaken for apologetic. Probably.

"I have to go. Page me if anything changes."

"But when are you going to pick him up?" Benji stood from the swing as Lou marched across the park toward the large tree. It would look like she left out the back gate.

"Soon," Lou called over her shoulder. "And you better leave now."

"Why?"

"Because those guys will come back." As soon as they pulled their frightened heads out of their asses.

She paused only long enough to make sure Benji was obediently jogging out of the park. The chain-link gate swung shut behind her, and she headed east, in the opposite direction of the cat callers.

With Benji out of sight, Lou slipped through the shade of the tree, thinking of her closet.

She hadn't wanted to wear body armor when meeting with the woman. Something about guns and ammo and looking like a warrior put women like Benji on edge. They wanted her to solve their problems, yes. Ride in on a white horse, certainly. But they wanted her to also look like a woman while she did it.

Her converted linen closet manifested around her and she placed one hand on the door, ready to push it open.

But then her bed creaked, shifting under the weight of a restless body.

Right.

For a moment she'd forgotten about Konstantine's claim on her apartment. Even though he'd nearly died and was in no shape to confront his enemy, she suddenly wanted to pitch him from her second-floor window into the pool below.

With a feeble attempt to suppress her irritation, she pressed her shoulders against the closet wall again and sighed through the darkness.

Unfinished wood materialized beneath her feet. Cold air licked up the side of her face. She reached up and pulled the string on the lightbulb suspended overhead.

A room came into focus around her. It smelled of sawdust. She'd built it herself two months ago, after her first encounter with Konstantine. She'd done a pretty good job of it, though a couple nails were crooked in places and one of the shelves slanted at an angle.

But she doubted anyone but her would notice it.

It was what sat on the shelves that would hold their attention.

She surveyed her secret stock pile. She didn't need the guns, the blades, or flamethrower for a stakeout. Grenades and tear gas were certainly overkill. She only needed some good body armor and enough firepower in case unexpected trouble arose.

She reached for her father's adjustable vest.

Despite the abuse it had taken in the last few years, it looked much like it had when she first took it from her parents' home a few days after they'd been murdered.

The vest was almost unusable. She knew that. But she couldn't bring herself to replace it.

*When will it be time to let go?* her father asked.

When a bullet punched through the worn Kevlar and stopped her heart. She wasn't sure she *could* let go before that day came.

In addition to the vest and some of her father's flannel shirts, she took his cut-resistant Kevlar sleeves which had to be resized later, but she'd found someone to do it.

The one she now slid over her black sweat-licking shirt and cut-resistant forearm guards.

Her father had worn it at the biggest size, the straps stretched fully extended. She wore it at the smallest, with the Velcro overlapping. Before she grew up and found a use for her father's vest, she would wear it on the nights she couldn't sleep. She'd put it on, tighten the straps, and crush it against her just to remember what it had felt like to have his arms around her. To be so completely engulfed in his strong arms and to feel safe.

Body armor on, cut resistant sleeves slid over each pale forearm, she checked her guns and ammo.

Good enough.

She exchanged her leather jacket for a larger Kevlar jacket preferred by bikers. Something large enough to fit over the vest.

The planks of her apartment creaked above. Konstantine was up and moving around now.

All the more reason to get going.

She pulled the string, extinguishing the lightbulb. For a moment she stood in the dark, hearing his feet gently slap the wood above. But then the dark softened, faded into the background and another piece of the world rushed up to replace it.

The smell of fish hit her first. Overpowering to the point of nausea. And then behind that, the ocean and breeze.

She emerged from the shadows and peered out. She was up high. On the second level of an enormous building, suspended on a wooden platform. It seemed as she was the only one up here, the wooden walkways bare in each direction. She peered over the railing and saw the concrete row below.

A warehouse? A man lifted enormous fish out of a wooden cart and threw them onto a conveyor belt.

She was in the fish market, not far from the beach.

The whole place reeked of fish left in the sun. Another man with sweat shining between his shoulder blades and the back of his neck sprayed a hose on the concrete floor, washing the remnants of guts toward the drain.

In another corner, Lou spotted Cam. He was the only blond in the sea of black-haired workers, most likely illegal immigrants who'd hit the Miami shore looking for a better life. Cam spoke low, but animatedly, chopping his open palm with this other hand, emphasizing some point to the man in front of him. Lou took him to be the foreman. He was in a dress shirt and loafers, not the gut-smeared work clothes of the men handling the fish.

Jason hovered a few paces back, leaning against a wooden post, aiming for casual but failing. His shifty gaze darted from Cam to the fish cart to the workers too quickly. When he uncrossed and crossed his ankles, Lou saw the silhouette of a gun.

They weren't the only ones watching.

An audience of seagulls had perched on the rafters, chattering away wildly as the man continued to hose down the fish guts. Lou suspected the gulls had infiltrated through the hole in the roof, a jagged mouth opened on blue sky in the southern corner of the building, facing the ocean. One more hurricane and surely this place would be lifted off its stilts and washed out to sea.

Oblivious to his audience, Cam stood in a tank top that reached nearly to his knees, his hairy pits flashing every time he raised his arms to point his finger at the man in front of him.

They were fighting, but Lou was too far to hear about what. She stepped into an adjacent shadow, trying to get a good look at the man, hoping that maybe this was the contact she was looking for. The next link in the chain. Or at the very least, a new lead should this one fall through.

She placed her foot on the next plank, heard the wood groan and crack.

The planks gave way under her weight, splinters tugging at her jacket as she crashed through, pulling down half the dilapidated walkway with her. She threw her arms out instinctively, trying to seize anything to stop her fall. A scrap of wood, a hanging beam. But her hands found only air.

The concrete floor rushed up to meet her.

# 13

King spread the glossy magazines on the white coverlet. He angled the magazine's shiny faces so Lucy could see what was advertised in each. Dresses. Cakes. Honeymoon vacations with bikini-clad women strolling on pristine white beaches, shielding their eyes from the sun with their hands. Marriage wasn't a billion-dollar industry for nothing. "Where do you want to start?"

With a shaking hand, she groped each magazine. Her moist fingers stuck to the pages even as she tried to push them aside. She settled on a thick catalogue advertising wedding dresses. The brunette on the cover was someone King recognized. A model for a makeup commercial or something. Or facewash. He couldn't be sure.

It was Lucy's own scent that had made him think of soap.

Someone had washed her hair for her, so she smelled of lilacs. King was betting on Naomi. And he also noticed the pillow. A large cushion with some sort of Tibetan design of spirals in rich orange, mauves, and gold.

"Where did you get that?" he asked, scratching at the beading along one seam.

Lucy paused in her flipping to follow King's gaze. "I woke up and it was here." Her eyes flicked to the foot of her bed.

"You don't know where it came from?"

"Oh, I do. It's mine. It's my meditation cushion. And there's this."

She turned and pointed at something King had missed upon entering the room with his magazines and jumbo coffee. A little wooden Buddha. Fat and happy, his hands over his head in a victorious pose. And in his upturned hands, some sort of cup, filled.

She pressed her thumb to Buddha's round belly. "Lou must've brought them from my apartment."

"That was nice of her." He said no more, but he thought plenty. *Why didn't she stay? Why didn't she tell you she loved you? Offer to sit with you for a while? Why did she have to come like a thief in the night?* He wondered if the visit was like the one she'd paid him a couple of days before. Another way to avoid whatever was going on in her apartment.

"I like this one," Lucy said. She turned the magazine so King could see. A plunging neckline in Art Deco style. A mermaid fit, or so description read. As if King knew dresses any better than he knew daytime soap operas.

"Too bad I don't have the cleavage to hold it up," she said, turning the page.

"What are you talking about!" He took the magazine and flipped back to the page, finding the dismissed dress. "It would be gorgeous on you."

He earmarked the page, creasing it between his thumb and forefinger.

She smiled. "You're sweet, Robert."

Her smile warmed him to his toes.

"What about flowers?" he asked, fishing for another magazine. "You need a bouquet."

"Do I?" she said with a laugh.

"Knowing you, you'll probably want something seasonal." If not, she might refuse flowers outright. He remembered the five-minute lecture she'd given him about commercially grown flowers the first time he'd gifted her with some red roses wrapped in cellophane.

She lay against the pillow, breathing hard as if flipping through magazines was proving too strenuous. "Sunflowers are in season. Lilies. Mums. Dah-dahlias."

"What color?" he asked, scribbling in the margins beside the mermaid dress.

"Fall colors. Red or burnt sienna. Robert—" she rasped.

The wheeze made him look up, alarm bells sounding in his head.

"You don't have to do all this. There's no point," she whispered.

"No point?"

She placed a clammy hand on his. "I know you love me. That's more than enough."

He scoffed, hoping it hid the fear welling up inside him. "I'm doing this for the rich inheritance."

She smiled, but didn't laugh. Her breath remained too high in her throat. Should he call someone?

"What flower will you pin to your suit?" she asked. "A sunflower is too large."

"I'll get a daisy or something like it. There's that yellow daisy with the black center. I've forgotten the name."

"A black-eyed Susan."

*Awful name,* he thought. "Or maybe I'll wear *only* a sunflower. Strategically placed. We can have one of those naked yoga weddings."

She laughed, but it devolved into coughing. He held the water out for her, helping her to sit up straighter.

The sight made his chest ache. The hateful voice he'd been carrying all morning rose up, volume to the max. *This is stupid. This is pointless. She's barely more than a bag of bones. She'd break the second you tried to push a ring onto her finger. This isn't what she wants.*

The voice had started as he'd walked through the French quarter that morning. From the moment he'd stopped into the corner market across from his apartment and scoured the magazine racks for *Bridal Boutique, Bridal Monthly. Brides-R-Us, The White Dress*, and every wedding magazine he could find, this relentless voice ragged him.

But it had been worth it when she took the first magazine from the pile, her shaking hand flipping open the first cover. The way she'd smiled. The strength in her voice as she patiently answered each of his questions. The laughter.

Stupid or not, she was enjoying herself. And even if the walls caved in on her tomorrow, squeezing the last breath from her chest, he wanted her to die excited about *something*.

Anything. No matter how stupid, commercial, or pointless. Anything to make these last moments the best they could be.

"This one's all about dresses," he says, seizing The White Dress from the slick pile. "Are you *sure* you want a mermaid dress?"

Red-faced but breathing, she motioned toward the slick pile. "I want to look at the cakes."

"Now we're talking."

King had purchased *two* magazines that focused on cake and food. It was true that he was thinner now than when he'd first seen her months ago, but he still loved food, as he always had. He'd lost nearly twenty pounds over the summer they spent together, walking the Tuileries Gardens, West bank and Eifel Tower together. Seeing the inside of an Egyptian pyramid by flashlight. The Parthenon and Coliseum.

She had a bucket list as well as anyone.

So they jumped naked into the Mediterranean. Kneeled in the temples of Kyoto. Dove the Great Barrier Reef on a clear day where the sea turtles and clown fish could be seen easily.

They'd worked on checking them off one by one, together. Saving tremendously on airfare and lodging. Sandwiching in as many excursions as she had the stamina for between her chemo treatments. Some days her spirit and body held up fine. Other nights, they agreed that movie and popcorn was better. But it was mostly King who had eaten the popcorn and watched the movie, while Lucy slept in the crook of his arm.

He worried that while all the walking and activity was great for him, maybe it had worn her out quicker. Would she have had more time if she'd rested? If she hadn't tried to push herself to squeeze the most out of the days she had left?

He wondered what his life might be like when she was gone…

He'd drank quite a bit before she'd came back into his life. Now, he drank no more than three drinks in one go. He wondered if it would come back—the weight and the drinking—once she was gone. *We hold so much of ourselves back for the ones we love.*

*Without her…Once she's gone…*

*Don't think of that.*

King wished he wasn't so big, so that he could lay beside her in the hospital bed, look at the magazines side by side. He would have to satisfy himself with turning the page, as she pointed out cake stands and decorations that worked well with a fall theme. A croquembouche.

"Do you think this was produced sustainably," she said, and pointed at a wooden pedestal on which a cake sat. Globs of chocolate icing decorated with orange and red leaves across three layers.

Her face pinched suddenly, and her hand tightened on the corners of the magazine.

"Are you okay?" he asked. His heart hammered in his chest, his stomach filling up with acrid bile.

She closed the magazine, eyes clamped shut. "I'm tired."

He pulled the magazine from her limp hands and gathered them up, placing in a neat pile next the wooden Buddha on the little table.

"We can pick this up another time." He shook the Styrofoam cup, rattling the ice. "Do you want more ice?"

She didn't answer.

"Lucy?"

She finally opened her eyes. They were bright with pain and fear. He pressed the call button before she even asked. Nurses entered a moment later. King stepped out of the way, clutching the cup of ice in his right hand, so they could fuss over her. Check the IV and the drugs.

Before they had to ask, he excused himself. He was too large to stand there gawking while others frantically worked. And it was just as well. The reality was his old claustrophobia had risen up to meet him. When Lucy had opened her blue eyes and revealed all her fear and pain, the walls of the hospital room had slid in closer. Four, maybe five inches. Even the ceiling seemed to press down from above. The air which had felt too cool one moment before, was suddenly hot. Way too hot. And instead of holding him up, the chair in which he sat seemed to pull him down.

He could never predict when his claustrophobia might arise. Often at night, he lay in his king-sized bed, staring at the ceiling. In those moments, he begged for sleep but the walls crept close. He would shove his pillows away. Open the French doors leading out to the covered balcony so a cool breeze could flow through his apartment. But often even the air and the moonlight weren't enough to relieve the mounting suffocation clawing at his chest and neck.

Only when he'd turned on the light did the walls of his bedroom seem to move back an inch.

Lying in the ruins of a collapsed building would do that to a man. Eleven DEA agents had gone into a building for drugs and a mob boss, and only King had come out alive. He'd been standing beneath a set of stairs when the bomb went off, bringing down the Westside brownstone they were searching. Brick after brick crashed down around him, until he was pinned under the rubble. Four days he laid in the

dark, trying to breathe, trying to stay alive.

Somehow he managed to keep breathing. He might have been pulled from the wreckage with all ten fingers and toes, but he hadn't escaped the rubble completely unscathed. His only company, the compressing darkness, was always with him now. And sometimes it liked to remind King that it was so.

King sank down into the plastic chair outside the hospital room. It was white and reminded him of an egg, whose shell had been emptied and cleaned before being placed on four metal legs.

He listened to the machines rattling in the room. To the rapid fire instructions spat between them.

He wondered if he should call Lou. Then decided against it. Two more nurses and a doctor rushed past him into Lucy's room.

The phone in his pocket buzzed. "Christ."

He fished the phone from his pocket, swearing as he worked his fingers into his coat pocket, getting seemingly stuck on corners that didn't exist.

He didn't recognize the number right away, but answered it. If he had been home, in the quiet calm of his apartment above Mel's shop, he would have let it go to voicemail. But any distraction, even a telemarketer, was welcome against the frantic commotion in the room behind him.

"King," he said.

"Robbie!" a deep vibrato greeted him. The kind of voice that rumbled up from the chest rather than from the nose or throat.

King new it instantly. "Sampson? How the hell are you?"

"I've been better, honestly. How are you?"

King tried not to listen to the hushed whispers echoing through the open door.

"I've been better too. What's going on?"

King heard the click of keys and knew that Sampson was typing something. "I heard you'd opened your own private practice. Is that true?"

"I did. But something came up and it's on hold at the moment."

*You'll have plenty of free time soon,* a hateful voice hissed. King shoved the snake beneath the water of his mind. *Enough to turn right back into the fat, alcoholic you were.*

"Just as well," Sampson went on. "In four months, I'll be leaving the force myself."

"Got retirement plans? A boat house in the Bahamas?"

The man laughed heartily. "I do love me some lime in the coconut. But no, no plans. Why, you looking for a partner? I wouldn't mind some investigative work. It's gotta be more interesting than Sudo-ku."

A nurse came out of Lucy's room, jogging right past him without a word. She cut into an adjacent room and reemerged with a box of some kind.

"You there?"

"Yeah, I'm here," King mumbled. But he was aware, if distantly, the way his mouth hung open, his eyes fixated on the nurse.

"If this is a bad time, I can call you back." Sampson's voice was so distant yet King saw him in his mind's eye. An ex-boxer like himself but they both had bellies now. Sampson as dark as he was fair. But a kinder, gentler man King had never known.

"There's nothing I can do unfortunately," King said. "So you might as well tell me why you called. Distract me."

King was certain that whatever Sampson might need, it wasn't post-retirement work.

"I called for a couple of reasons. First, you should watch your back."

"Who wants to kill me now?" King chuckled, but the sound was hollow. He was pantomiming a conversation now. He was relieved to find he could still do it when necessary.

"We don't know. But 24 of our agents have disappeared this week."

"Field agents?"

"Yeah. And some undercover. It's not unheard of for undercovers to go dark, but the ones we've confirmed missed their check-ins. We wouldn't think anything of it except—"

"—except 24 is a lot."

"In 48 hours."

King whistled. "That is mighty damn suspicious."

Sampson agreed. "We don't know if this has anything to do with Brasso's disappearance. We haven't made a connection yet."

Brasso. King knew exactly where *he* was. After a brief stint in a forced isolation in a Siberian shipping container, he'd received free one-way passage to La Loon, courtesy of Louie Thorne.

Just thinking of Brasso made King's jaw jump.

He may have saved King from the wreckage of a collapsed building, but apparently that hadn't been enough to inoculate him against betrayal. Brasso almost put a bullet in King himself—if Lou had given him the chance.

King heard a chair squeak through the line and wondered if he'd missed something Sampson had said. He tried to imagine the other man in the hustle and bustle of the St. Louis Headquarters.

The last time he'd visited that building was three months ago, with Lou in tow. They'd slipped right through the shadow of an oak tree up into Brasso's office, trying to get a sense of how deep the man's betrayal ran.

Where was Sampson in the building? In one of the cloistered offices? Or was he on the main floor, in the thick of it. An office with a closed door, he suspected, given the silence on the other end. That wouldn't have been possible if he'd been in the center of the fury that consumed the floor.

And the office itself? Sampson had been a military man and as neat as they come. No doubt all the trash was in the waste bin. The surface of the desk clear of everything but a computer and maybe a coffee cup. Behind him on a windowsill, a few pictures of his two grown kids and wife.

Doreen would've added something nice to the place. A rug. Maybe a plant.

"I want you to keep your eyes open," Sampson said, offering King solid ground again.

"I'm not a field agent anymore, Sammy," King pointed out, hoping to recover the thread of the conversation he may have dropped. "No one is going to come looking for me."

That was a damned lie. He'd done away with that illusion when his very own partner offered him a case—only with the intention of dumping his chained body in the river for the fishes to nibble on. And he hadn't cut Lou from his life, and with that one, who knew what the hell would come knocking.

"Keep your eyes and ears open," Sampson said.

"You said you called about a couple of things. What else?"

Silence stretched on the phone.

"Did I lose you?" King asked, his heart tapping out a strange rhythm. *Danger*, it said. *Danger*.

"Nothing serious," Sampson said, and King knew it for the bold faced lie that it was. "But I'd like to tell you in person. You free on Friday?"

# 14

Lou managed to get her body into an upright position before her boots hit the fish cart. Her momentum was more than the dead weight of the fish. Like a seesaw, her end went down and the fish went up. But the motion was enough to cushion the worst of her fall, absorbing her momentum. If she'd crashed through the landing a foot or so to the right or left, it would've been a different story.

She stumbled back a step with the shifting cart beneath her boots, knees shaking. Her balance was compromised. The back of her ankles hit the lip of the cart. This was enough to buck her off the other side.

She hit hard.

The unforgiving concrete floor bit her elbow. It sang, sharp pain ricocheting up the funny bone into her neck. She rolled under the conveyor belt, seeking shelter in its shadow. Before she slipped two fat tuna slapped against the floor an inch from her face. Their watery eyes wide-open, mouth parted in a pantomime of surprise. The tail slapping concrete splashed water into her face.

She recovered in the darkness of a closet. She didn't know what closet, and she didn't care as she ran her hands over her wet face. She reeked of fish. Her face. Her hands. Her clothes were wet too, no doubt from when she'd tried to break her own fall. She wiped at her cargo pants and snatched a shirt off a hanger above her to dab at her face.

She pat herself down, checking to make sure all the working parts were present and accounted for.

Only the elbow throbbed. It was a hell of a time to realize that this Kevlar jacket didn't have reinforced elbows like her leather jacket did. But the pain was tolerable. She could work with that.

Splinters in her hair and the reeking scent of fish clinging to her, she would have to push that aside. She still had her guns and her bullets. And if she was lucky, her target.

The closet door creaked open, slowly spilling light into the space. Her entrance must've been louder than she thought.

Lou pressed deeper into the darkness, and right out the other side. No doubt the closet would be searched and some tenant confused and frightened. She probably cost someone a decent night's sleep.

She was back in the fish house a moment later.

A man screamed. Too close. So close her ears rang with it. She turned just as Jason, wide-eyed reached for the gun tucked into the back of his jeans. She's appeared right beside him without meaning to. What had he been doing? Squatting in a dark corner while everyone else tried to solve the mystery of the falling woman?

Before he could get his gun up, Lou grabbed his elbow, pushing down to lock his hands at his side, making it impossible to pull the weapon at that angle. She freed her own Beretta and yanked him through the dark.

A heartbeat later, her boots hit the dirt beside her Nova Scotian paradise. It was dark.

"What—" Jason began, his wide fearful eyes sliding from her face to his.

She didn't have time to play with him, especially since he wasn't the man she wanted. She wanted Cam.

She put the Beretta under his chin, watched his eyes double in size and pulled the trigger. The silencer kept the report from ricocheting through her head, splitting her ear drums. But the sudden explosion of brains and blood was unpleasant. The smell was gamey to her, like a deer skinned and gutted, ready for processing.

His body dropped like a sack of concrete and she released his elbow. One look at the crumpled body and a cursory glance at the endless wilderness to ensure she hadn't been seen, and she was off again, squeezing herself back through the darkness.

She emerged on the upper level of the fish house. She cursed her compass and the darkness. Hadn't they learned their lesson? Were they looking for a second dramatic entrance?

The gulls certainly hadn't. Squawking, they took flight in a flurry of white and gray, causing a whirlwind of feathers and bird shit to rain down on the commotion below.

All eyes turned skyward, but the birds offered surprisingly good cover. After all, no one wanted their face pointing upward as shit and feathers rained down.

She spotted Cam immediately. He had his pistol out and pointed upward, a phone pressed to his ear. No matter who he was calling, it was likely in Lou's best interest that she end that call.

Lou had a chance to press herself into the corner of the upper loft, finding darkness again and slipping down to shadow cast by the processing machinery to his right.

What she hadn't realized was that the foreman had his back.

She registered the gun only a second before it went off. She moved, but not enough. It tore through the side of the Kevlar jacket, no doubt skimming the vest beneath. A second bullet bit into her upper arm. She didn't have time to consider if the artery there had been severed before he was taking aim again. The third bullet hit her square in the gut. It was like a fist to the stomach, knocking her back into the machine. The vest absorbed the bullet, but it hurt like hell. A big, ugly bruise would sit purple over the bone tomorrow.

She swore, fury rising in her like a pissed off snake.

Cam, startled by the chaos was raising his own gun. His face a twin expression of the defiant and frightened foreman beside him.

Lou came to depend on the fact that men rarely aimed for a woman's face, at least straightaway. But they would eventually, when enough bullets to the torso didn't seem to slow her down.

If she didn't do something, she would lose her brains all over this machine.

She seized both the foreman and Cam by their shirts and yanked them toward her. An overzealous tug that sent both men crashing into her, pulled off their feet in surprise. The three of them slammed into the side of the machine. Its metal duct popped and creaked. Lou felt the force of it ripple through her back and set fire to her wounds. She pinched her eyes shut for an instant against her burning arm. But the darkness swallowed the groan bubbling up between her lips.

As it opened its mouth and swallowed the trio, she wondered what would happen to the men if she were to let go in this infinite dark. Would they simply cease to exist? Or exist forever? Perhaps reaching for her, grabbing at her like phantoms each time she tried to pass through the in-between.

The world opened again and she hit the dirt on her hands and knees. Panting.

Lou was losing blood from the arm. The Kevlar was sticking to her skin. But she couldn't tell if it was a superficial blood loss, or if the artery had indeed been sliced. One was a flesh wound. The other could end her life.

With two men against her, she couldn't stop to remove the jacket and inspect the wound. She could only hazard a guess. She was losing blood and her arm was going numb. Neither sign was good.

She couldn't keep both men alive—and herself.

The first thing she did was take Jason's gun from the dewy grass three inches from his hand and put two bullets in the back of the foreman's head before he could recover from the slip. The shock of the sudden night and calm pool stretching out before him had been distraction enough. He hadn't even seen the bullet coming.

He fell beside Jason, another heap of gore.

Cam still had his gun.

"Fucking shit!" His mind was obviously divided. It didn't look like he could decide if it was better to stare at the two bodies on the ground between them, or to keep his gaze trained on Lou. A third factor snatched at his mind too—the sudden and bewildering change in scenery always baffled her prey.

Lou trained her Beretta on the man. He took a step back, the heel of his combat boots catching on Jason's limp, outstretched hand. He stumbled and fell. His ass hit the cold, hard ground.

It reminded her instantly of Castle, one of Konstantine's mules who she'd brought to a similar lake.

But this man wasn't the squabbling, squealer that Castle had been. He was ready for her. At last, Cam seemed to realize he had a gun too and lifted it, pointing the gun's black eye right between her own.

She slipped through the shadows and reappeared behind him under the cover of the giant oak. A swift kick to the back pitched him forward onto his hands and knees. His face inches from the two bodies. She went to pull the other gun with her left hand and find she couldn't. It was cold and limp at her side.

Bad news.

Cam vomited onto the bodies. A pile of brains inches from your face will do that. She let his stomach run its course, taking the precious moment to run her own inventory. Darkness crowded in on the corners of her vision and the cold in her arm was spreading toward her chest.

She'd better make this quick. She pressed her gun to the back of Cam's head.

"Who do you deal to?" she said. Her voice was as cold and flat as ever.

"Fuck you."

She pressed the barrel of the gun to his right shoulder, wedging it between the shoulder blade and spine. She pulled the trigger.

The bullet blasted through the shoulder muscle, beneath the clavicle and hit the foreman's skull cap on the other side. Something was spit into the water.

Bone fragments possibly. Or a chunk of brain.

Cam howled.

He rolled sideways, instead of on top of the bodies. The bullets weren't a particularly large caliber. She suspected she could get as many as five in him before the cause was lost. Especially if she stuck to the outer fringe of the extremities. Fingers. Toes. The meat of the upper arm and thigh, assuming she didn't hit any arteries. He wouldn't talk if he bled out.

Lou spoke over the howling and cursing. "Your shipments come through Miami's ports. You process them and hand them over to *who*?"

"Fuck you!"

Lou's teeth began to chatter. She clenched her teeth to stop it which only caused her whole jaw to tremble. She shot Cam both in the right arm and the right foot. "It'll be three bullets next t-time."

Embarrassed by the chattering teeth, she pressed the barrel to the side of his face.

"This one will be in your cheek."

"Fallon!" he screamed. "Bruno Fallon."

"W-who else?" Because she knew he had two distributors that took in the Miami port shipments.

"What the—"

She shot the gun into the air and he bleated like

a sheep.

"Paulie Kraninski! Bruno Fallon and Paulie Kraninski."

"Where d-do they send it?" A tremble in her left arm joined the tremble in her jaw. She lowered the gun. She hoped he thought her lenient rather than suspect the truth. She couldn't hold up the gun anymore. All feeling had gone out of that side of her body.

*Hurry Lou-blue,* her father warned. *You'll black out in two minutes. Three tops. Get somewhere safe.*

"Kran sends his shit up through Atlanta. And Fallon through Dallas."

"Thank you," she whispered.

And then shot him through the head.

"Thank you?" she murmured to herself. She laughed, a bewildered, off-kilter sound.

It was hard to drag the men into the water with one hand. And she didn't want to make multiple trips. So there was a stupidly comic moment when she had three men in the water, but was trying to get a hold of each while they slid beneath the surface.

But she managed to pull them beneath the nighttime waters and find blood-red water rushing in.

When she broke the surface of Blood Lake, Lou

found she couldn't hold all three men. She released two of the water-soaked corpses and lifeguard dragged the third toward the shore.

Dragging a wet corpse was even harder than dragging a dry one.

She didn't even have the corpse out of the water when the leaves rustled. Something thrashed through the thick jungle foliage on her right. It would be here in seconds.

She dropped the body, which turned out to be Jason's, onto the soggy shore and surveyed the nightmare landscape.

The two moons hung in the purple sky and apart from the ripples she'd created swimming to shore, Blood Lake was still in the quiet evening.

Of course, it was always a quiet evening in La Loon. Every time Lou had visited this strange place, the sky was the same color, the moons hanging in the same position. She had no idea if some version of the sun rose and set on this place. She often wondered if this part of Jabbers' world was like Alaska. For months at a time, everything traveled the sky in the exact same arc.

The beast emerged through the trees liquid fast. Her lithe, black body contracting and expanding, like an enormous cottonmouth snake. But she was no snake. Not with her body as big as an elephant's, her six legs, and taloned feet. Nor with the terrifying mouth that opened and released a blood-curdling screech. The air vibrated with its assault.

Jabbers darted forward, and once upon a time Lou would have pulled her knife or her gun then, anything to remind the creature that she wasn't prey. The mangled scar tissue on her shoulder showed just how indiscriminate the beast was when it came to fresh meat.

But Jabbers only bounded past her, playfully pouncing on Jason's limp body the way a fox pounces outside a rabbit hole.

Dizziness overtook Lou. The world tilted and she went down, her knees hitting the soggy earth at the water's edge. Her hands hit the mud.

She wasn't sure if it was the exertion of dragging the men, or if the seeping bullet wound itself—*I must've hit the artery after all*—but now she understood she'd overdone it.

Bloody water lapping at her backside and hips. She struggled to breathe.

A large black head rubbed against the side of her face. It struck Lou as very cat-like gesture. The way felines will rub their heads against a leg.

Another nudge, harder this time and then the

sound of sniffing. Nostrils as large as a dragon's, inhaling the scent of Lou's bloody arm. A tongue the color of vanilla ice cream licked the wound, blood smearing across its surface like strawberry syrup.

In this way, apart from the deceiving black fabric she wore, Lou realized just how much blood she was losing. And how incredibly appealing a fresh kill must be compared to the soggy corpse several feet down the bank.

She'd been stupid to lower her guard. Stupid to think that her own bleeding body on the shore wasn't enough to tempt the beast. She should pull her gun. She could protect herself but her limbs were so heavy and darkness crowded in on the edges of her vision.

And the beast was fast.

Another hard nudge and Lou hit the water with her back, sinking. Blood red water overtook her.

And then she was through the other side. Breaking through the starlit waters a galaxy away.

She dragged herself to shore, feeling the breath tighten in her chest as if a belt were being pulled tight against it. She couldn't seem to get enough air into her lungs. Or blood into the heart.

What just happened?

Had the beast really shoved her back into the water? And she hadn't crawled in after her. Hadn't gobbled her up like a wonton in some sweet and sour soup.

If not to eat her, why?

She couldn't follow this train of thought very far. Her mind blurred at the edges and her arms shook violently as she hauled her torso onto the blood-soaked grass where bits of brain and remnants of skull dried in the lakeside grass.

She'd have to clean that later. If there was a later.

There was only the briefest experience of grass. Of cold earth and the scent of dirt. But it was quickly replaced by wooden walls and a hard, flat stone against Lou's back.

No, not stone. Wood. A wooden wall, wooden bench. A closet? What kind of closet has a bench?

All she could do was sit in the dark, breathing. She wondered if she would die like this. Would someone open a closet and find her rotting corpse. She hoped it wasn't a child.

"You may begin whenever you are ready," a man said.

Lou caught the scent of his aftershave.

"Begin what?" she croaked. It was hard to speak. She realized straight ahead was a curtain, not a wall like the panels surrounding her. But the box itself was too dark to make out more. Except there was a voice coming through a small hatchwork window, the pattern too intricate to reveal who was on the other

side.

"Is this your first time?"

"My first?"

"It isn't a problem. You simply begin by saying 'forgive me father, for I have sinned. And then tell me what you did wrong."

"There's no such thing as sin," Lou said into the dark, her eyes fluttering closed.

The man laughed. "There is no evil in your world?"

"More than average, I think."

"If you have nothing to confess—"

"Confess," she whispered, her voice rasping. Then she realized where she was. Her mother Courtney had been an ex-Catholic. And while Lou had only gone to the stone church in their hometown on Christmas and Easter, she knew about confession.

She asked the compass for somewhere safe. Somewhere quiet. And this is where it brought her. Like the universe was offering her a chance to ask forgiveness before she departed this world.

She smiled, laying her head back against the unforgiving wood.

The priest misinterpreted her swelling silence.

"Sometimes it is difficult to know where to begin. Maybe we simply feel that something is wrong or—"

"I know what's wrong," she managed. All feeling left her hand and the gun slipped from her fingers and clattered to the floor of the confessional. "I'm bleeding to death."

"What?" The priest's alarm was instant.

But Lou couldn't worry about that now. Her body was so cold that she couldn't move her fingers or her arms. Nor could she break her fall as she pitched forward, careening through the curtain.

# 15

Nico entered the large warehouse, his bootsteps reverberating up to the high ceilings. His men, because who was left was *his* now, stood against the walls, out of the way of center floor.

Eight men sat on their knees with black sacks over their heads, their hands tied behind their backs sat center stage. Nico had learned this technique from his captors in Russia. In the work camp, they used all manner of intimidation to lord over the men kept there. They stripped them naked, whipped them, starved them, blocked out their vision with blindfolds. Restrained them with ropes or suspended them in the air. It might seem counter intuitive, but Nico understood there was something especially cruel about blindfolding.

The darkness heightened the fear.

It was warfare of the mind. No one could torture a man like the mind itself could. And the blindfold was only the first step in unleashing that tethered mind. Without the outer world to distract it, the mind turned on itself.

So he was not surprised that two of the eight men were openly weeping as they sat on their knees, head hung.

Only three were perfectly still, listening and waiting as their training had instructed. The other three were near hyperventilation. The sacks over their faces compressed and expanded with each panicked breath. Nico wouldn't let them suffer for long.

He crossed the large space to the man standing in its center. A camera tripod set up before him. This man, Jonathan, wasn't one of the ones that Nico trusted implicitly. There were several such men, hanging around in the dark of this warehouse two kilometers outside of Florence, further down the bend in the Arno than Ponte Vecchio.

Nico had killed those who were openly loyal to Martinelli's bastard. He'd put a bullet between every pair of eyes. But the silence was contagious. Quickly, they'd stopped fighting him and fell in line. That was how it should be. But Nico was certain that was for the sake of their own lives or families, and not out of any true loyalty to Nico.

If he was lucky, Konstantine was dead now.

Bled to death in the arms of the bitch who tried to save him. Nico had pumped enough bullets in his guts to have done the job. And if not, that knife in the back should've done the job. But Nico had lived in the labor camps a long time. He understood that some men were simply harder to kill. And he was open to the possibility that Konstantine was such a man. And perhaps also the bitch.

If they lived, and if Konstantine intended to return with his dog to reclaim the Ravengers, he had a plan for that too.

"When are we going live?" Nico asked the cameraman. He repressed the urge to put his thumb to his mouth and chew on the meat of it. It was a habit from childhood and one that had always risen with his nervousness. But this was no time to show weakness.

All eyes followed him around the room, assessing him. After all, if one mutiny could be pulled off, so could another. If any heart in this warehouse had such ambitions, Nico's assault might be encouraging rather than a deterrent.

The man paused drawing on this thick cigar. "Six minutes before the broadcast is up and running."

"And you're going to seize their stations. I want

this live."

The cameraman only nodded, silver smoke pouring out of his nostrils the way smoke pours from the mouth of a dragon.

"Everyone into position!" he shouted over the soft conversation that had steadily grown with his back turned. Eight men from the wall crossed the concrete floor and came to stand behind the black-sacked captives.

"Four minutes," the cameraman murmured, fidgeting with the black machine on top of his tripod.

"Ready?" Nico shouted again and the men standing behind the kneelers lifted their blades, showing that they were in fact in position and ready. No doubt the men kneeling expected a bullet between the eyes. A quick executioner death given the positions in which they were forced. But Nico had a flair for the dramatic. And he wanted his message to the agencies that would hunt them to be very clear.

If this move didn't rid him of his enemies, and convert the rest to allies, he wasn't sure what would.

"Ninety seconds."

The man removed the lens cap from the machine and adjusted it. Once satisfied with the camera's setup, he plugged a small microphone into the side of the machine before passing it over to Nico.

"More light, please!" he called up to the rafters.

And until that moment, Nico had forgotten about the men up there, working the spotlights that set their little stage.

Bright light filtered down on the kneeling men. It looked like a Broadway play ready to begin.

"Very good," the cameraman said. He adjusted the lens one more time. "Sixty seconds."

He pulled the cigar from his mouth, and wiping its burning end across the bottom of his boot, left a smear of grey ash in its tread. He tucked the fat roll behind his large ear and leaned down into the camera.

Waiting.

Nico tried to still the hammering of his heart. Nico struggled to tell the difference between fear and excitement, but he suspected this one was the latter. He needed only make sure it was not mistaken in his voice.

"Ten, nine, eight, seven…"

The cameraman held up his hand, showing all five fingers. Then four, then three…

The men at the corners of the room froze.

Then the cameraman was holding up only a fist, which he lowered, and Nico understood it was now his time to speak into the microphone poised before his dry lips.

"For years, the Americans have waged war against us. They call it the War on Drugs. But we know better. This is the war on poverty. The war against those who dare to rise above their circumstances. Those who want to feed their families, warm their homes, send their children to good schools. The system abandoned them, so they created a new system—and were punished for it. You blame drugs for destroying families, destroying lives. But it is your own greed. Your own unwillingness to invest in the people around you…That is what is destroying the world."

Nico wet his lips, took a breath. He motioned for the men to remove the black sacks from the kneeling man's heads.

"You send your dogs after us. But we are not afraid."

Nico waved his hand, the signal. And eight pale throats were stretched like sheets before the knives slid across them. A red mouth split open on each, blood bubbling up and over. The men squawked like chickens in the hen house.

"We will tolerate your tyranny no longer." Nico put his mouth close to the microphone. He spoke in the clearest English he could, enunciating each word carefully. "I am Paolo Konstantine. You will hear from me again, very soon."

# 16

King sat on the balcony overlooking Royal Street. The ferns lining his patio waved in a gentle breeze. The sweat on the back of his neck chilled and offered some relief from the heat of the day. A trash truck beeped as it backed up toward the alley to seize a dumpster there.

He'd tried working inside, preferring the air conditioning and overhead fans to the mugginess of the day. But the walls wouldn't let up. The heat spiked. It was like trying to breathe with a blanket over his face. Opening the balcony doors to let in the breeze hadn't been enough to loosen the crushing hold the walls had on his heart yet. He understood it wasn't really the heat of the day wearing him down.

Every time he thought of Lucy, of the scare they'd had the morning before, it felt as if a fist squeezed his heart. He'd managed to linger in the hospital for hours, a parade of nurses and four different doctors, six trips from the room to perform this or that test. All of it had yielded only a "stable" condition.

The doctor told him vaguely about spiking compounds in the blood and stresses to her heart. Nothing which really meant anything to King except, of course, the three things he already knew.

One: Lucy was dying.

Two: They were running out of time.

Three: There wasn't a damn thing he could do about it.

He carried this heavy reality with him as he moved his work space out onto the balcony. The sunlight, the people, the elevation, and open space, all of it helped. A little.

At least he'd salvaged most of the afternoon. He'd removed six more marks against Lou from the databases he'd swept. Three that were her handiwork without question, known drug mules plucked from a park in New York, a subway stop in Boston, and outside a corner store in Detroit. And three that *might* have been Lou. He worried he was abusing his privilege. Was keeping his friend's daughter safe—Lucy's niece—away from the public eye really enough reason to destroy evidence? It wasn't evidence of a crime *exactly*. A couple keystrokes here and a video deleted there. Any threads that could lead back to her if someone decided to start digging.

And what if someone caught on to what he was doing? The dummy IP addresses he used to crack the system would defer suspicion only to a certain extent. If anyone was remotely as skilled as he was—and he wasn't even top shelf talent—they could find him easy enough. Then what?

*You know what*, he thought. Lou would put a bullet in the unfortunate soul and call it a day.

Sneakers on his kitchen floor caught his ear.

"Okay," Piper called out. She walked out onto the balcony with a glass pitcher of Mel's sweet tea in her right fist and two glasses stacked on one another in the other. "Two glasses of sweet tea as requested."

She put the pitcher on the outdoor table and flipped the glasses over. She poured them each a tall glass, making sure one of the lemon wedges slopped out into King's glass.

"Thanks, kid," he said, squinting at her through the sunshine.

"It's the least I could do. Thanks for covering for me earlier." Piper gave him a sheepish grin. "Mel would've killed me."

King had opened the storeroom, looking for the register tape Mel had asked for and had come upon Piper in the passionate embrace of another girl. The one had a high, sideways ponytail of black curls spilling down over one shoulder.

The girl was ready to laugh. King saw the embarrassed grin and barely repressed giggles threatening to erupt from her. Piper must've seen it too, because she'd clamped one hand over the girl's mouth. King could only stare at Piper's ruddy red nose and swollen lips for a moment, before reaching over and plucking a white roll of register tape off the storeroom shelf.

He'd closed the door without saying a word, replacing the tape while Mel continued giving her tarot reading behind the velvet curtain, none the wiser.

"I doubt she would've killed you," King said, taking a deep drink of the tea. Ice clinked against his front teeth until he pulled his upper lip down to shield them. "A lecture maybe."

"She hates it when I use the stockroom as a make-out closet."

King barked a laugh. "I didn't realize this was a common occurrence."

"Only if there's no one in the store." Piper gave a sheepish grin.

"Mel will appreciate that you put the customers first." He balanced the cool glass against his knee.

Piper didn't seem to hear. At least, she'd already turned to her laptop in front of her, a large archaic machine that probably cost her no more than a couple hundred bucks from a local pawn shop. The laptop's fan sounded as if it were about to take off, simply lift the laptop off the table and fly it away over the Quarter's streets.

"So what am I looking up first?" Piper asked.

King had been covering Mel's expenses by giving Piper grunt work through the summer and into the fall. Most of it was reading news stories for suspicious activity. Anything on the drug trade or border control. Politicians suspected of any connections. Missing persons. But that was before he realized he could crack the DEA's and FBI's private servers.

Piper took a deep drink of her tea, crunching ice between her teeth. "Come on. What has our girl gotten into lately?"

King snorted. *Our girl.*

"I want you to find out who carries mermaid wedding dresses in town. Probably a size six or eight. He pulled the magazine that Lucy had flipped through from his bag at his feet and handed it over to Piper, opening it up to the dog-eared page.

"You're going to marry her!" Piper exclaimed, taking the magazine. It fell open across the keyboard of her laptop, right to the earmarked dress page.

"If she'll have me," King said.

Piper's face screwed up. "You're going to marry, *Lou*?"

"No!" King shouted, perhaps too forcefully. "I'm talking about Lucy."

Piper put a hand over her heart, her silver rings catching the sunlight. Prismatic light danced on the tabletop. "Whew. My goddess. Okay. Right."

King wasn't sure how to take this. Did Piper think he was too old for Lou? He would've agreed with her there. But any other disqualification would've hurt.

"Would you be sad if Lou got married?" King asked, teasing her.

"Uh, yeah. You know she's my dream girl."

"You seemed to be doing just fine in the storeroom earlier."

"Vanessa? Oh, we're friends."

King snorted, the sound of it echoing in his tea glass. "I'd hate to see how you treat your enemies."

King wouldn't ask the wildly inappropriate question *how many women have you slept with Piper?* He tried to do the math in his head. How many women had he seen around the shop this year alone? A dozen at least, since January. And he'd seen her in Jackson Square a few times, kissing one girl or another in passing, as he left Café du Monde with his sack of beignets and coffee.

Had she really slept with them all?

"You have a lot of friends," King said, cautiously, as Piper continued to clack away at the keyboard, scribbling names of dress shops in town on the top of the yellow legal pad he'd given her. The black ink pressed hard into the page.

Piper shrugged. "I'm good company."

That could mean any of a hundred things, he supposed. And he had seen a core group of the girls over and over again. Return customers were usually pleased customers.

Customers.

"Do they pay you?" he asked.

Piper's mouth fell open. "Hey! Just because I'm capitalizing on my youth and good looks doesn't mean I'm a prostitute, man. Geez."

"I'm sorry. It's none of my business."

"Damn right. And what have you got against prostitutes? Whatever a woman wants to do with her body is her business."

"Of course it is," he said, offering no protest.

And feeling like he'd just stepped in a massive pile of dog shit, added, "And I like prostitutes."

Piper's eyebrows shot up. "TMI, man."

"They are great sources of information."

She pulled out her cell phone and started dialing the first number on her list. King could hear the ringing across the table.

"Hi, yeah. Can you tell me if you carry any mermaids? What color?" Piper's lips turned down. She looked at King and then seemed to think better of it. "Uh…one sec."

She frowned at the dress in the magazine. She squinted at the fine print below the model, describing the dress. "Uh, cream maybe. Yeah, no. Not white. What sizes are available?"

Piper leaned back in her chair, waiting for the woman to check the colors they had available.

"What are you supposed to be doing?" she asked him, turning the cell phone up so that the mouthpiece was pointed toward the sky over her head.

He was supposed to be scanning the databases for more evidence of Lou's hunt. "I don't know. I can't focus today."

Piper looked ready to say something but she pivoted the phone over her mouth again and began to speak to the shopkeeper again. "Yep. Ready." She grabbed the pen, scrawling notes. "Awesome. How much?" Her eyes bulged, and she whistled. "And the other two?"

More scribbling.

He watched her write and wondered if he was a fool. Of course he was. What use did dresses and flowers and all that have now? Lucy might not even see the end of the week. And she was bone tired and in so much pain. Why would King drag her from her bed, put her in a dress and make her play some part? This was his own desperation shining through, as if marrying her will tie her to this world—and to him.

But she'd been so happy looking through the magazines, talking about cake. It had been the brightest he'd seen her eyes in weeks. Maybe clinging to the hope this would make her happy did make him a fool. But frankly, he didn't know what else to do with himself between now and visiting hours.

King turned on his own laptop.

"Yeah, thanks for your time." Piper terminated the call and started dialing the second number on her list.

When she finished, he'd have her start on the flowers. He would do the cake and food himself. He wondered if Café du Monde could do a croquembouche out of beignets. A small one. What else…

A photographer?

His dark screen finally lit with his welcome page. A search engine that compiled the daily news. He was halfway through typing *New Orleans Wedding Photographers* when the banner changed to the bright red *Breaking News!*

He clicked it without thinking and saw a face he recognized.

Paolo Konstantine. Martinelli's bastard son stared back at him from the screen.

A polished news anchor with swept blond hair speaks to the camera. King expands the video with a double click of his mouse. "Authorities say they have identified the man responsible for the on-camera slaughter of eight federal agents. While the man's face is never seen on camera…"

King sat back in his chair, watching the blonde rewrite a story worthy of the news. Sensationalism at its best. But now that he's seen it, he couldn't take it back. He googled Konstantine, and found that the man's face was the leading story on over twenty online news sites, with more and more updates pouring in. *Trending* with an upward arrow appeared by his name.

And he thought Lou had problems before…

"Did you hear what I said?" Piper asked, tapping her pen against the legal pad.

King reluctantly pulled himself from his thoughts. "Sorry."

"I said I've got over twenty dresses here. Should I stop now or call the other three shops?"

"Twenty is plenty," he said. He fished his wallet out of his back pocket and offered Piper the plastic card. "Why don't you take one of your lady friends dress shopping. Pick one about Lucy's size and shape."

"The dress?"

"The girl," he said.

"Nah," Piper said, plucking the plastic from between his fingers. "I can't take someone wedding dress shopping. It sends the wrong message."

"How will you know how they fit?"

Piper tore the dress from the magazine and folded it into eighths before slipping it into her own Teenage Turtle wallet with King's credit card. "I'll try it on myself."

"Try to keep it under $2500. And if in doubt, get it a little larger rather than smaller. We can always tailor it down, not the other way around," he said, as Piper saluted and started down the fire escape on the side of the balcony. He had no idea why she liked to climb up and down that thing so much. King's back and shoulders ached just looking at it.

He returned his interest to the computer screen and Konstantine's face. A myriad of portraits from every conceivable angle. The internet darling, a forward facing death glare.

King wondered if his efforts to protect Lou might prove pointless after all.

There were some things you couldn't prepare for.

# 17

Lou's eyes flew open. She sat up in bed. Bed. Lou turned toward the skyline and saw it was night. The pool shone two stories below, its spotlights ominous in the dark. The sparkling water seeming to beckon unwary swimmers into its depth. Someone had replaced the petunias with mums in patio planters and cut back the creeping morning glory entwined with the No Lifeguard On Duty sign.

Stretching out beyond the pool and its walled garden was the St. Louis skyline. The arch cut the sky with a delicate whoosh. Lights shimmered like candles from distant windows.

Ice clinked in a glass.

She turned and saw Konstantine sitting on her sofa. His arm draped lazily across the back of it, a chilled glass of water perched on top of his thigh.

He watched her with a guarded expression. "Dare I ask what happened to you?"

Memories bobbed up from the inky depths of her mind. Benji on a park swing. A wooden walkway collapsing beneath her. The scream of gulls. Cam on his knees in front of her, hate screwing up his snarling face.

"I'm not sure," she said. And she wasn't. She didn't have the whole story anyway. She vaguely recalled the melodious voice of a priest in the confession box. And all her strength leaving her at once. But then what?

"You appeared here about four hours ago," he said, those liquid eyes remaining unreadable. "Were you in a hospital?"

She frowned. "Hospital?"

He pointed at her. No. At the wrist resting on her coverlet. Encircling the small, bird-like bones was a white hospital bracelet. *Boston University Hospital.* The new bracelet wasn't the only change. Her Kevlar jacket, father's vest, and every gun were gone. Even her underwear. She had only the scrubs, the hospital bracelet and the gauze covering her upper left arm.

"Fuck," she swore. "Did I look like this when I showed up?"

"I haven't touched you. You appeared in the bed, as you are now. If I hadn't been sitting here, I would have thought you'd come home and put yourself to bed."

She noted the novel open and face down on the sofa cushion beside him. He was more than halfway through. Of course, she had no television, laptop or radio in the apartment. What else could he do with his time except perhaps plot his revenge against Nico.

"The priest must've called 911," she muttered, throwing back the cover and placing her feet on the cool wooden floor.

His face at last revealed emotion. His right eyebrow hiking itself up onto his forehead. "You were with a priest?"

"I must've slipped back after the surgery," she added. She clearly wore enough gauze to suggest medical intervention. And she doubted she slipped away while on an operating table. All the bright lights shining down on her would have made it impossible. But the moment they took her back to her room to rest? Turned down the lights and adjusted the IVs? No doubt.

And at least they hadn't known who she was. *Jane Doe* was printed in place of where a name should be on the bracelet.

She stood, and a wave of dizziness seized her. She swayed on her feet.

And then he was there. His arms under hers.

"Where are you trying to go?" he asked. The heat from his breath was on her face.

"I need my vest," she said. She hoped the priest had had the good sense to remove most of the armor before the paramedics arrived. He would've had to if he'd tried to staunch the wound until help arrived.

"It will have to wait."

"My father's vest—"

"You won't ever wear it again if you're dead," he said.

She froze against him. Her limbs were like sacks of wet sand. Absolutely useless. It was the relentless gravity of the room that wouldn't let go of her.

"You're bleeding," he said softly into her hair. She realized how rigid his body was against hers. And the breath between his lips was thin and strained.

He smelled like her soap.

She pulled away from him under the pretense of inspecting her arm. She stood there in the center of the apartment, her back to him. She lifted the scrub sleeve to inspect the wound, but found only gauze soaked through with bright red blood. "This is why I can't wear white."

He laughed. A short chuckle in his throat. "I

can't imagine it's your color."

She frowned. "I love white t-shirts."

She wanted to say more. About how clean a white t-shirt felt. More than that. It had also been her father's favorite. He seemed to have only two outfits in her memory. The black t-shirt beneath his adjustable vest. Black cargo pants and boots. Or a white t-shirt and jeans, which he wore on the weekends when he helped her mother around the house. Cutting the lawn. Pulling weeds. Repairing a fence.

She squeezed her eyes shut against the memory of him.

Since the truth had come out in June, and the story of Brasso's betrayal splashed every paper and magazine for a week at least, it had been easier to think of him. A cold stone settled in the pit of her stomach the night he died, and it hadn't loosened for the fourteen years that followed. Until the world knew again what she'd always known. Jack Thorne was a good man who didn't deserve what happened to him. The truth brought her peace.

But sometimes, when she wasn't expecting it— like this very moment—a memory would emerge, bright and beautiful and it would suck all the air from her body.

Those moments were hard and she suspected that as long as she lived, she would have them.

She preferred this to the alternative—to forgetting the face of her father.

She often stared at the photo of her father, now safely hidden between the kitchen utensil tray, and retraced the lines of his face. His strong jaw with the scar in the chin that Lucy said came from a motorbike accident when he was fifteen.

*He hit a stump and went clear over the handlebars!*

Those bushy brows and scruffy cheeks. She'd gladly give up an hour to this practice of remembering, if it meant he wouldn't become a shadowy figure in her mind.

Lou pushed back thoughts of her father and turned her attention again to the gauze on her skin. It was easy to remove once she worked her nail beneath. It was too soaked through to adhere to her skin properly. No matter. She'd use her own kit to replace it. She'd obviously popped a stitch or something.

She turned toward the window to get a better look at the wound in the light.

Konstantine whistled.

She understood why.

Her arm was black and blue and swollen from shoulder to elbow.

The bullet hadn't nicked the artery as she'd feared but had split the flesh in her upper arm completely, no doubt giving the look of a hotdog that had been sliced down the center, exposing the vulnerable inner meat within. They would've had to use a few internal sutures to close the gaping wound. Those would dissolve out of sight without her ever seeing them. But the tight sutures snaking across the surface of her bicep were seeping blood.

Crimson bubbled up between the black nylon and she could see that one stitch in the middle had popped and frayed. Its snapped end sticking up from the puckered flesh. What had she done to snap it, she had no idea. Lay on it maybe, add too much pressure to the arm. It would have had to be a significant force.

She understood why she'd bled so much now. This was a nasty flesh wound that would scar horribly.

"You need to rest your arm," Konstantine said, interrupting her assessment. "Do you have a sling?"

She leveled a cold stare at his face.

He held his hands up in surrender. "I'm not a doctor."

"If you want to play doctor, get my kit," she said. It wasn't until these words were out of her mouth that she realized their implication. If Konstantine had taken them perversely, she didn't know because he'd already walked out of the room, his back to her as he walked down the hall.

He appeared carrying her large box of medical supplies.

She sat on the edge of the bed, elbows resting on her knees as he placed the kit beside her right leg.

He popped off the lid, revealing the topmost tray of silver tools, packets of medicinal cream and bandages.

She pointed at what she needed. "Those pliers, the peroxide and the gauze."

He fished each item out with deft fingers. She noted the bruises on the back of his hands had faded from the purple to yellow.

She handed him the old bloody gauze and took the peroxide. "There's old towels under the second tray."

He handed her a faded green scrap of cloth, which she pressed against her arm, just under the wound. It was hard to clean up this particular part of her arm. It wasn't on her dominant side, which helped. But it seemed impossible to hold the cloth under the wound and pour the peroxide at the same time.

"I'll do it," he said and he already had the white cap off the brown bottle and was kneeling over her.

Cold liquid hit the wound and burned like hell. The fizz and pop of the solution pricked her ears. But she'd felt worse. The burn was little more than irritating and she knew to save her real annoyance for what was to come.

"There's a lighter in the second tray. Top left."

He hesitated, but only until she gave him another cold stare. Then he was handing over the orange lighter.

"I want you to pinch the two snapped lines together long enough for me to light them."

He didn't move.

"If you pinch the nylon together so that some of it sits above the pliers, I can melt it back together. This will prevent it from pulling at the wound. Grab the pliers too."

She watched him rummage through the trays. The light from the window fell across his neck and jaw. She realized she was staring and turned away.

The wound was ugly.

"Here, pinch them together."

He hesitated.

"You'll have to come closer than that," she said,

calmly. Her voice was utterly emotionless. And it remained so even as he had to scoot forward, placing himself between her legs.

She swallowed. "I'll squeeze the wound together and you clamp the wires."

"Okay," he said, licking his lips.

She added the slightest pressure to either side of the wound where the nylon had snapped, and the wound gaped open.

When the wires were overlapping, he clamped them together. His eyes were very green in the light and fixed in concentration on her arm. She caught herself staring at his full mouth, the scruff around his lips. She wanted to rake her fingernails over it. Maybe bite his lower lip hard enough to make it bleed.

Instead she said, "Hold it. Twist the ends together if you can."

He did as she struck the metal on the lighter with her thumb until the orange-yellow frame sprung up.

She lit the ends and watched them evaporate in a puff of smoke.

When he removed the pliers, the black nylon lay fused over her skin once more. But when she bent to pick up the towel from the floor beside her left foot, she heard the slight *pop* and saw a fresh trickle of blood spring down her left forearm, rolling along the crease in her arm. The wound looked like a bloody mouth, opening to speak.

"Or not," she said. Damn. She had no choice but to restitch it.

She sighed and motioned for the box. He leaned over her right leg, his abdomen pressing into her thigh. It sent a deep clenching thrill up the inside of her leg, centering below her navel.

"Skaggs black?" he asked. And he turned toward her, making her glaringly aware of how close their faces were. And she knew he knew it too. Despite his calm mask and uninterested expression, she could see the pulse jumping in his throat.

"That will do," she said, hoping her own throat wasn't betraying her. And if it was, so what of it?

I could fuck him, she thought. She wanted to. But here, in her own apartment in her own bed, with someone who knew her name and her history…

It was a sobering effect, the light that removed all shadows. The desire died away almost instantly.

Her back straightened as she accepted the little paper packet.

She tore open the white packet and tapped its contents out onto the back of her scrubs, using the top of her right thigh as a sort of table. A curved needle was already attached to the black nylon. And the string was coated in antimicrobial agents, or so said the packaging. So no need to worry about using the peroxide again.

"Do you need anesthesia or—" he began.

She inserted the needle through her skin before he could finish. It was Konstantine, not herself, that hissed, rocking back onto his heels.

"Mio dio," he said.

Lou didn't know much Italian, but knew this was a swear of one kind or another.

"You can look away if you're squeamish," she told him.

He didn't. Instead he said, "What the hell happened?"

"I was shot."

"How?"

"A bullet ejected from a gun and I happened to be in its way."

Whatever he wanted to say next, he dropped it.

She glanced past him at the green digital clock on her stove. It was nearly one in the morning. "After I'm done you can go to bed."

He laughed but understood a dismissal when he heard it. He repacked her kit and carried it out of the room, leaving only the bit of gauze and tape she needed to redress the wound. With his exit, he took that wall of heat and her hyperawareness of his body in relation to hers. It was as if someone had opened
the window and let the night breeze wash in over her.

When he returned he said, "How do you get those supplies? Some of them are for doctors only."

"I take them from medical supply stores or pharmacies." How many times had she slipped into some dark supply storeroom at night, stuffing her bag with gauze, tape, needles and bottles of disinfectant.

"You're a thief?" he asked. He smiled as he was amused.

"I leave cash on the counter." *Usually*.

Unless she knew that pharmacy was owned by a mob, which sometimes she targeted, or if the pharmaceutical company was Satan incarnate. Then she took without care.

She stood and crossed to the kitchen. Tossing the suture needle into the trash underneath, she washed her hands in the sink and added the gauze Konstantine had left aside for her.

"Go to sleep," she told him. "You're healing."

She motioned to her bed.

He shook his head. "You're more wounded than I am now. You take the bed."

She didn't want to tell him she couldn't. That the pillows, sheets and all of it smelled like him. That the idea of sleeping in the apartment where he also slept—freely, of her own will—was like agreeing to

something.

But he'd already tucked a cushion under his head and turned away from her, offering the long plane of his back in the light from the window.

And the fact remained that she did need rest.

It wasn't only the pain wracking her body. Now that the danger had passed, her body ached. Every muscle had grown stiff and unforgiving. *Dragging three corpses across worlds will do that do you...*

And there was the fact that Lucy was on her radar.

The compass inside her whirred softly, a tug urging her to go and visit the woman again. It wasn't the firehouse alarm that had woken her weeks ago. The night Lucy's health turned a corner, Lou hadn't been fully awake before she found herself kneeling down and scooping her aunt off the floor.

A hop-skip-and-jump away and she'd delivered the woman to the hospital she'd never visit for herself.

*The woman.* Already her mind was taking steps to distance herself from the inevitable. As if Lucy wasn't the one who'd wrapped her arms around her the night her parents died. As if reducing her to nothing, to no one, could lessen this blow.

It was Lucy who had assured her that her parents were gone—irrevocably gone—but that she wasn't alone.

*I can never replace what you've lost,* her aunt had said. How strange she had seemed at first. This hippie with bleached hair in a long flowing skirt and arms as defined as any man's. *But I can give you a home and love you and help you in a way they couldn't.*

She had meant slipping of course. Not only the fact that she was now offering Lou room and board and an alternative to six years in the foster care system.

But she couldn't see Lucy now. Not looking the way she did, shot and bleeding. It would only upset her. Make her worry.

She pulled back the covers and slid between the sheets. She leaned across the mattress and felt the plastic slats of the blinds. With restless fingers, she pried them apart, one by one, welcoming more and more light into the bed.

It had been a while since she'd tried to sleep in this bed at night. It was easier to sleep from dawn until the late afternoon, when the sunlight was strongest. She could fall into deep slumber then, without any fear that dreams of the men she hunted may deliver her to their bedrooms.

But it was more than that.

Her nighttime habits had also taken over, hadn't they? It was easier to hunt by night. Under the cover of nightfall, stalking her prey was almost too easy. It was when she tried to do it during daylight hours. When they themselves may be more alert, but also the shadows against her. Shadows she could work, true. And it was only the light against dark that projected them. And yet, night was her natural ally. She didn't need a shadow when she was hunting under the cover of night. The world itself had become a shadow for her.

She let her back soften into the mattress, welcoming the support against her aching body. But she found a spot she could lay in.

She didn't think she could sleep though. Not only because a man lay less than two feet from her, his skin wrapped in the moonlight. The back of his neck a tuft of black hair.

But she had to try. Fighting sleep would only make healing harder.

"How did you survive?" Konstantine asked.

His voice was far too intimate in the darkness. Not full volume, but enough above a whisper to be clear.

"I slipped into a confessional. I guess the priest took pity on me and called an ambulance." *And I'll take pity on him if he still has my father's vest.*

"Not tonight," Konstantine said, turning over on the sofa. The coils creaked beneath him. His eyes shone like onyx in the dark. "The night Angelo came to your house, how did you survive?"

In her mind, Lou heard the quick *blat-blat-blat* of gunfire. Saw the strobe lights flash in the window and knew her mother was dead. Saw the side gate fly open and a ghostly hand shoving aside a lilac bush. Petals the colors of bruises rained down on the lawn. That glimpse of the phantom illuminated by the motion lights before her father lifted her off the ground and threw her into the water knowing it would save her.

Her back arched instinctively. Fourteen years separated that moment and this one, but she still felt the cold water knocking the air out of her, before sucking her down, enclosing her limbs like tendrils of seaweed. That unforgettable image of her father turning and running away, his white shirt an ethereal haze, he himself a target drawing the gunfire away from her.

"We were talking in the backyard when they came," she said. "He threw me into the pool."

"Ah, yes. Like in the bay when you took Ryanson. Your father knew you could exit through the water?"

"Yes."

"What happened when you came back?" If he had looked too interested. If he had come up onto his elbow, turned this into some slumber party share time, she would have shut down.

But he'd closed his eyes.

Dark lashes spread across his cheeks and serene light shined on his skin.

She wouldn't give him all of it.

Wouldn't recount for him what it was like rising out of Blood Lake with the full weight of her terror on her shoulders. Wouldn't tell him how she'd hidden on that strange shore until her terror of the place overtook her and then she tried to go home.

But it hadn't been their pool she'd crawled out of. It had been a river. And then a bathtub that had been left to fill while its owner stepped out of the room for a book or glass of wine. Then it had at last been a pool, but not hers. Rather an Olympic pool in a closed gym. She cried herself hoarse on the shallow steps, the eerie glow of the water not frightening as it always had.

She had a new fear. And it had eclipsed her world.

Finally, she made it home to find it crawling with officers and not one of them was her father. They'd wrapped her in a beach towel and sat her on the front step with a glass of water she never touched.

She understood now that her blind panic was partly to blame. And also the idea of defying her father. He had wanted her away, wanted her safe. Her compass wanted this also. Both of these factors stacked against her. And so when it came time to return—a third strike. She had been aiming for her parents. Trying to let the compass take her to the arms she wanted most.

But they weren't there anymore. That connection had been severed.

A tether snapped.

"Why does Nico want to kill you?" she asked.

She wanted the conversation to steer away from her now. Far away.

His eyes opened again, and light reflected in those ink-black pools. "Padre warned me this would happen. Nico was jealous of me since we were boys. When we were children he would hit me, push me around and Padre always put a stop to it. He never did that for other boys. I think that only made Nico hate me more. One day he broke my hand with a hammer."

She said nothing.

"Padre tied him to a post in the courtyard behind the church and beat him for it. He made everyone watch. I'm certain we've been enemies since."

"Padre must have known he was fueling the rivalry."

He was silent for a while. Finally he said, "Whenever Padre had a problem, he would ask me what I thought even though my suggestions were often ridiculous. For example, he once asked me how could he bring in something very large through the city without anyone seeing it. And I told him to put it inside an elephant."

He smiled to himself.

"This was ridiculous, of course," he added.

"Padre and all the other men had laughed. But then his face lit up and he cried, 'Santa Maria Cristo!' He used the statues in the parade to hide the guns. They were carried through the streets right to his church and no one knew the difference. He always listened to me. Encouraged my ideas."

"I imagine intelligence is hard to come by in the criminal world," she said.

He didn't laugh. She noticed.

Finally he said, "I would argue that intelligence is very common is the criminal world. We must know your rules well enough to break them. And we must know the minds of men, so we can control them."

Silence hung in the air for a long time.

"There is a blanket in the closet," she said, before turning away.

# 18

Lou woke before Konstantine. It wasn't dawn. She had at least an hour or two of night on her side. The pain in her arm made it hard to sleep. It wasn't only the pain keeping her awake.

She hadn't slept so near a man, not since she was a child. When her mother was away on their annual sisters-only vacation, when they left their husbands and children at home and retreated to somewhere tropical—once the Virgin Islands, another time, an all-inclusive resort in Mexico—she would sleep with her father then.

She would climb up onto their elevated four-poster bed with much difficulty and he would let her watch television while he did paperwork that he hadn't finished on this or that case during the day. She would wake hours later, to find the popcorn bowl moved, and she herself tucked into her side of the king-sized bed, while he snored softly beside her.

It was too vulnerable, sleeping beside someone. Sex was easier.

From time to time, she found men while hunting. Never the men she hunted. Someone who was simply in the right place at the right time. Someone who walked up to her, and said hello while she tracked this or that man. Someone who'd smiled the right way. Someone who'd noticed her in a world where she moved mostly unnoticed.

She'd let them take her back to their place. But she didn't tolerate wine, conversation, or any of the tactics that they seemed to think she needed. They gave her names. Numbers. She gave them nothing.

She'd never seen a man more than once. Never taken them back to her apartment. And sure as hell had never brought them food. She couldn't imagine lying down beside them, and closing her eyes. There was always the chance a knife would slice her throat or a gun would be pressed to the side of her head. So no, she hadn't slept beside a man since Jack Thorne died.

Yet here he was. Konstantine. His chest rising and falling with each relaxed breath. His cheek on her pillow.

*Of all the men in the world...*

*It's done,* her father said. *If it's done, no point in worrying it like a bone. You're only punishing yourself twice.*

She slid from her bed and grabbed her black boots. Still wearing her scrubs, she stepped inside the closet and closed the door behind her.

The first stop was a thrift store. She exchanged the scrubs for camo pants and Ramones t-shirt. A black hoodie befitting the chilly September night. A black sports bra with one of its cups missing, the other easily removed. Socks for her feet which she laced her boots over. Had she come during business hours, this ensemble would have cost her $13. She took a twenty from the pocket in her boot and put it on the counter.

The first thing she did to every pair of boots she bought was sew an inner pocket into the tongue. Something tight enough to hold a few compressed bills without them slipping loose.

When she needed two hands for guns, purses or backpacks were impossible. Even fishing money from a bra was too much trouble, often shifting and disappearing in this or that corner of the fabric.

She wasn't fit to see the priest, but hopefully she wouldn't see him. Get in, get out. Avoid the formalities.

She stepped out of the parking lot light spilling from a display window of the thrift store and into a changing room outfitted with a thin black curtain. When she emerged, she was in what looked like a ticket booth. Did churches have ticket booths?

She supposed this one did. And a cash register. But the room was locked, so unless she wanted to bust the handle, she was forced to slip again. This time she emerged behind a great stone pillar reaching up to the tremendous ceiling above.

A prism of color danced across the blood-colored carpet running between the pews toward a suspended figure of Christ on the cross. She stepped into the light and looked up. A stained-glass ceiling spraying reds, blues and yellows. Emerald greens and the white wings of an angel. Mary holding a child, as the angels bore her on high. The first light of dawn.

"Can I help you?" a voice called.

A man approached her.

He wore the black clothes and white collar of a priest. He was bald on top and what was left covered the flesh from his ears down.

He stopped three feet from her and confusion seized his face. "It's you!" he said. With part terror and part excitement.

"Are you the one who found me?" she asked, shifting in her boots as the socks she'd hastily pulled on began to slide down. They were too small. A small price to pay for keeping Konstantine asleep and

avoiding more slumber party chitchat.

"Yes," he said. He raised a shaking hand as if to touch her face and then froze, dropping it. "How did you survive?"

She realized now what she'd forgotten. Her sunglasses which she saw perfectly in her mind's eye on the glass coffee table back home.

If she had been wearing them, he likely wouldn't have seen the hard, uncompromising glare that met him when he'd reached out to touch her. She knew her gaze was hard. She'd heard more than one person comment on the way she seemed to look through them. Benji had said that when she smiled it didn't reach her eyes. Lucy had said much the same. *I feel like you smile only to please me, Louie. Never because you're happy.*

When conversation was unavoidable, it was best if she wore sunglasses.

"Thank you," she said and smiled, hoping that at least some of it crossed the plains of her cheeks and achieved a facsimile of sincerity. "But you have something of mine."

It was part question, part hope.

And it was enough to kick the priest into motion. "Oh yes! I have it all. I'm so glad you came back
because, heaven help me, I honestly didn't know what to do with all of it. Follow me."

The two of them, utterly alone at this hour, moved silently through the dim church.

She didn't ask why he was the only one here. She had no right to question why the good father couldn't sleep at night.

At the end of a short stone hallway, he pulled a collection of keys from his wrist.

A loud clanking sound released and he pushed the door wide, flipping a switch on the wall. It illuminated a small office. A desk that was very tidy but also quite full of books and papers in need of reviewing.

The priest went around the side of the desk and bent under it, slowly retrieving one thing or another from the darkness beneath.

Her holster. The guns. Blades lined up one after another on the tabletop.

Then at last, the vest.

Something in Lou's chest loosened when she saw it. Though blood soaked as it was.

"Thank you," she said. "For keeping it safe."

Then she wasted no time slipping the weapons into place where she could. The priest stood silent, watching her every movement as if she were an elegant dancer on stage.

"You really are just a girl, aren't you?" His mouth hung in wonder. "Forgive me, young woman."

"What did you think I was?" She put her arms through the holster, moving quite slowly with the left arm as to not pop another stitch while the flesh was swollen tight.

"I'm sending an angel ahead of you to guard you along the way and to bring you to the place I have prepared."

Lou froze. *The place I have prepared*. She thought of La Loon instantly. That nightmare standing between her world and what?

"Exodus 23:20."

"I don't know the Bible," Lou said, checking to make sure everything was secure. The knives in their holsters and the guns in theirs. Not the vest though. She would simply have to put it on or carry it. And there would be no walking around in public tonight. As every piece of metal she wore stood in plain sight.

"Angels," he said. "I'm speaking of angels."

She searched his face. But there was no teasing there.

She gestured at the guns, the knives. "Do I look like an angel?"

"Angels are the warriors of God. And you simply appeared."

Irritation nipped at the back of her neck. "I'm not an angel."

His face screwed up with genuine concern. "Why?"

"I have too much to answer for."

"Don't forget this." He handed her something she'd forgotten she'd been wearing. Her German watch. The international pager that Lucy had given her several birthdays ago, under the pretense that she should be able to reach her niece if she needed her.

She clicked the small button on the side of the device and its digital face blinked to life. Four pages. One from Benji, a thank you no doubt. And three from King.

"I have to go," she told the priest. One page from King would have been enough. Three…

"Godspeed," he said, his eyes wide with wonder. "I hope we meet again."

*Careful what you wish for.* Lou stepped into the corner of his room and pressed her back into the shadow.

A dramatic exit, she knew, that would only fuel his superstitions. But it was rare that Louie had a chance to enjoy herself.

# 19

King looks at the cell phone in his hand again and sighs. Would paging her a fourth time really matter? If she didn't answer the first three pages, it was either because she wouldn't or couldn't. If the first reason, it pissed him off. But that voice in the back of his head was quick to point out the ridiculousness. *She owes you nothing. She isn't going to come running just because you've given her a page, Robbie.* Maybe there were women in the world who responded that way, but he understood Lou Thorne wasn't the kind to run at his beck and call.

If she wasn't answering because she couldn't— well, that was a whole other bag of shit.

He squeezed his eyes shut and exhaled slowly. "At least have the decency to die after we put her in the ground."

"I'm trying," a woman said.

King looked up from his socked white feet and met the eyes of Lou Thorne. She stood armored, clutching a vest in her fist. He recognized it was one of the old, outdated vests they used in the DEA SWAT teams. He wondered if that was Jack's vest, the one that had never ended up in inventory after his service weapon and all other equipment had been reclaimed.

"Coming or going?" he asked.

She glanced at the vest in her hand and seemed to note the guns and knives for the first time. "I'm not hunting tonight."

Hunting. King laughed. "This is your usual evening attire, is it? I guess I will cancel that Macy's gift card for your birthday then."

This was meant as a joke, but she wasn't laughing. She seemed only interested in getting him back on track. "You paged."

Right to it then. King ran a hand through his hair. "Do you, by chance, still have Paolo Konstantine stowed away in your apartment?"

There. The smallest twitch in her arm and a stiffening of her neck.

Before she could put a bullet in him, he added. "It was a guess. I haven't been snooping."

Her shoulders didn't relax. "Good guess."

That's a yes then. "I'll hazard another guess that you haven't seen the news in the last 48 hours."

She frowned. "What's happened?"

He sank onto his red leather sofa and used the remote control to turn off the fan overhead. She propped the vest against the side of his coffee table and took a seat on the cushion beside him as he powered up his laptop.

The page he'd viewed last was still up and running, so he simply refreshed the page and then clicked the arrow that restarted the newscast.

She watched it without speaking. When it was over and the screen was dark again, she said, "Is there more?"

"Not public, no."

"What's un-public?" she asked.

It took him three tries to get onto the DEA server. They were changing things up then. A televised beheading can do that. King could crack it, but admittedly, they were making it harder. He filed this warning in the back of his mind, along with the idea that he should change his IPs more frequently and then found what he was looking for.

He hesitated for a moment before playing this death tape. Then he realized how ridiculous he was being. Trying to shield Lou Thorne from the sight of slaughter was like trying to prepare a carcass out of the tiger's sight, lest he disturb its tender sensibilities. There was nothing on this tape she hadn't seen with her own eyes—or caused for that matter.

He pushed play.

And watched as eight men forced onto their knees had their throats slit for the camera. He turned away from the screen and watched her reaction for the last line "I am Paolo Konstantine. You will hear from me again, very soon."

He saw what he wanted, loosing a breath he hadn't realized he was holding. "It's not Konstantine on the tape is it?"

"It's Nico Agostino," she said. "I told you there's a turf war over the Ravengers."

King didn't recognize the name. He grabbed the yellow legal pad off the coffee table and scribbled. He didn't have it in him to ask her how she spelled it. Augustino?

She glanced at his page. "You spelled it wrong."

And corrected him.

King tried to recall what he knew of the Ravengers and the man who ruled them. The last time King had seen Konstantine in the flesh, he was tied up on Ryanson' boat, about to be drilled to death by another gang member.

*What interesting friends you have*, he thought but he didn't speak. She seemed deep in her own thoughts.

When he couldn't stand the silence, he said. "It looks like Agostino wants to remove Konstantine from the field completely, not just from the drug trade."

She was cold beside him. No warmth radiating from her. A chill ran down his spine.

"It looks like it," she says.

"I can't believe you missed."

She leveled him with a frosty stare.

He raised his hands in surrender. "I'm sure it couldn't have been helped."

She gestured toward the screen. "What does this mean for Konstantine?"

"Three of those agents were British Intelligence, but the other five were ours. So I suspect that the great US of A will be rushing in, guns blazing soon."

"Konstantine will have to stay out of sight until his name is cleared."

King laughed. "Do you think they'll just let him go? A drug lord? Once they realize he isn't the man they want, I'm sure they'll find something else to arrest him for."

She considered this.

King swallowed all the comments he knew were

uncalled for. *What would your father think of you shacking up with a drug lord?* First of all, it wasn't King's business what Lou did or didn't do with any man in her life, and two, he knew better than to bring up Jack Thorne. He glanced at the vest propped against his coffee table.

"What about me?" she asked, meeting his gaze directly.

The strange question startled him out of his thoughts. "What about you?"

"Has my name turned up?"

"No," he said, perhaps too quickly.

Her gaze hardened.

"I've been watching and listening to the wire," he said, trying to infuse his voice with indifferent calm again. But it wasn't working. Throwing the ball back into her court would be better. "Did you end up in a hospital by chance?"

She blinked. The briefest fluttering of eyelids.

"I wondered if that was you. Unnamed woman brought in for several gunshot wounds. Which arm was it?"

He reached out to brush her left arm, but she was already up and across the room, standing in the center with the vest in her hand.

"I'm sorry," he said, hoping he hadn't gone too far. Now was not the time to push her away. "Is that why you're taking the night off?"

"I'll be ready when it's time to take out Nico."

His anger, surprisingly furious, rose suddenly. "So are you going to take on half the world to protect Konstantine with only one of your arms in decent shape? That sounds *brilliant*. See where that gets you."

He expected her to storm off then. Like a scolded teenager, slamming the door as she went. But instead her hard gaze seemed to soften into something like curiosity.

"How's Lucy?" she asked.

So that was how she was going to play it?

"You would know if you visited her."

"Sure thing, grandpa."

"I'm marrying her."

Lou laughed. "A lot of good that will do you."

"She needs something to look forward to. Something to hold on to."

Her laugh cut short. "Wedding dresses or cakes or any of that bullshit? That's what you think women hold on to."

"Some women."

"Says the divorced man who's been single for at least the last ten years."

"At least I'm spending time with her! At least I'm soaking up every second I have with her before she's gone from the face of the earth! And when she is, all you'll have left is your regret."

Lou moved the vest to the other hand. And for a horrible minute King thought it was so she could pull her gun and put a bullet between his eyes.

But she didn't. She was adjusting for the pain, some wound, old or new, was her giving her grief.

"Congrats on your engagement."

She delivered this with all the enthusiasm of someone declaring their imminent death. Then she was gone.

## 20

Nico sat in the front row pew of his father's church, Santi Augusti al monte. He stared up at the figure of Christ, with the tears upon his face for all the misery of the world. Or perhaps it was not Christ he regarded with his upturned face. But the face of his own father. A face of misery, despair.

It wasn't Nico's father who had built this church. That was done by friars in the 1400s. But he himself had commandeered it from the mob boss with whom he'd apprenticed. Padre told him stories of Bellini when Nico was a little boy and how much Padre had learned from the hard man—*what to do right and what to do better.*

As a boy, Nico had no doubts that he would inherit this empire. He was secure in his father's love. That was until Konstantine arrived.

He remembered the day everything changed, standing on the stone steps of this church beside his father. Padre had a package for Konstantine, no more than eight or nine years old, to carry across town.

*I can do it, papa*, Nico had said. He was four years older than the boy. Surely at thirteen he was more capable than the green-eyed brat in his American sneakers.

*No*, his father had said. *I need someone clever for this.*

Had Konstantine heard these words, Nico would have likely attacked him on the street before the kid could get any ideas. But he was already running down the street through a cloud of pigeons, the brown paper package tucked under his arm. His father had spoken to him and him alone.

*Who is clever now, papa?*

The life Padre Leo built for more than forty years had been seized by the very son he cast out. His legacy business turned over to the hands he wanted most never to touch it. How would God have felt, if Adam had returned triumph to reclaim the Garden of Eden?

Of course, perhaps it would be easier to forgive the seizure of a mere garden.

Unless it was also worth more than three billion dollars.

The casinos, the firearms, heroin fields in Afghanistan. The cocaine pumping into Europe. A network of thousands of loyal men and women the world over. And all of it run by a single man. Paolo

Konstantine. Every protocol, every decision, run by him first. As if he were their god.

Reclaiming his father's life work was only the beginning. Once he repaid those few who dared to elevate him to his rightful place, he would be unstoppable. Whole markets had been left untouched and Nico was going to change that.

Humans. Sexual exploitation. An untapped market that Konstantine nor his father dared to harness. People were a commodity that could push the Ravengers' three billion to eight billion or higher. Look at the Russians. Worth nearly ten billion and why? How did the Americans put it?

Sex sells.

And why not? People were so easy to acquire. So many displaced from their countries every day. War, famine or drought—a dozen reasons. It was no trouble at all to make them disappear, especially the children and women.

Narcotics had to be grown or manufactured. They took time. But people? They could turn a profit almost immediately. And their shelf-life was better. A drug offered only a single use. Put black tar in the veins or powder up the nose and that was it. More had to be ordered, made, shipped.

But one woman could be used over and over and over again. All night, every night for years. She could bring in twice as much revenue as a gram of cocaine if a businessman like Nico spread her right. And she could be shipped too—anywhere to fill the demand. A whorehouse in Atlanta. In Budapest.

Perhaps Konstantine nor his father hadn't seen the possibilities. Or they didn't have the stomach for such an enterprise, but Nico was stronger and smarter. He would expand the Ravengers holdings in all the ways these two pathetic men couldn't.

The steps across the stone floor echoed behind him. He cocked his head slightly, turning at the hint of danger. But it was only Gigi. A lanky boy of fourteen. Nico sat up at the sight of him, excited.

"Did you find what I asked for?" Nico said, leaning back against the pew.

The boy slung the black backpack off his shoulders and squat down on the floor to scrounge through it. "Yeah. Can we talk here?"

He blinked up at Nico from his place on the floor. Nico swept the church, eyes peering into every shadowed corner. But his orders had been followed. No one had approached him today as he sought guidance from his father in the nave. Perhaps they would have worried more if they'd known what was in his fevered heart. That he hadn't in fact been seeking Padre Leo's approval at all but had been basking in the self-righteous pleasure of knowing he'd accomplished the very thing that his father denied him.

The plan he fulfilled after ten long years of dreaming in the work camp. *He* manifested this moment. And he knew it. Every time the bullwhip was brought down across his back and his blood spilled on Russian soil. Every time a boot slid between his ribs or a fist made his ears ring. He thought of his father, thought of the moment he would pull this empire out from beneath him. His only regret was that he hadn't been able to do it looking in the old man's eyes.

But Konstantine was a lovely consolation prize. Seeing him fall, in some ways, would be even sweeter.

"I found these," the boy said.

"Yes," Nico said, placing an arm along the back of the wooden pew. "What do you have for me?"

The boy pulled out a paper folder with two pockets, one on each side. He removed out a jumble of photographs with trembling hands, and handed them over to Nico. Pointing over the top of the photo as he shuffled through.

"He has a whole collection of photographs, just of her."

"Seems obsessive," Nico notes. But he understood why. It wasn't only that the woman was beautiful, it was her strange talent. What was it about the darkness that made you want to look closer? "When were these taken?"

The boy took the top photo and flipped it over, showing the date stamped on the back. "Most of them are dated about three months ago. But some are even older. I think he started his collection years ago."

Nico looked at him expectantly.

The boy cleared his throat. "I ran these photos to find the matching face. There were no names but Konstantine wrote something on the back."

Nico turned the photograph over and read Konstantine's small script "Lou. It's a man's name. Perhaps it isn't for her."

"Is it true what they are saying about her?"

Nico regarded the boy's round face. It was still a boy's face in every regard, even if his voice had changed. Soft round cheeks and eyes. No hint of facial hair.

"What do they say?"

"She captures men like a spider and eats them."

Nico smiled. The boy had the good sense to look
embarrassed.

"Yeah, I don't believe that," the boy said, pulling himself up as if to make himself taller. "I think she's like a ninja or something. She saved Konstantine's life. Twice now."

Nico gave him a hard glare and the boy fell silent, his eyes downcast.

Nico then regarded the photos dreamily. The woman clad in black standing in a shadowed bar, her hair pulled up off her neck, exposing a tender stretch of flesh. He could slit that pretty throat easily. He needed only a way to pin her dark wings to the floor long enough to do it.

He thought of the strange room that Konstantine built outside of town and smiled. *Had that been your intention, brother? To betray her? Trap her and bleed her dry? Or perhaps only to keep her all to yourself...*

If the woman was his only remaining ally, Nico could fix that. Once she knew what he was, and his intentions for her, she would turn on him. Then perhaps he wouldn't even have to put the bullet between his eyes himself.

That had been his mistake after all.

He should have simply shot Konstantine in the head while he could. When he saw Konstantine, he would kill him quickly. If the woman didn't beat him to it.

"That is all," he said to the boy. The boy hesitated for a moment, clearly expecting payment. But one wolfish glance from Nico sent him running from the church without another word.

Now what to do about the woman. Nico looked at the granulated image of the woman watching someone else. A man perhaps. It was hard to tell, even though the unwavering gaze, a hunter's gaze, was easy enough to recognize.

No matter what his father said, he was no fool. He knew that assets and allies would be what carried him through—carried his vision to completion.

Nico had a long, hard road ahead of him. It seemed a waste to destroy a creature so unique and valuable.

If only he could turn her against Konstantine. If only he could offer her what no one else could. He would simply have to figure out what her desire was. People were easy like that. Particularly women. Special talents and bloodthirst aside, she was a woman.

An offer she couldn't refuse, he mused. And a reason to turn against Konstantine so that she wouldn't stand between Nico and what needed to be done.

He settled against the pew, his shoulder blades rubbing against the cold wood. He looked defiantly into the face of the weeping Christ. The tears of a father who could only watch his wayward children and wait.

The bright image of the padded room flashed unbidden in Nico's mind. With all its bright, unwave-ring light.

*Yes*, that was how he would do it, how he would change her mind and make her see the truth of it.

A dog, no matter who was master, still loved the hunt.

She could be trained like any other.

# 21

Konstantine heard the door to the closet click closed. He turned onto his side. Her blankets were bright with moonlight, tousled but empty. He rolled onto his back with a sigh, the sofa springs creaking. He placed one hand beneath his head.

The ceiling above collected long shadows from the room.

His body ached, but he had healed most of his wounds in the last few days, hidden here in her apartment. He should be grateful for her sanctuary. He seriously doubted she'd ever offered such a place to a man before. To women, perhaps. He'd followed her movements closely leading up to their encounter in June and since. Never too close to be noticed. But he was curious.

He wanted to know everything about this woman, how she lived her life, how she supported herself.

As foolish as it sounded, he wanted her. His urge to woo her was like any urge to woo a woman.

But he understood that dinners, flowers, and myriad of attention and declarations would be not only ridiculous, but were likely to be met with a blade to the throat.

And simply showing her his erection—even if unintentional—hadn't worked in his favor either. He had his eye open for the opportunity, certainly, but was unsure what the opportunity might look like.

So he'd taken to watching her instead. To get a sense of anyone, one must look at what they do with their time. What they cared about.

She enjoyed slaughtering men. But that would hardly make a fitting gift. Gifting a lioness with a pig when she could bring home the gazelle was insulting. But what else did she love?

The aunt, to be sure. And also the retired DEA agent in New Orleans who lived above some occult shop in the French Quarter. But most of her time was given over to hunting mules.

To his surprise, it had a symmetry. A rhythm that suited her.

She didn't go for the highest men in charge, those who would be simply replaced with another power-hungry mind. She went for the workers. The reliable soldiers who got the work done. Those on whom the bosses relied to exert the will—those, who if missing, brought production lines and shipments to a grinding halt.

It was brilliant.

Many of her targets were his own men and she had cost him more than enough trouble and money. But he was not her only target. She seemed to target all the drug cartels indiscriminately. And the Ravengers were far from the only one in business.

True she once focused solely on the Martinellis and their intricate connections. But since his brothers and father were dead, it seemed her only ambition to undo their influence brick by brick.

For that reason it had been easy to step in and offer a bargain to his late father's cousin, a partnership that had merged the Martinelli empires with Padre Leo's Ravengers. This is what Padre Leo himself had wanted—though he had had no idea of Lou Thorne's part in this acquisition. How she had all but gutted the operation from the inside out, so that by the time Konstantine arrived on cousin Giuliani's step, the deal was done.

And by appearing as an ally he had prevented a bloody takeover between their two tribes. He let Giuliani Russo run his cartel and Konstantine focused on the Ravengers.

What Lou knew of this arrangement, he had no idea.

Her time seemed mostly focused on dismantling the Mexican cartels in the last month or so. It was their drug lords she purged from the streets. And with their sixty percent market share on America's unquenchable demand, Konstantine couldn't be upset by that.

And what if what she desired was the Ravengers? If in exchange for her body and soul, he must give her the 3.3 billion dollar empire, lock and key?

Could he betray Padre Leo? A man who'd protected him and entrusted him to look after his legacy in exchange for the woman he desired?

He wasn't sure.

And he feared that day, that decision, may be rounding on him sooner than he'd like.

Yet he couldn't handle her the way he would any problem—decisively and directly.

To do so surely meant chasing her back into the shadows, and away from him. He didn't think she was interested in business alliances.

If she carried her father's ideology in her own mind, she meant to undo the entire drug trade.

Including his own. And if that was what it took to have her…

He sighed into the empty apartment, looking at the future with unease.

A flash of light caught his eye. He sat up on his elbows, searching for the source.

It was the island cabinet. The light shining through the trim would've been impossible to see, if he hadn't been lying in the dark.

The light clicked off and Konstantine repressed the urge to feign sleep.

A moment later, the closet door popped open and she strode inside. Her boots moving soundlessly across the wooden floor. *La sua leonessa. No wonder the men never hear you coming.*

She entered the kitchen and pulled a glass down from a cabinet shelf. He listened to the faucet run. The filling glass caught the moonlight from the windows.

He wondered what it would be like. To have a home with this woman. To hear her moving about it in this way, dressing, showering, cooking… knowing that she belonged to him.

He would settle for belonging to her.

*What a pathetic romantic you are*, he chided himself.

She stared down at him, water glass in her hand,

the side of her leg pressing into the sofa.

He met her gaze from the flat of his back, silently praying she would sit on the end of the sofa. That she would put a hand on his thigh. Or better yet, put down the glass and climb on top of him completely, letting the weight of her body sink onto his.

She only stood there. "Nico fucking hates you."

He laughed, surprised to hear such a filthy word in such a pretty mouth. "I'm aware, mia cara."

"Are you *aware* he beheaded eight agents on live television and gave you all the credit?" she asked with an arched brow. "You're on the news."

His laughter died. He swung his legs off the sofa, throwing himself onto his feet. "*Dannazione*! I need to make some calls."

She took a long drink of the water, her eyebrow arching.

"Please," he added. "If you are not currently engaged."

She finished her water and put the glass on the coffee table.

She went to the picture hanging on the wall and removed it. Konstantine was unsure if he should act surprised, indifferent, or sorry.

Apparently, a reaction was unnecessary.

"You've been snooping."

"My apologies," he said, and hope she noted the

sincerity in his voice. "I was bored."

She snorted. "And the most interesting thing you found?"

"An armory where your cookware should be."

She stiffened. "You think women should be cooks."

"And men. We are all responsible for feeding ourselves, aren't we?"

The safe popped open and she removed three magazines and two pistols. She put the ammo in the pockets of her black cargo pants and then the gun in the waistband of the small of her back.

"Are you eyeing the guns or my cash?" she asked as she closed the safe and put the picture back in place. "You have plenty of both."

Did she know how much he had at his disposal? Cash and assets? "You think I'm rich?"

"Oh, you have a few billion," she said, flicking her eyes up to meet his. "Likely more if those casinos you built in Singapore take off soon."

She stepped past him to the closet, leaving the door open.

He only looked at her. How had she come by that information? He wondered. It wasn't printed anywhere. Only his accountants knew those numbers. The men who looked at the proverbial books. He ran an imaginary list through his mind and wondered who might have gone missing or had an arm twisted.

Of course, it was fair play. He'd been learning all he could about her, too.

She holstered one of the guns. Konstantine assumed the other pistol was for him, but she kept it.

"Can I have a gun?" he asked.

"No."

"Don't trust me with a gun?"

"No one touches my guns."

"At least it isn't personal."

"Are you coming?" she asked, beckoning him into the waiting closet. "I thought this was urgent."

He slid into the dark beside her. Chest to chest, he could feel the heat from her body radiating over his skin. She turned her head to reach for the door and something brushed his cheek. Hair? He wanted to lean in, and make sure. Find her lips in the darkness and press her back against the wall of the closet. He was sure she could brace her knees against the wood as he entered her.

"Where are the people you need to call? What city?" Her breath was hot on his face. Intimate. Voices in the dark always were.

"New York," he said, squeezing the words out, feeling the fire in his face and the desire throbbing below his belt.

With his body pressed full frontal against hers, it was almost too much. He could feel the erection forming. The building pulse. And if he didn't shift himself away to create space, she was surely going to notice it as well.

But it wasn't Konstantine that leaned in close. She pressed her body against his, pinning him against the wall. He wanted to reach out, wrap his arms around her, take a fistful of her hair, but she'd pinned his arms in place with the weight of her. He shouldn't have been surprised by how strong she was. He'd seen her lift and drop men twice his size with ease. But feeling her uncompromising grip on him was different.

An edge of panic entered his mind.

Then they were falling backwards through space. He felt as if a rug had been yanked out from under him. The momentary panic grew. The sensation of weightlessness followed by compression in his head.

Then the world was beneath them again.

At some point, her hand had snaked around his hip, holding him in place. Again the urge to wrap his fists up in her hair rose. But before reason could be overruled, she released him and stepped out of the closet into a dim bedroom.

Two double beds side by side, a nightstand between. A desk with stationery. Not a bedroom exactly. The name of a chain hotel printed across the top of the stationery. He heard a metal *clank-clack* and realized she was locking the door no doubt leading to a hallway.

"Hurry," she said, nodding toward the phone. "Local calls are free."

"We are in New York?"

"Yes. Be sure to dial 1 or you'll confuse the desk clerk. This room isn't checked out."

Konstantine picked up the beige phone and pressed the key to connect him to the outside world. The dial tone greeted him.

"I'll come back," she said.

And when he turned to ask her where she intended to go, the closet door was already closing behind her.

Just as well. He would feel strange conducting business under her watchful eye.

He dialed his friends in New York.

He'd already considered which men he would contact when this happened. After all, Konstantine had been expecting this. Not Nico necessarily. But bloody succession was always possible when the leader of a crime faction died. Padre Leo had prepared him for this moment. And now Konstantine had to wonder if part of that preparation was against Nico himself.

*Keeping secrets from me, Padre?*

Mario Ricci picked up on the third ring. His New York accent was comically thick. "Who the hell is this?"

The unknown number calling his personal emergency line no doubt had startled the man.

"Ciao, Mario," Konstantine said, nervously twining his fingers up in the phone's cord.

"Konstantine!" the man said with a relieved sigh. "I wondered if I was gonna be hearin' from you. I was starting to think you were dead."

"No, amico mio. Not yet." Konstantine wet his lips, his eyes falling on the cheap hotel print across the room. A photocopy of a boat sailing down river beneath a soft blue sky. "No doubt you know why I'm calling."

"Oh yeah," said the man with a dry chuckle.

"Your pretty face is all over the news right now.
Congrats my friend, you're a celebrity."

"In our business, that isn't such a good thing."

"Tell me about it. So what's the plan?"

"I will handle the press," he said. "I need your help with something else."

"A trip to Florence to kick Agostino's ass, maybe?"

Konstantine laughed. "Word does travel fast."

"Especially when you got two ears and an asshole pressed to the ground."

"I can offer you two million in exchange for your men and time, Ricci."

"Aww, that's sweet," Ricci said and Konstantine heard the refusal coming. His pulse quickened.

"But you don't need to do that. Padre already cut a check for 2.5 million if I helped you."

*So you did expect this Padre.* And the old man had set up protections. Konstantine's throat tightened at the news. That a man such as Padre would ever pay him such kindness. A man who had owed him nothing.

"Padre is very trusting to cut you a check so early," Konstantine said. "And you're a good man for admitting to receiving it."

Ricci laughed, a hearty chuckle that no doubt jostled the man's large belly. "Yeah, well, I don't know about *trusting*. He cut Tommy Romano 3.5 million to put a bullet in my head if I *didn't* help you or if I didn't fess up to the money. And you know that chump bastard's been looking for a reason since I married his ex-wife."

He didn't know. But now he did.

"Besides this seems to be the day for calling in favors. When it rains, it pours," Ricci went on. Konstantine heard the flint of lighter strike once, twice, and then the sharp inhale. A cigarette or a cigar.

"What do you mean?"

"You ain't heard? Conway's distribution chain is fucked. Two of his guys disappeared down in Miami and there's a warehouse in the fishing district that had forty three bullets—43—pried out of the walls and machines. A fucking mess. The Cubans were going on about a devil coming to claim souls, but Conway thinks it was Hendrix fucking with him. I swear those two are gonna kill each other before the year is out. Anyway, he's got nobody at the docks so Conway asked me to send a couple of my guys down until they can get it sorted. Until then, a ton of cocaine is just sitting in the gulf."

Konstantine thought of Lou, naked, stepping from the closet. The heart-stopping sight of her wet hair stuck to her cheek. Konstantine suspected he knew what might have happened in the fish house.

Ricci coughed. "So when you want to move against Agostino?"

"When can you be ready?"

"Tomorrow? I'll call my guys at the jetway and get us some birds to put in the air. I don't know what Tommy Romano's got, but I know he's bringing something smart. Can you hold off that long? They's huntin' you pretty hard."

"I can wait until tomorrow."

"Good. Meet me at the Charlie's tomorrow at 1:00. And don't get caught on the way here."

Konstantine thanked him and ended the phone call. Six million to secure his succession. And no doubt more, tucked away with this or that hand in case Konstantine had needed the help. The list that Padre had made him memorize in the event of an emergency…it hadn't been so random after all. The men and women selected were those who Padre knew and trusted best from decades of working together, but they were also hands that he'd deliberately greased.

*You are still looking out for me, Padre. Grazie.*

Melancholy crushed his chest.

"You sure you can trust them?" Lou asked. He looked up to see her leaning against the wall. He wasn't sure how long she had been there, watching and listening.

"Padre trusted them, and that is enough for me."

He expected her to laugh at that, but she didn't. Then he remembered the aunt and the New Orleans ex-cop. Perhaps Lou knew something of inheriting help herself.

"Are violent successions really so common in your world?" she asked.

Konstantine stood, his bones creaking. "We even have a name for it. *Dispute resolution.* And yes, in addition to forming alliances, it's good money."

"Is it only about money for you?" she asked.

Her face was dangerously calm.

He smiled. "No. There are some things I want more."

# 22

King had just put in the order for his beignet croquembouche, assured by the manager that it could be ready in 48 hours when the cellphone in his pocket went off. At that moment, the world stopped and began spinning in reverse.

He didn't remember running back to his apartment, getting in his car or racing to the cancer center. He became somewhat aware of himself halfway down the hallway to Lucy's room, pushing through the swarm of nurses and patients.

When he reached her room, his heart faltered.

It was empty.

"Mr. King," a voice said.

He turned and found Naomi standing there. Her braids pulled behind her head and secured with a tie. For a horrible moment, he felt the walls closing in on him, felt his lungs compress, threatening to explode. *She's trying to figure out how to tell me Lucy is dead Lucy is dead Lucy is dea—*

"She just got out of surgery," she said quietly.

"Is she—" His breath was tightening in his chest.

He should've brought his damned inhaler.

"Her heart is having a real hard time with it all, but the surgery went fine," Naomi said, taking his two pale hands in her dark ones and squeezing them hard. Too hard. But enough to bring him back to his own body and this time and place. The walls moved back. He drew his first real breath. "They might keep her up there tonight, have more eyes on her."

"Can I visit?"

"Not until they're sure she's stable. I'm sorry."

"When will they know if she's stable?" he asked, grateful for her cool hands. It kept him steady in a room that started to spin around him.

"An hour, maybe two."

"I'll wait."

She gave his hands another squeeze. "I'll come find you in the cafeteria if I hear something."

He thanked her. Walking toward the cafeteria was a much calmer affair than his entrance had been.

When he got there, and smelled the food wafting from the hot bar, his stomach turned. But he walked up to the counter and ordered a large black coffee, served to him in a paper cup too thin to protect his hand from the heat. He removed his cell phone from his pocket and laid it on the tabletop beside the steaming cup.

Then he did nothing. He was unaware of any thoughts trailing through his mind.

In their place seemed to be a general anxiety. A low-grade buzz that filled every bit of space in his mind and allowed for no other ideas to materialize.

He stared into the inky black of his coffee for who knew how long, looking at a reflection he didn't recognize. The hollowed-out eyes with deep purple bags beneath. A part of his mind understood it was his own reflection, but still more disbelieved it.

He reached into the pocket of his black duster and found his wallet. His fingers fished out the white card with a number printed on the back. He almost had it memorized now, but didn't trust himself not to screw it up while his mind was a million miles away. Robotically, he punched the number for the fifth time in the last 24 hours and pressed the # key to designate this was an emergency.

Lou may hate hospitals, but she would come. She had to come.

The coffee was cold when she showed up, sliding into the booth seat opposite of him. Her eyes hidden behind mirrored sunglasses and her leather jacket sat evenly on her shoulders. He couldn't tell if she was packing, but suspected so. If her arm was a wreck from her run-in the other night, there was no evidence of it. She moved as if no part of her body ailed her. Which is a hell of lot more than King could say for himself. Half the time he walked bent slightly at the waist, because his low back was so stiff.

Even if his heart wasn't collapsing in his chest, the ache in every joint would ail him.

"Is she dead?" Lou asked as last. He hadn't realized until she'd spoken that he had been silent for several minutes, looking into his black coffee without acknowledging her arrival.

"She's in critical care," he said. His voice cracked. He took a sip of coffee, cold and disgusting, but enough to wet his pipes. "Her heart is giving out under the strain of…of everything."

"Have they let you see her?"

"No."

"I'll take you," she said, her palms pressing flat to the table.

"No," he said, perhaps too quickly. "They don't want us in the way. I'm sure they have their reasons. We'd only prevent them from doing their job."

"Which is what?" Lou asked. He searched her face for cruelty or sarcasm. But it was only his own eyes staring back at him in the reflection.

"Keeping her alive as long as they can."

"Maybe she doesn't want to be alive anymore."

King's hands curled into fists. The blood red knuckled turned white. "That's not for you to decide."

Lou looked ready to speak. But then her lips flattened. Finally she said, "Konstantine is about to move against Agostino. He's working with the Ricci family."

King knew the name. They'd tried to nab the Riccis in the 70s. All the good it did them. They were slick snakes.

"Did you know they have a word for it? Dispute resolution."

"Yeah," he said. "That's how the old, powerful families stay in power. And they rely on the alliances of other groups to maintain that power."

"Who knew thugs were so aristocratic," she said.

"Don't you think this is the wrong time?" he asked.

"For what?"

"To be running off to Italy for a gunfight. You should be here. You should be with her."

"I offered to take you there and you said no."

"Can't you holster your bullshit long enough to tell her goodbye! Properly!"

He was screaming. Sweat slid down the side of his face.

Lou was perfectly impassive in the face of his anger. She only said, "Are you looking to join her? When is the last time you took your blood pressure medicine?"

He'd actually been removed from the medicine after the last checkup. The doctor had been pleased with his weight loss and new exercise routine.

"What do you want from me, King?" she said. Not petulance. Again that utter calm which in its own way was more infuriating than if she'd yell at him. Slap him across the face. Anything. Show any damn emotion.

"I want you to stay with her! I want you to show her you give a damn! That woman raised you, kept you out of foster care and now she's *dying*, and you can't even take the time to make sure she doesn't die alone."

He expected her to leave then. To get up, walk through the lunch room and disappear around some dark corner.

Instead she said, "You've made a lot of assumptions."

"Fucking hell." He fell back against the booth's back.

"Maybe she doesn't want me to see her like that.
Doesn't want me to remember her that way."

His breath hitched. "You need to do what's right! You need to make this easy for her!"

"Easy for her or easy for you?"

And at this she did rise and exit the booth. He watched her go, her long lean steps and the jacket shifting over her shoulders as she went.

# 23

After a bowl of ramen in a busy Tokyo street annex, Lou spent the early hours of the day walking the streets of Paris. She stood outside a macron shop and saw the little wafers made of almond paste. It was too early to buy Lucy a half-dozen to enjoy with a cup of earl grey. And knowing King, he'd been trying to shove food down her throat for days.

*He's figuring out how to let her go. Just like you.*

Lou shook these thoughts from her head as she wandered past Notre Dame, over Pont Neuf. A batobus slid silently down the river, its lights casting shadows along the flanking cobblestone banks. She stepped up behind a stone pillar and out onto the streets of London. She hadn't intentionally chosen such a place. But the mere thought of Lucy had brought her here.

She remembered a ninth grade social studies report, where she was expected to write about the history of a city of her choice. Lou had chosen

London because it was the birthplace of so many books and writers she loved—even more so after her parents' death, when there were days that felt as if books were all that she had left. Any world was better than the shattered world in which she lived.

At the first mention of the report, Lucy had been delighted.

*Well let's go see it*, Lucy said and the next thing Lou knew, she was stepping out of her aunt's cramped Oak Park linen closet and into Piccadilly Circus, with the red double decker buses and funny black taxi cabs whirring by.

Lucy had always been able to surprise her like that.

In the beginning, Lou was certain that her ability to travel through the dark or water was a curse. Something to mitigate and endure. But Lucy had been the first to show her the magic of it. The power of it. The freedom.

*There isn't a place in this world you can't go, Louie*, her aunt had told her in those early days. *You just have to know where you want to be.*

"You gave me this freedom," she murmured. Her chest compressed painfully.

A boy pushing a bike with a flat tire clipped Lou, setting her wounded arm on fire.

"Sorry, love. I didn't see you there." He flinched at her cold expression. "You all right?"

Rather than answer him, she headed toward the National Gallery, to the other side of Nelson's Column.

"Sorry!" he shouted after her.

The bright pain faded to a steady throb, to an unpleasant heat. She refused to take off the jacket and inspect the wound. Not only because of the guns it hid, but because of the muggy, damp quality to the early morning air. One press of her watch told her it was only 4:30 in the morning. Most of the shops were not yet open, and the world was mostly quiet in the early dark. A few people were hurrying across town trying to make their jobs. Or those catching early flights or trains out of the city.

Such as the mother marching past the Gallery steps with her red roller bag in tow as well as two children, a boy and a girl, with matching suitcases. The girl gave Lou a long, hard, fearless look. And Lou couldn't suppress a smile in the face of that defiant chin.

When she could no longer feel her fingers, and knew no more calm could be gathered by wandering, Lou bled into the building's shadow and emerged from the corner of a hospital room.

A machine clicked and beeped. The sound of something being pressurized and released in turn.

Her aunt seemed to know the moment that she'd entered. Her eyes fluttering open and her head turning toward her with much effort.

"Hi, Lou-blue," the old woman croaked. And she did look quite old now. Her blue eyes brighter than Louie could ever recall seeing them, as if the last of her light had gathered there.

"Hi," Lou managed. Though the smell of the place was already pressing in on her. The smell, in its way more offensive than any blood or brain matter sprayed on her. In its way a perversion.

"I miss you," Lucy said.

Lou would often say nothing to this sort of remark, but it seemed cruel now. "I miss you too." And she found that once she said it, it was true. She missed the woman her aunt was. The caustic wit. The benevolent goddess energy, always visibly straining to accept some new horror that Lou had committed. Her patience. Her reassuring presence.

"I just went to London and Paris," Lou told her. "Our old haunts."

"I miss traveling," Lucy said with a dry-lipped smile.

Lou saw too much of the bones in her face. She

considered sitting but there were no chairs in this room. This wasn't a room that welcomed visitors. So they'd come that far then. It was time.

"If you could go anywhere in the world right now—" Lou began. But she didn't have to finish.

"Somewhere warm. I'm always so cold now. No matter how many extra blankets they pile on me, I'm always cold."

Lou slipped her cold London-chilled hand into her aunt's and found that it must be true. Somehow the frail grip was icy.

"Maui maybe," her aunt mumbled, pinching her eyes closed.

"How long do you have?" Lou asked, hoping her voice wouldn't betray her. But her heart hammered hard in her chest. She could feel it pressing against the bottom of her throat, making her voice thin.

Death, which had always been so familiar to her, was a stranger again. Someone she didn't know knocked on the door. The death she knew was a firecracker. A whirling dervish. Fast, violent, and quick. This death was larger. It slid into a room, took up all the available space. It wouldn't leave. It ate up the heat and joy. It lingered like a revolting grease smeared on the mind that if touched, you were

reminded of it all over again.

"On the machines?" she asked. "Oh we could stretch this on for a while, I think. Maybe weeks."

"Off the machine?" Lou asked.

Lucy met her eyes, considered her face with a mix of hope and fear. "A few hours at best."

"Maui's sunset is in an hour," Lou said. She counted the machines in the room. Counted the tubes running from her aunt's paper-thin skin. And when she was done assessing the situation, she caught her aunt staring.

"Yes." She searched Lou's face, looking almost as if it weren't real. "Yes, take me to see the sunset."

Lou, as carefully as possible, unhooked each cord and tube and machine tying her aunt to this place. Then she crossed the room and turned off the light.

In pitch blackness, there was a terrifying moment when she thought she'd touch Lucy and find her already dead. Or already gone. Maybe slipping away accidentally, leaving Lou to search the world for her.

The silence of the room without the monitor was deafening.

But then a bony hand seized her forearm with surprising strength and tried to pull herself up.

"Don't," Lou commanded. "Let me."

She threw back all the blankets but one and slipped her good arm under the woman's knees. Frail arms went around her neck and then they were through.

The first thing Lou heard was the chatter of birds, a raucous in the trees. A few fell silent at their shocking arrival, but then went right on with their conversation as if to say *oh it's only you?*

Lou stepped out of the woods with Lucy in her arms. She was heartbreakingly light as Lou's boots sank in the sand. But Lou kept them both upright as she carried her down the strip of beach to the water's edge. She placed her on the sand a foot from the waves, so the water could only reach her toes, but climb no higher.

Lucy laughed with delight. "Oh yes. This is so much better. We should've come sooner."

Lou stood over her awkwardly as Lucy removed her socks.

"A hospital in no place to die. Sit with me, Lou."

Lou obeyed, plopping down onto the sand beside her. She was confident that they wouldn't be disturbed. Not only because they were the only souls for as far as the eye could see. But this was a private beach belonging to a billionaire. And he was at a Geneva technology convention or so said all the papers. If someone did come to ruin her aunt's last few moments in this world—Lou would handle it.

Her aunt took a deep breath and inhaled. The wind from the ocean blowing back the hair from her face. For a long time they said nothing. They only looked out over the western horizon at the sun dipping lower with each breath. Waves crashed on the sand enveloping them. Eventually Lou had to take off her boots and roll up the end of her cargo pants so that they wouldn't soak through with salt water. These were her best boots. She wanted them dry if and when she faced Nico.

Lou glanced at her aunt once or twice from the corner of her eye, wondering if the woman would drop off at any moment. And Lucy noticed.

Smiling, she said, "No, I'm not dead yet."

Lou snorted.

"I'd forgotten how beautiful the world can be," Lucy said, her hospital blanket whipping around her.

Lou realized suddenly that she wore only a paper gown under it. "Are you cold?"

"No. The sand is nice and warm. It's like sitting on a loaf of freshly baked bread straight from the oven. Mmmm."

Lou drew circles in the sand between her legs. She found it easier to focus on the sand than on the woman beside her.

Finally Lucy said, "I've often thought of this moment. The moment of death is a big deal in Buddhism, you know. How your mental state is at the moment you pass will impact your future life."

Lou didn't interrupt her.

"So I had all of this planned bullshit I was going to say to you. Things I thought that would help us both let go. I was going to apologize if I gave you the impression that I wanted you to be anything other than what you are. And I was going to find a way to help you and King not be so angry. Because of course anger and guilt are part of it."

She thought of King's twisted, grieved face in the cafeteria earlier.

"And now?" Lou asked, throat tight.

"Now…" She turned and looked at Lou's face with intense regard. She reached up and cupped her cheeks. "Now I only want you to know that you're loved, Louie. You've always been loved. And I hope that I see you again. In the next life."

Tears were pulled from her eyes by the relentless wind rolling off the ocean. Lucy wiped them away with her thumbs.

"I just—" Lou began but her voice broke. "Thank you."

Lucy smiled but said nothing.

"You taught me not to be afraid of slipping, and you taught me how to listen to my compass. I hope—I just hope you don't regret what I chose to do with it."

Lucy brushed the hair back from Lou's face. "You helped me too. Before you, it was only me."

The sunset bled from orange to pink, their hands clasped.

"I know you will find your way. I really do believe that." Lucy said, squeezing her hands. "You should believe it too."

Lou put her arms around her aunt, and kissed her bald, scarf-wrapped head.

"What do you want to come back as?" Lou asked, pulling away and untangling herself from the embrace.

"What?"

"You believe in reincarnation, don't you?"

"Oh, yes." She thought for a moment. "Something that can fly. I've always loved cardinals."

Lou laughed. "They don't live very long."

"You're right. So perhaps a cardinal, then a crow. Before making my way back to human again."

"A man or woman?"

Lucy snorted. "A woman of course."

They watched what was left of the light dip lower behind the horizon, that false line implying there was an end to it all.

They knew better.

# 24

A hand squeezed King's shoulder, waking him with a start. The cold coffee shook with the movement, rippling its black syrup surface. Lou stood there, looking down at him in her mirrored sunglasses. But her jacket was gone. And her shoes. Her pants were rolled up to the mid-shin, with sand clinging to her feet and toes. He stared at this, bewildered.

"Hurry up," Lou said as if they'd been in the middle of something.

"Where the hell have you been?" he asked, rubbing his eyes. "Fiji?"

"With Lucy, come on."

King's heart took off like a rabbit, kicking hard in its fear. To echo this was the pounding of feet. He looked across the cafeteria in time to see four or five white coats rush by.

"We need to move," Lou said and looked ready to haul King out of the booth if he didn't move himself.

"What the hell have you done!" he screamed.

And then Lou did haul him from the booth, pulling him toward the shadow where the walls met.

His rage built, ready to release its fury on her, but then the world tilted. The rollercoaster dropped and that squeezing sensation forced all thought from his mind and air from his lungs.

A orange-pink world rushed up to meet them.

Birds of every conceivable color darted in the branches above, chattering as loudly as any pack of monkeys. Through the canopy of thick foliage, thin sunbeams hit the forest floor.

The temperature shift was enormous. The cool, humid air that held New Orleans in its grip was replaced with the balmy warmth King always associated with beaches.

And sure enough, when Lou pushed back the low branches, she revealed a gorgeous beach. Pale, clean sand and aquamarine waters tinged with the orange of sunset. For a moment, King could only stand there, marveling at the beauty of white crests rolling gently onto the dusky shore. They had only a few minutes left of sunset he was sure. For a moment he'd forgotten why he was so angry, so alarmed, until he saw a small figure wrapped in the cancer center's pink blanket. Then it came rushing back.

He crossed the beach in no time at all, coming down onto his knees beside her.

"We have to get you back to the hospital," he said. His voice was strained, strident.

"This is where she wants to be," Lou said.

"She's confused!" King screamed. He pounded a fist into the sand. "Half the time she calls me Jack! She doesn't know what she's saying."

"Robert," Lucy said calmly. "Look at me."

King blinked.

"Look at me," she said again, reaching a hand up to cup his cheek and force him to meet her eyes.

King obliged her.

"I don't want to die in a hospital bed."

He desperately searched her eyes for the glaze of pain. That look of confusion that often overtook her when her veins were full of the medications keeping her alive and comfortable.

"One hour on this beach is worth a hundred days in that room," she said, running a thumb over his shaven cheek.

"What happens when it gets cold and dark," he said finally, transitioning from his knees to his butt in the sand.

"Lou will get us more blankets. Build us a fire. Roast me a marshmallow," Lucy said, with a broad smile. "I'd love a roasted marshmallow. And a good beer."

Lou stood up, brushing much of the sand off her feet before forcing them back into her boots. Then she marched back into the woods, leaving them alone.

"You can't eat that stuff," King said, doubtfully. "I've been trying to feed you crap for weeks."

Lucy shrugged, her blue eyes bright in the sunset. "Maybe I want to be alone with a handsome man."

He leaned in and kissed her then, but he had no illusions about where this was going. The last thing this woman needed was his weight on top of her. But it seemed enough to hold her in the crook of his arm and place kisses on her scarved head.

He wanted to ask about the wedding. Tell her about the dress that Piper found and the croquembouche that had been ordered. But all of that seemed so ridiculous now as she sat curled up at his side.

"Are you sure you don't want to go back?" he asked.

She squeezed his hand. It was a weak grip. "I've had enough of that place. I want to die breathing fresh air."

King said nothing else on the subject. Instead he
only took off his long duster and threw it over her shoulders, adding another layer to the blanket around her. The last of the sun gave its way to twilight.

"She will be okay," Lucy said finally. She squeezed his hand again. "And you will be too."

"You have a lot of faith in me."

"In both of you."

King's heart hurt. "And if I fail? What if she's dead before she's thirty?"

"Ah, well the best of us die young, I suppose," she said. And he knew she was only trying to lighten the subject. She was right to do it. Now wasn't the time to speak of death. Or reminding her of all that she wouldn't get to see.

She searched his face as these thoughts rolled him like ocean waves.

"Nothing is good nor bad," she said. Her words had a strange lyric quality to it. He was sure she was reciting something. "It is only the mind that makes it so."

"More Buddhist bullshit?" he asked. He hated how the anger clipped his words. But he wasn't sure he could hide it any better than he was.

"It's okay to be angry," she told him. She cupped his face and ran a thumb over each of his cheeks
again. "But I have no regrets, Robert. I'm glad I came
back for you."

The words unleashed a stream from him. "I'm sorry I didn't come to you sooner. I had every excuse. I could've said I wanted to see how you and the kid were doing. I could've—"

She covered his mouth with hers. He relaxed into the kiss, trying to enjoy it. It was hard. Part of it was the smell. Though they'd brought her out of the hospital and into the world, she smelled of death. That acrid medicinal taste clung to her dry lips. And that scent filled him with terror. Irrational, claustrophobic terror. But he willed himself to remain in place and to kiss this woman.

When she pulled back she smiled. "Do you remember that time I made you go to Yuri's naked hot yoga class with me?"

"As if I'll ever forget. I've never been asked to put my face so close to my own junk before."

She laughed. "And you fell!"

"Because I looked ahead at the woman in front of me doing that moon pose…"

"Half moon."

"It wasn't her moon I was looking at."

Lucy laughed. When was the last time he'd heard her laugh like this? Maybe the fresh air was better for her.

He went on, hoping to milk this drop of joy for all it was worth. "It's a shame you weren't ahead of me. I would've liked to seen you from that angle. I feel bad for the guy who was behind me."

They fell into laughter then. And it felt good. It felt so good that those remnants of anger receded. He was sure they would appear again soon, rising up some dark and ugly night to remind him of all his regrets. But for now, Lucy was in his arms. She was laughing, and the night had bloomed beautiful around them.

Lou seemed determined to keep herself busy. King was vaguely aware of her comings and goings as they continued to sit, watching the sky darken. But her deliveries were endless. She brought new meaning to the idea *move heaven and earth for you.*

Though heaven and earth in this instance was a pile of wood for the fire. Kindling and a striker. A pile of blankets that she arranged for Lucy beside it, making a pallet big enough for the two of them—Lou herself got a low beach chair.

And she didn't stop there. She showed up with a large pizza and a six-pack of beer. Pillows, which King recognized as those she'd brought to the hospital room. When it was all said and done, it was quite the beach party. The only thing they were missing was someone on guitar.

Lou used a bottle opener to pop off the cap from a frosty bottle.

"Soft Parade!" Lucy cried softly, with a bright smile, accepting the bottle from her niece. The firelight danced in her eyes. "I love this beer. Perfect for a warm night like this. Have you ever had it, Robert?"

King admitted that he did not.

He watched the women talk, reminiscing about ridiculous times, about good times. Lou followed her lead, smiling at all the right moments though from time to time, King caught a glimpse of hollow distance in that gaze.

No one spoke of death. Of dying. King himself added to the conversation where he could, adding his own adventures with Lucy to the proverbial pyre.

Lou continued to deliver wood and feed the fire well into the night.

"Do you have any regrets," Lou asked her aunt, throwing another log onto the fire. This one was wrapped in yellow twine and King wondered who she'd stolen if from and if he cared.

"You'd love it if I gave you a kill list," Lucy laughed. The words were delivered sweetly, no hint of anger or cruelty. And King could tell that Louie was relieved by this. "But no. I have only one regret. I'm sorry that I didn't marry you, Robert."

She placed a hand on his knee and squeezed it. She snuggled deeper into the crook of his arm.

Without a word, Lou rose from her chair and disappeared through the woods. King wondered if it was to give them a bit of time alone. If she'd read some signal in Lucy's tone, or if the affection going between them had simply left her uncomfortable.

But a moment later, she reappeared.

Lou emerged from the forest edge with a man in tow. For a wretched moment, King thought *Konstantine. Lord help us, she's brought Konstantine here*.

But when the man stepped into the firelight, it wasn't the Italian at all. This man was much older and stately in his black robes.

The priest looked nervously from Lou to the couple cuddled together by the fire. "She tells me that you would like to be married?"

# 25

Konstantine was restless. He stared out at the river, counting how many ferry crossings the old-fashioned boat made, overloaded with tourists and the occasional starburst flash of a camera sparking from the opposite bank. Families wandered up and down the boardwalk, one child holding a bright red balloon that bounced and bobbed as she skipped between her parents.

He knew he should feel only gratitude. Her apartment, however small, was his sanctuary. Nico had nearly killed him. No matter what counter measures had been necessary, Konstantine would have had to hide until he was strong enough to retaliate.

And what better place? No one knew this place or this woman. Not really. He'd circulated and encouraged overblown tales meant to keep his men alert and in awe of their supposed alliance. But none knew her name or her real identity. Unless…

If Nico was smart, he would go through Konstantine's possessions, leaving no mattress or safe unturned. Given enough time, and he had been given enough time, he would likely find the photos. That was a possibility—and a threat.

All the information his old servant Julio has drummed up on her, in his initial quest to learn her identity—birth certificates, news reports regarding the murder of her parents, and school records—he'd burned it all.

But he hadn't had it in him to burn the photographs.

On the nights when he craved her so badly, sometimes sitting at his desk in his dark alcove, a glass of Chianti at hand, he would thumb through the photographs. No matter how grainy, the sight of her was enough to put his mind at ease.

Or if she did something to anger him…

When she killed his best port liaison in Jersey, for example. He'd received the call the next morning that four distributors had gotten nervous and rescinded their shipments when Wallie Rambo never answered their calls nor gave them the information for the drop point.

Some of the men thought Wallie had bailed. After all, he had quite a few gambling debts and had angered a local card shark.

But Konstantine knew who had plucked him

from the dark, and it was no card shark.

It cost quite a bit of money and time to reconfigure the distribution line to his liking. Good, trustworthy men were hard to find in this business. And despite his penchant for gambling, Rambo was reliable, and did as he was told.

In those moments when he found his anger and frustration rise, he need only look at the photographs, see the strong outline of her determined jaw and remember who she was. What she really was to him.

Their destiny was so much bigger than either of their minor schemes and he understood that.

Her gift had brought her to him, long before she could have known who he was. No matter what else they were doing in this world, they were tied together for a greater purpose.

Konstantine understood this.

And Padre Leo had taught him patience. Some things cannot be rushed.

*Look at this great cathedral*, Padre had said. Konstantine could still see Padre's black pants and a black dress shirt that was open at the collar, a gold chain at his neck.

They'd been decorating the church for Christmas and Padre had pulled Konstantine aside from the other boys when he heard him complaining about how long the work was taking. It felt as if they'd been decorating for days, and just when Konstantine thought they were done, another heap of red ribbons or garlands would appear.

*She is beautiful, isn't she?*

As a boy Konstantine knew nothing of beauty. But he'd loved the high ceilings. The magic of a mosaic that had lasted centuries.

*It took six hundred years for this church to become as you see it*, Padre had said. *Remember that, passerotto.*

*You cannot rush greatness. You must be patient. You must build it brick by brick—*

A sharp sound yanked Konstantine from his memories. He turned away from the window, expecting the closet to open. But it didn't. Then he heard a sound that he would recognize anywhere.

A fist connecting. And it came from that secret room beneath the kitchen island.

He was across the apartment before thinking. Then he had the latch flicked open and was descending the stairs.

Lou must not have heard him as her fist repeatedly connected with the wooden post over and over again.

He seized her wrist mid-swing and she redirected easily.

But he'd expected this. He'd seen enough rage in violent men to know how they reacted if you dared interrupt them.

What he hadn't been expecting was the momen-tum. Though he'd seized her other wrist, deflecting the blow, her forward movement had thrown them both into the wall at the bottom of the stairs. They stood beneath the halo of lamplight. He held her wrists so she wouldn't strike him.

To his surprise, she let him.

With each breath her body grew softer against his, until she was simply leaning against him. He was pinned against the wall under the weight of her.

She looked so slight and no more than 5'7 or maybe 5'8. But she was solid muscle and he supposed that made up the weight. Or maybe it was something in that gift of hers. Perhaps gravity was different for this one.

He loosened his grip on her wrists cautiously.

"What happened?" he breathed into her hair.

At first she didn't speak. And he considered that she might not answer him at all.

Then she said, "She was sick for a long time and didn't tell me."

He understood then. He'd known about the aunt's illness. Tracking her had been easy compared to the woman now leaning all her weight against him. Lucy Thorne wasn't a ghost. She had as many public records as anyone, including some private ones, which Konstantine had accessed with ease.

He thought of Padre, of how again it seemed like this woman's life echoed and intersected his own. Padre too had hidden his illness until nothing could be done but say goodbye.

Konstantine turned her wrist so he could inspect the damage. The knuckles were split and bloody, but on a whole, it looked all right. He wondered how often she might have rages like this, and how conditioned her hands must be as a result.

"Did you get to say goodbye?" he asked softly, running one thumb over the back of her hand.

She nodded.

"Good," he said, finding his voice dangerously calm. He was hiding his own emotions well enough. He hoped. When he felt more in control of himself, he said, "We should clean this up."

She mounted the stairs without a word, taking all that heat and weight of the moment with her. Konstantine turned off the light behind them.

She was already sitting on the edge of her bed,

the kit open before her, cleaning the wound by the time he latched the island door closed.

He knelt before her and helped her wrap the hand carefully. Then it was done.

As soon as he fastened the lid back onto the box, she pulled him into the bed with her.

She rolled him onto his back easily, her legs sliding down on either side of his waist. It felt even more delicious than he'd always imagined it would. Her muscles shifting. Her heat.

She wanted him. He could see it in her eyes, a look of hunger as easy to identify as his own. But it wasn't tender. It bordered fury.

His eyes slid over her body, his hands on each of her hips. He wanted his hands to be right here when she slid herself down onto him. He had only to undress her first. He reached for the hem of her shirt but she slammed his wrists back into the mattress, pinning them on either side of his head.

He was fine with this. He would give every ounce of control to this woman, if she wanted it. Whatever she needed to trust him.

But when he met her eyes again, tears stood out in the lashes.

He bucked her forward with his hips and flipped

her over. She hit her side, then her back, until he was

rolling her away from him.

Her tight ass pressed into that perfect seat of his lap and his arms went around her.

He lay still, holding her against him as snug as that vest she wore. "If you need to take care of—"

"—it's done," she said. Despite her tears, her voice remained perfectly steady.

"It's dangerous to fight when you aren't yourself," he said.

Her power and abilities would be his greatest ally in the fight against Nico and his army, but he wouldn't want her to truly endanger herself. He knew firsthand that pain in the heart and mind were more crippling than pain in one's body.

She remained motionless in his arms. So warm. He thought of kissing her neck. Her hair. Of sliding the hand on her abdomen down to find that place where her legs met.

He didn't.

*You must build it, brick by brick.*

"With so many bastards in one place," she said, her neck luminous in the moonlight pouring over his shoulder. Her breath hot on his arm. "I'll be more *myself* than you can stand."

# 26

Lou rose from the bed without making a sound. Konstantine never woke. He'd fallen asleep where she'd left him, on his back in her bed. Lou however couldn't sleep. Not because she didn't understand what was happening between them, but because she wasn't sure she had enough sense left to be cautious. She'd almost slept with him. And she would have if not for the sudden, bright memory of Lucy's dying face flashing across the screen of her mind.

Her bony hand cupping her cheek. *Forgive me, Louie.*

The last thing she would ever say.

By now, no doubt, they'd found her body in the hospital room where she'd returned her. She'd placed the body back into an empty bed just after sunrise Hawaii time, and pressed the call button. She didn't wait to see who would come, or if this was even the correct room.

What they would think of the sand, of the smell of smoke in the dead woman's hair, and her lack of shoes…Lou didn't know. She took the blankets and departed, certain King would fill in the gaps sooner or later.

He'd insisted on being returned to his apartment where he could change and wash the smell of smoke from his hair and errant sand from his body. He thought if it looked as if they had both been to the beach, it might've been enough for them to push an inquiry, even if there was no way they could prove anything.

So shower first, and then he would return to the hospital, prepared to receive the news he already knew was coming.

She suspected that it was possible he could've been tied up at the cancer center for a while with some kind of bureaucratic bullshit. But he should be at his apartment by now.

Lou stepped into her converted linen closet and let her compass whirl in the dark, searching for King.

When it locked onto him, and the walls melted away, she wasn't greeted by his familiar red couch or beast of an armoire. Not by his king-sized bed nor his tiny bathroom.

It wasn't his apartment at all.

She emerged from the shadows onto the street.

A woman screamed, immediately falling into giggles, one hand on her chest.

"Christ," she said, her voice high. "I didn't see you."

She wobbled past Lou with her plastic cup, her heels unsteady beneath her.

She read the street sign, the corner of St. Peter and Bourbon. She took one look at the neon bar sign, noted the thudding bass blaring through the open door, vibrating her chest, and knew exactly where King was.

The doorman motioned her forward. She didn't bother. Rounding a corner, she took the alley in. Alley to the bathroom. Bathroom into the bar itself.

It was easy to spot King.

Mostly because he was such a massive man. Another because he was making a fool of himself.

A man beside him was talking shit and King had turned on his stool to eye him with a wrathful gaze. Before Lou could even cross the dim bar and reach him, the basket of pickle chips had been overturned, and the first punch thrown.

A brown beer bottle was knocked over, pouring frothy booze over the lip of the wooden bar.

She reached him in four long strides, stepping between him and the other man. It was a man in a leather jacket with his fingers wrapped in fingerless studded leather gloves.

He was at least a hundred pounds lighter than King. He was built like a soccer player. Tall, thin.

When Lou stepped between them, she gave King her back. She'd hoped that at least he wouldn't hit her.

When the biker threw his second punch, Lou was there to intercept it. She deflected it with her rotating wrist and struck the man in his throat. His eyes bulged, both hands going to his neck.

Before his anger overrode his surprise, she gave him a swift kick in the knee to think about. He toppled.

Lou turned, ready to haul King from the bar and was greeted with a fist. She moved at the last moment, sparing her face from the wild hook. But because she'd stepped back, she'd put her wounded shoulder right in the path of his blow.

Her arm sang. Furious, waves of pain radiating up her arm, she seized him with her good arm and yanked him from the bar. She didn't head toward the exit, but rather the bathrooms. As piss-scented and filthy as they were, they were far darker than the streets.

King howled the whole time. Hellbent on defending his honor.

"What the hell did you do that for?" he screamed. "I was fine. I was handling it fine."

He no doubt had more to say but the slip swallowed his words whole.

When they appeared in his apartment, the first thing King did was fall to his hands and knees and puke on his rug.

The acrid scent of sour vomit and booze bloomed in the room. Lou opened the balcony door, hoping the breeze would overcome it. Watching him sit back on his heels, his eyes glazed, she realized how drunk he was. Quite. And a man his size didn't get drunk like that quickly.

"Did you go back to the hospital?" she asked.

"No," he shouted. She wasn't sure if this was on purpose or if he had no idea how loud his voice was.

"Why?"

"Because I didn't have my car," he said, even louder. "I didn't have a car. It's still in the parking lot. I drove to the center yesterday. And it's still there."

"So you went to the bar instead? Because it was walking distance?"

"So what if I did? What if I *fucking* did!"

No doubt he'd been drinking all day. He smelled like it. He looked like it. What time did bars in the French quarter open? She had no idea. But she was sure that he'd been there when someone unlocked the door.

Drunk revelers stumbled through the streets, their laughter rising up through the window, mingling with the whine of a violin.

King seemed to regard the vomit on the rug as if he wasn't sure how it'd gotten there. Then he threw up onto the carpet again.

"What the hell is all this?" Mel appeared in the kitchen, closing the door to the apartment behind her. "What is he going on about?"

"He's drunk," Lou said.

"I'm not drunk," King said.

"The hell you aren't. And in my house!"

Mel saw the vomit and wrinkled her nose. "What in the world would Miss Lucy think of you carrying on like this?"

King laughed. Laughed, maniacally until the rolling laughter gave over to tears and he covered his face with his hands.

"The hell," Mel murmured. She looked to Lou, hoping for answers. Lou noted her fortune teller get-up. The long purple skirt. The scarf tied around her head and gold bangles on her wrist. The deep kohl lining each eye.

"Lucy is dead," Lou said, finding the words foreign on her tongue. Her grief made the words heavy and unreal in her mouth.

Melandra's rage softened. "I see now."

Lou couldn't bear to look at the concerned face. "I'll go get his car."

"No need," Mel said, going to the freezer and fetching a frozen bag of peas. "I'll send Piper to get it. Can you help me get him onto the couch?"

Lou lifted him and plopped him on the sofa.

Mel looked a little surprised. "Thanks." She placed the peas over the worst part of King's swelling face.

Lou couldn't stay here. Not with the scent of vomit, not with Mel's concerned, mournful face. She turned to leave, and a bony hand caught her wrist.

Her instinct was to swing. To throw a fist into whatever wanted to pull her back into the misery. But she'd already done that to Konstantine tonight. Now having seen King do the same, it left a taste in her mouth. If she'd looked half as ridiculous as he had, she'd never lose control again.

"You going to be all right?" Mel asked. The hold on her wrist loosened. "Is there anything you need?"

Yes. She wanted to choke the life out of a man. Any bottom-feeding scumbag would do.

"I'll be fine," she said and turned before Mel could see her grimace.

Mel let her go. "I'll look out for Mr. King. Take care of yourself."

Lou gave some sort of noncommittal nod, only somewhat aware of the room around her. Already her thirst, her desire had risen up in her. Her nerves seemed to thrum with it. Every fiber in her being begging for some kind of release from the anguish plucking at her nerves. The whine filling her mind like razorblades on guitar strings.

She stepped into the shadows of the armoire and out again. She wasn't sure where the darkness would take her. Where she wanted to go. She only knew she couldn't be near King and all his anguish. And she sure as hell couldn't be go back to her apartment to face Konstantine and all his desire.

People with their fucking feelings. She didn't even want to deal with her own.

No, she needed a distraction. A nice, dangerous distraction that would take up all the space in her mind.

A kitchen materialized from nothing.

A gleaming surface held pots and pans. Dishes ready to be served. She expected people in little white uniforms, familiar chef's attire to appear any moment. Instead the prep table was lined with white bricks. Rows and rows of white bricks wrapped in clear plastic.

Then she heard the male voices. The angry arguing. She crossed the grimy tile of the kitchen, checking the gun at her side. She marched right down the center aisle. *Reckless*, her mind breathed, as it searched for nonexistent shadows.

She pulled the gun with her bad arm and it burned.

*Reckless*.

Still she marched forward.

And then there they were, two men arguing so fiercely amongst themselves that neither of them saw her. At first.

"This isn't enough!" the one screamed, his broad back to her. His bomber jacket bouncing with exaggerated fury. "Where's the rest of it?"

"Tony, I fuckin' told you. This is all he gave me. Call him and ask him yourself. This is all there is."

"But I paid for twice as much, at least. If there's no dope then give me my fucking money back!"

The bomber jacket shoved the shorter man. By pushing him out of the line of view, it revealed him for who he was. A squat Asian man, maybe no more than 5'5, 5'4. His eyes wide at the sudden push. But his new angle gave him a full view of Lou, approaching from behind.

"Don't be looking like a scared little bitch, Po. You aren't going to fool me with shit again. Looking behind me, trying to get me to turn and then when I turn around, you fucking bolt like a pony at the track. No way. Fool me once and all that shit."

Tony pulled his gun and pointed it at the man named, Po.

"But—" Po began.

Lou seized Tony by the back of his leather jacket with her free hand, her good hand, and with the other, opened the freezer. Po stood stunned, and unmoving as Lou dragged the howling man into the freezing dark. The cold didn't last.

His knees hit the dirt.

Lou wasn't sure if they always toppled like because she released them so abruptly after the slip, or if slipping through the dark was such a dizzying affair. King had complained about it once, but she herself had no problem emerging from the dark on her own two feet, head clear, and the night calm around her. Unless of course she'd been shot, or was dying. She supposed that was true.

But she hadn't even put a scratch on Tony. Yet.

She should change that.

Her right hook crashed into the side of the man's face. Her knuckles slid along the jaw bone finally connecting with the mouth. The lip split over the teeth. It swelled instantly, blood pooling in the crack.

She waited. She stood there waiting for him to retaliate. She *wanted* him to retaliate.

*Not in my name, Lou.* Lucy's plea rang through her mind the second before Tony's fist connected with her gut, winding her. She went down on one knee.

His leg rose, and she knew he meant to kick her in the face.

She let herself fall. Fall through the dark and appear three feet behind him in a moonlit patch that seemed made for her.

His foot connected with earth with more force than he'd expected and he was pitched forward. His arms waved comically trying to reestablish control. She kicked him in the tailbone, and he cried out. His back arched furiously as he threw back his head and howled his pain.

*Why do you pick fights?* Lucy asked.

It was the aunt she remembered best in her mind's eye. No more than 42 maybe. Lou was fourteen and halfway through her first year in a new school.

*There are better ways to deal with your anger*, Lucy told her after she picked her up from school on the principal's orders and walked her down to the city bus stop. They did public transport to and from school at Lucy's insistence. *No slipping in school.*

Apparently, kneeing a guy during gym was also forbidden.

"He slapped my ass."

"Language."

"He *assaulted* me," Lou had said. "Be glad all I did was knee him."

Lucy's silence after that had weighed on her. Gave her mind such a wild and menacing playground within which to dream up the possible insults she must be composing for her niece in her mind. Lou had braced herself for her rejection. For her cold regard. But on the bus, halfway to their Oak Park apartment Lucy said, "Fighting isn't an appropriate way to dispel your anger."

"Don't start up about yoga again."

"No, not yoga," Lucy agreed. "I have something
else in mind."

The next day she'd dropped Lou off at an aikido
dojo on Chicago's east side and Lou took to it like a bird to the air.

But all the training in the world hadn't seemed to prepare her for this. For the moment when her life was thrown into the pool again.

She was drowning.

She was falling through and there was no one to pull her out.

Nowhere to go but down.

And now, thinking of her aunt's calm face, the fight left Lou. Her heart sank to irretrievable depths and with the last of her fury, she seized Tony by the back of his neck and hauled him up. She threw him into the lake with one great shove. He hit the water the way Lou must've hit the water that June night her father saved her life. Mouth open in surprise. Arms out as if to break a fall. An ugly splash that had winded her.

She marched through the water after him. And just as his head surfaced, she was on him.

She wrapped her legs around his body and pulled him down, squeezing the way an octopus with its many tentacles must squeeze its prey before pulling the food to its beak for rendering.

The water warmed. Turned the color of blood.

And then there they were on the other side.

Tony's reaction was one she'd seen a hundred times. Blind, abject terror. He flailed in the water. He screamed at the terrible landscape. He followed her to shore howling, as if she were his salvation instead of the person who'd condemned him to die in this place.

Then the familiar screech she'd come to expect broke open the sky.

The beast bounded around her, circling her twice and swiping at her stomach with its head as if in greeting. Then she chased after Tony the way a puppy chased after his master. But when she caught him, the sounds that emitted from his mouth couldn't be mistaken for play.

Lou sank onto the embankment, and put her face in her hands. She wiped the water away, and smoothed her hair back from her face. She'd lost her sunglasses. It was hard to give a shit about sunglasses when Lucy was dead.

She breathed, head between her knees. When the world stopped spinning, she shrugged off the leather jacket to give her burning arm a good look. It was swollen, the flesh pinched red between the black wire. But it was not bleeding, not oozing puss.

She heard Jabbers behind her but didn't bother to turn. "Fucking eat me. Put me out of my misery."

She wouldn't.

The beast had saved her life by shoving her into the water before she'd blacked out. Lou understood that now. She'd known it was smart, possessing an intelligence of some kind. But now she suspected the walking nightmare had even more than she imagined.

It understood that she came and went by the water. And it understood that somehow, on the other side, there was a possibility that she could heal.

It sniffed Lou's wounded arm, and sneezed.

Lou cringed, using the water to rinse the wound. "Hope you don't have some horrible tropical disease in your snot."

The monster sat on its haunches beside her. Its white tongue licked the blood from its snout before chewing the guts from the webbing in its feet.

Then it slid into the water, paddling a circle before diving underneath. Lou only watched, catching her breath, taking in the eternal twilight and double moons.

Seemingly tired of water play, the beast crawled onto the shore again, once more taking a seat beside her, reclining on all fours and licking what can only
be called forearms

Lou reached out and touched the cool, damp flesh. The beast made a sound, not unlike purring.

"Who needs retail therapy, when I've got you," Lou said, patting that reptilian snout.

And then, just as she had on the night her father died, Lou cried herself hoarse on the banks of La Loon.

# 27

King woke on his red sofa, staring up at a long patch of sunlight across his ceiling. At first all he could taste was the burning, citrus taste of booze, like maybe salt and lime had been left in his mouth all night to putrefy. He smacked his lips a few times and found the moisture gone.

He sat up and the world spun. His arm shot out and grabbed the first thing he could find—which turned out to be his enormous coffee table. He held its smooth surface with a weak grip until the room stopped spinning and came into focus again. The large armoire in the corner, cherry wood that looked especially red in the light pouring through the open balcony. Sunshine glittering across his white bedspread in the adjacent bedroom. The quiet kitchen with a water glass sitting half full beside the silver basin.

A leather jacket on a hanger, hanging from the trim above his bedroom door. Its hook was placed so that the weight kept it steady despite the slight swing in the breeze.

Lou was sitting in his leather armchair. Beside her rest his record player on its stand and a stack of vinyls leaning against it. Their fraying cardboard edges reminded him of how old, how *vulnerable* they were. His eyes slid to the Bob Dylan vinyl where he kept his weed and a half-used pack of rolling papers.

Seeing Lou in the chair, flipping through one of the bridal magazines that had no doubt been on his coffee table, and those records—all of it brought Lucy to mind.

Was that really only three months ago?

The way she had stretched on his red leather sofa, an icy glass of sweet tea balanced on her bare knee. Her body was ethereal in the moonlight sparkling through the open balcony door. It was if she'd never left him if he overlooked the longer hair. What would he give to rewind it to those three months and start all over again? And how much more, to go back twelve years…

A wave of sadness slammed into his chest. A fist seized his heart and squeezed.

He wiped at his eyes with balled fists. Doing so made his knuckles burn, reminding him of the split flesh from the night before.

"Are you still drunk?" Lou asked, closing the bridal magazine and tossing it to the floor with disgust. He saw she was sporting her own bloodied knuckles.

*What a pair we make*, he thought.

"No," King croaked. "Unfortunately. I hope to change that very soon."

"Your landlady will kill you if you do," she said. Her mirrored sunglasses were up on her head and she regarded him with Jack's unflinching eyes. But the glasses looked different. Maybe she got a second pair.

"Is that your jacket?" he asked, pointing at his bedroom door. It hung from a hanger balanced precipitously on the top of the frame.

"It got wet," she said, as if this explained everything.

Then more of the room came into focus. The dried vomit in the rug. His bloody knuckles which burned as he flexed and balled his hands in turn.

Dead. Lucy was dead.

She'd died in his arms on a beach in Maui. And as fucking romantic as that sounded, it didn't spare him an ounce of the grief.

Then he was crying. *Really* crying, his whole body convulsing. He hadn't cried like this when his parents died, nor his beloved grandfather. Not even Jack, whose death had hurt his heart in a way none had before.

Before he knew it, Lou was pressing his red rescue inhaler into one of his hands, pushing against the knuckles until he unballed his fist and accepted it.

She was shoving a bottle of Jack into the other.

He laughed, a strangled, humorless sound, when he saw it. "Where the hell did this come from?"

She didn't seem to hear him. She was fishing his cell phone from the kitchen island and handing it to him. "Your phone has gone off several times. You've got messages."

King put down the bottle of Jack on the coffee table and accepted the phone.

He did have messages, so many that his screen looked like an emergency. Red flags blaring at him from several icons.

He listened to each one in turn, informing Lou of its contents.

"Piper got my car and parked it in the alley."

"They found Lucy and want to know if I want to see her before they send her to the morgue." His voice cracked and broke on that last one.

The last voicemail was from Sampson informing him that he would be visiting him today at

approximately eleven. His tone was grave.

King squinted at the green clock on his stove. 10:53. "Shit."

The fire escape rattled the same moment as Melandra blew into the apartment. "Mr. King, get up. There's a cop looking for you."

Before he could process this, Lou had crossed the room, snatched her leather jacket from the hanger and disappeared into his bedroom.

"What did he look like?" King asked. But he didn't need her answer. In the same instance, one finely clad leg stepped onto his balcony followed by another. The spit-shone black shoes. The uncreased navy blue dress pants. A nice cotton, collared shirt tucked into the pants. A gray mustache trimmed and clean.

Sampson hadn't aged a day since King saw him last.

"What did I tell you?" Melandra started before Sampson could even cross through the open balcony. One hand was on her hip, the other pointed a fierce finger at the man's face. "I will call the law on you, do you hear me? I want to see your damn warrant!"

Sampson held both hands out in front of him, palms out in surrender. Or they would be, if the left hadn't been clutching a manila folder.

"Mel, it's all right," King said. He would've said this even if it wasn't. He was desperate for some quiet with the throbbing headache splitting his brains in half. It was the headache, no doubt. But crying hadn't helped. "Sampson and I are friends. And we had an appointment."

Without missing a beat Sampson said, "We do."

With no target, Mel threw up her hands in exasperation. And perhaps that would have been the end of it had she not spotted the bottle of Jack on King's coffee table.

She yelped and snatched it up with one clawed fist. "No, sir!" She shook the bottle at him, brown liquid sloshing against its sides until it was King's turn to hold up his hands in surrender.

"It was from…a gift," he quickly corrected, dropping Lou's name from the sentence. "I didn't drink any."

Something flashed in her eyes and King suspected she knew what he'd meant to say, but she arched her brow all the same. "Who gives half-drunk bottles as gifts, King, I can't say."

But she took the bottle and left him alone with Sampson.

"A spirited woman," Sampson said, in obvious admiration.

And King laughed at the unintentional pun. Because surely he hadn't meant Mel's penchant for cards and conversing with the dead. Instead he said, "You have no idea."

Sampson glanced around the apartment. "Nice place you have here, Robert."

"Thank you. But I don't think you came all the way from St. Louis to compliment my paint job. What's going on?"

"I needed to talk to you," he began.

"Obviously."

"And it wasn't something that should've happened over the phone." Sampson regarded him with dark eyes. "Lest it be admissible in a court of law."

King's heart stopped on a dime. When he recovered he said, "I would offer you a drink, but I'm afraid Mel took it away. Water?"

"No, thank you."

Sampson took a seat in the leather chair that Lou had just vacated.

"If we are talking court, do I need to ask you to lift your shirt for a wire?" King asked solemnly.

Sampson didn't even look offended. He untucked his nice collared shirt and showed his tight brown belly. Swaths of grey hair covered his chest, but no wire.

"Who is investigating me?" King asked.

"I am."

"Are you serious?"

"As of this morning," he said and tapped the folder against his leg.

"May I ask what *for*?"

"We know that you signed onto the server and accessed unpublished information."

King's heart sank. Now he *really* wished that Mel had left the bottle behind.

"Though looking at you, I can hardly believe it," Sampson said, ramrod straight from the leather chair. He'd always had impeccable posture from years of band followed by a military career, he'd once told King.

"Why do you say that?" King asked, wondering if he should lawyer up. And if so, with who? Someone expensive no doubt.

"Robert, you look like hell."

"I've had a rough 24 hours," King said, lying back against the cushions.

"How rough."

"My wife died."

*My wife.*

"I'm sorry. I didn't realize you were married."

"It wasn't finalized," he admitted. "She'd been sick in the hospital. There was a priest but no marriage certificate. I'm not sure it would hold in court." King knew he was rambling. But focusing on the bullshit details that didn't matter felt better than looking too closely at the raw reality. Lucy was gone. Lucy was gone and she wasn't coming back.

Tears stung his eyes.

"None of that matters if you loved her."

"I do. I did." His voice cracked.

Sampson said nothing. Puzzlement danced across his face. King saw his conflict, his desire to push forward with his business in coming here, warring against the decency of not kicking a man while he was down.

King wanted him gone. And if the man had flown from St. Louis to talk to him, he wasn't leaving until he'd done what he'd come to do.

"How bad is it?" King asked.

"That's what I came to ask you," Sampson said.

King said nothing.

"I can see now that this isn't a good time, and I'm real sorry about that," Sampson began. "But you've got to talk to me. Tell me what is going on."

"I needed some information," King said.

"About Paolo Konstantine?"

"Just an old man's curiosity," King insisted. "Go on and call me an Uncle, but it's not like I was using it maliciously."

"What does Louie Thorne have to do with all this?"

The mention of her name made King's blood freeze in his veins. Had he really been so careless? He thought he'd done a good job of entering and exiting the server using different IPs and encrypted lines. Whatever emotion played across his face Sampson must've seen it.

"Isn't she Jack's daughter?"

Of course he made the connection. Because Sampson knew Jack too. Knew how much the grunt had meant to King when he was flying high in the St. Louis unit, in the peak of their glory days before his murder and the slander of his good name had brought everything crashing down around them.

And hadn't it been Sampson himself who had testified on King's behalf, vouching that no matter what Jack may have done, no matter how many connections formed with the Martinelli cartel, King was innocent of all wrong doing.

"To help you along," Sampson said, his face somewhere between masked and sympathetic. "I'll tell you what I did. I compiled every search conducted on our server in the last ninety days and what I found was a whole lot of people were checking on the name Louie Thorne. Or sometimes Lou Thorne and once in a while Lucy Thorne, who turns out, is Jack's sister and a woman you've been visiting at the New Orleans Cancer Center nearly every day over a month. And I take it she's the wife you are referring to?"

King tried to control his exhale.

"What's going on, Robbie?" Now Sampson's face was genuine concern. "What are you doing? Is this for your P.I. business?"

"If I told you," King said, running a hand over his weathered face. "You wouldn't believe me."

When had he gotten so damn old? His head ached. His back and neck ached. His hand knuckles were the color of a split plum.

"Try me," Sampson said. "Because I've been tasked with detailing every suspicious log-in for the last ninety days and I need to have a good damn excuse for this. The department is on high alert over this Konstantine mess. There's a real possibility that innocent people like yourself will get caught in the crossfire if we aren't careful. They want to cover their asses and they want to blame someone. You know how it goes. And this is suspicious as hell, so give me something you can float on here or you're going down with the ship."

King looked up and saw Lou leaning in the doorway of his bedroom.

Shock ran through his body and his surprised jolt must have alarmed Sampson as well. He was on his feet, holding the manila folder down at his side as his right hand snaked toward the small of his back. So he was packing. Weren't they all these days...

King had thought she'd left. That she'd simply taken the leather jacket she now wore and had slipped through some shadowed corner of his bedroom, or perhaps from beneath his bed. But here she was, mirrored sunglasses and all.

"Won't you introduce us?" she said.

King finally found his voice. "I don't believe you've met Jack's daughter, Lou. Lou this is Sampson. He worked with your old man back in St. Louis."

Sampson couldn't contain his surprise. And King understood full and well. The creature standing before him was like something out of the jungle. Her entire leather-clad presence from head-to-toe. No wonder she blended with the underworld so well. She looked cut from the same cloth. And for anyone who'd hunted danger in the dark, they knew dangerous when they saw it. When it stood before them, the urge to reach for the gun was high.

But Lou was offering her hand. She was saying hello.

Sampson found his voice at last. "It's nice to see you again. You're…all grown up."

King arched an eyebrow at the other man but Sampson didn't seem to notice. And he couldn't read Lou's eyes either behind those sunglasses.

Lou was speaking. "It's my fault that he keeps searching your database."

King's skin chilled. Sampson was a do-gooder. He stood on the right-side of the law. And though that made him a trustworthy man, it didn't mean he could be trusted with the truth.

If Lou saw his panicked expression, she continued as if she hadn't.

"The Italian crime factions thought they won when my dad's name was publicly trashed," she said. "When he was exonerated, they became angry. They've made threats, tried to track me down. King knew they were looking into your servers. And he wanted to make sure there was nothing there that could lead them to me."

King was holding his breath. It was a damn good lie. It was a damn good lie because it wasn't exactly a lie at all. The criminals were trying to crack the server. He was sure they were pissed when Jack was elevated to hero status again. And no doubt more than one drug lord would love to know this woman's real name and how to find her.

Sampson was trying to detect a lie, King could see it in his searching expression. But he couldn't find one.

"They threaten you?" he asked, finally.

"Almost every day." Another truth. Sampson didn't need to know that those threats usually came delivered from fear, at knifepoint.

"Why haven't you reported it? You could have asked for protection?"

It took considerable control for King not to burst out laughing. Louie Thorne, in need of their protection?

"Do you think I can trust the DEA after what Brasso did to my father?" she said.

Sampson was the first to avert his eyes.

"I see," he said finally.

"King was just trying to protect me."

More truth, though King wouldn't have been able to say it from his own lips without dipping the words in guilt first. He wanted to honor Jack and Lucy, but it wasn't enough.

He flexed his hand and saw fresh blood spring up between the malformed scabs. Sampson was looking at his busted hand too, no doubt drawing his own conclusions.

"I've got all I need. I'll leave you to your grief," Sampson said. "I'm sorry I came at such a bad time. And I'm sorry for your loss."

He hesitated at the balcony door. "King. One more thing?"

With much effort, King dragged himself from the sofa and followed Sampson out onto the balcony. He pulled the door shut behind them.

"*That's* Louie Thorne?" Sampson asked, his face overrun with disbelief.

King wasn't sure if this was a real question or verbal processing. "Yeah. Makes you feel old doesn't it?"

"I remember her at the picnics. Quiet. Liked her books."

"Still quiet," King said, unsure where this was going.

"You've got to stop logging on," Sampson said.

"They're in frenzy over this Konstantine bullshit."

"All right." He held up his bloody knuckles. "I'm in need of a break anyway."

"And you should keep track of the threats," Sampson added. "In case this all ends up in court, you'll want proof that she's been threatened."

As if Louie Thorne would ever let it get that far. "It's good advice, Sammy."

He was staring at the closed balcony door. "Is she all right?"

"What do you mean?"

Sampson touched the side of his head and raised his eyebrows. "What happened to Jack, well, that'd mess up anybody. And she was there that night."

"Does she seem crazy to you?" King asked, genuinely curious. He wondered what the rest of the world saw when they looked at Lou.

"No," Sampson said, shaking his head. "No, she seems smart. Charming. But Ted Bundy had been charming too."

King laughed. The jab was too close not to strike him funny. "She's not eating people or fucking their corpses. I assure you."

But King was sure that Lou had surpassed Bundy's body count years ago.

"Well, look after her," Sampson said. He frowned at King. "And yourself, Robbie."

"I'm trying."

Sampson squeezed his shoulder and climbed onto the fire escape with the folder tucked under his arm. "I'll be in touch if anything develops with this."

"You know you can use the front door. Mel won't bite. Probably."

Sampson only laughed. "My momma didn't raise no fool."

King listened to the fire escape rattle with the large man's descent before he stepped back into the apartment and closed the balcony door.

"You're not being careful." Lou leaned against his bedroom door, watching him carefully.

King snorted. It was all he could muster in the form of humor. His heart wasn't in it. His heart, in fact, was nowhere to be found. "Maybe that's why Lucy linked us up. She wanted you to babysit an old, stupid, man."

*Lucy.* Just her name, the thought of her, as light as a dry corn husk in his arms. He pinched his eyes closed and pressed his thumbs into his temples.

This hurt. And it was going to hurt for a long time.

"You can't go on the server anymore," Lou said.

"No shit."

"There's another way. I don't know how it works, but I know he's good at it."

"Him who?"

"Sober up and I'll introduce you."

# 28

Konstantine tried not to pace the apartment. He had one hour before his rendezvous with Ricci. Tonight he would be back in Florence. Tonight he would face Nico and… what? Would he win? With Lou by his side, his victory was assured. He'd seen her on the boat with the senator, exacting her revenge. She'd dropped a man with every bullet. Nico's army would be nothing against her, especially with his borrowed New York army behind them.

And yet…

Something ate at his stomach. There was an unease inside him that he didn't trust.

*God speaks to us when we listen,* his mother had said. *But only when we listen.*

His mind turned over the possibilities. All the ways the plan could go sideways.

The closet door burst open with more force than he'd come to expect from Lou.

An enormous man emerged first, Lou bursting in after him. Konstantine froze beside the rumpled bed, composing himself. He knew his outward appearance was calm, dignified. He'd practiced it enough to know how the expression felt on his face even when he himself couldn't see it. But his heart hammered.

Lou turned her dark eyes on him, arching an eyebrow. "I see you're ready to go."

"We have one hour," he said, hoping she hadn't forgotten that he would need her to transport him. She seemed nonplussed by this news. He took this for affirmation that she hadn't lost track of time.

But then why was the cop here. *Ex-cop*, he thought. This man had gone through the police academy, served several years on the Minneapolis force before being promoted to detective. Ten years later he applied for and was accepted by the Drug Enforcement Agency and began his career in St. Louis. He left the city only once, when an injury sidelined him and it was during that teaching exile he met Louie's father.

He'd been married once before for eight years, was a decorated hero, a minor boxing champion in his 20s. And he had liked to drink.

That was all Konstantine knew of the man standing before him.

He gave the man a once over, appraising him as politely as possible and concluded that whatever else might be true, the drinking was not such a thing of the past.

He looked rough.

Though his hair was recently washed and slicked back from his face. His eyes were dark with circles beneath and he had the posture of an old man. No, a *defeated* man. Even when he saw Konstantine and tried to pull himself up to his full height, it didn't quite leave him.

Perhaps it wasn't the drinking or the age. Perhaps, Konstantine realized, what he was looking at was grief.

"Robert King," he said and extended his hand.

"Paolo Konstantine," he said and accepted the shake. Neither man tried to overpower the other or squeeze too hard.

For a moment, neither of them knew what to do with their bodies. They hovered as Lou disappeared down the hall to the bathroom and emerged changed. Fresh black cargo pants and a new black shirt. Her feet were bare on the wood floor and her hair pulled back to reveal her neck, keeping all strands from her face.

Konstantine couldn't help but watch her move, admiring the shift and sway of her body. Whatever grief she felt for her dead aunt was tucked neatly away in a corner of her heart for now.

Konstantine knew King was watching him, watching Lou. "Lou says that you're good with computers."

"I have a bit of talent," he said.

Lou snorted as she opened the safe. She threw guns and ammo over her shoulder onto the bed. "Who knew Italian men were so modest."

"You're the one who gave the proof of Jack's innocence?" the large man said, slowly sinking onto the sofa.

"Yes." Konstantine mirrored him, taking a seat on the side of Lou's bed, far enough that a pistol wouldn't hit him in the face.

"I've been monitoring servers and databases, trying to erase anything that linked to Lou. But it looks like they're on to me. Is there a way to do it *without* being noticed?"

"Of course," Konstantine said. "I will be happy to show you."

"Can you get a computer in New York?" she asked.

"Ricci will give me whatever I need. I'm sure a laptop will be no problem. But if you intend to do this tutorial before—" He let his words hang in the air.

"If you're busy—" King started.

"Konstantine will probably die tonight," Lou said as casually as one says *we're expecting thunderstorms.* "It's now or never."

"All right," King said. "When do we leave?"

"Now," she said. "I'll take Konstantine first and then I'll be back for you."

King looked ready to object but she was already stepping into the closet. Konstantine didn't hesitate. It wasn't only the opportunity to step into the dark with this beautiful creature again, to feel her hard body against his, it was also his eagerness to begin. He'd felt like an eternity, not days had passed in that apartment.

He tried to relish it, every shift of muscle under his hand as he embraced her.

"Ready?" she asked and he knew her lips were quite close to his. Oh the temptation. But he was no fool.

The world shifted into view. They stepped out from under an overhang, some back-alley stoop with an added layer of shadow from the adjacent dumpster. She left Konstantine on this back stoop of Charlie's Chinese House and was gone again before he could thank her.

He rang the bell. A slot slid open revealing only black eyes. "Tell Ricci that his 1:00 is here."

The slot closed and Konstantine was left alone in the garbage-reeking alley for a moment to compose himself. He heard the hobbled steps of Ricci sound before the door opened on the round, joyous man.

"Hey! You're early! But it's all right, it's all right. Get in here!"

He ushered Konstantine in with a pat on his back.

"Who the hell are you?"

King stood awkwardly in the alley.

"He is with me," Konstantine said.

The two men exchanged looks as King gave a solemn smile.

"Is this guy okay?" Ricci asked. He'd lowered his voice for Konstantine's ears only. "I'm getting cop vibes."

King burped loudly and excused himself.

"Or maybe he's the town drunk," Ricci added.

"He is a cop, but he's one of my cops." He slapped Ricci's shoulder. "And he and I need to conduct a bit of business before we leave for Florence."

Ricci shrugged. "All right. You can use the Jade room until Buddy gives us the go. You remember Buddy? He's Karlene's boy. Anyway he runs the airfield, everything that goes in and out goes through Buddy now. So when he says we're clear to fly, then we'll take a little drive down to the airfield, and we're off."

Konstantine thanked him.

They followed Ricci through the kitchen and maze of hallways of Charlie's Chinese House. They passed the open door of an office and Konstantine paused.

"Can I borrow a computer?" Konstantine asked, gazing into what no doubt masqueraded as a restaurant manager's office. Wood paneling on all four walls and a great wooden desk. A tray with receipts stacked and a rubber band tying them all together like a fat roll of cash. A black box that looked like a walkie-talkie. But Konstantine wondered if it was a police scanner. Perhaps he had both squirreled away in there somewhere.

"Sure, sure."

Ricci stepped into the office and fished a key out of a ceramic tray on his desk. It looked like one

of those misshapen creations that children gave their parents from art class. He tried to remember how old Ricci's daughters were now. Teenagers, perhaps? Maybe the eldest ready for college. He couldn't
recall.

The key opened a cabinet and after a brief search, the man found what he was looking for.

Ricci handed over the laptop, wrapping the snake-like charger cord around and around its square body. "It's a dummy. So if we gotta burn it after, it's fine. Can I get you anything to drink or eat while you're waiting?"

Konstantine was in fact starving despite his nerves. He told Ricci as much. "I'll have Valerie bring something in for you guys. Go on and get comfortable. I'll make sure nobody else bothers you while you do your business."

The Jade room was probably named so for its emerald green wall paper and the gold flourishes in Chinese design that ran vertically along the walls. A large red table with carved dragon legs sat in the center of the room, flanked by wooden pillars the same color.

He pulled out a chair and sat while King did the same.

"Tell me," Konstantine began. "Does…our mutual friend often leave you alone with people you do not know?"

He wanted this to mean more than it did. That she trusted him not to harm this man—whatever he was to her. Or perhaps she trusted the man's ability to protect himself, should it come to it. Though one look at his bloodshot eyes and purple circles told him that perhaps that was not true. At least not today.

But again this only gave Konstantine hope. That maybe, with time, she could grow to trust him.

"At least this isn't a Siberian shipping container," the man mumbled taking in the emerald wallpaper and golden accents.

Konstantine didn't know what to think of this. He searched for footing in the conversation.

"Did she say anything?" He hoped the question sounded casual. He kept his gaze on the screen as he created the cloaking he would use to show the old man a few tricks.

"She told me to stay with you until she got back. She's going to pop in and check on—" Here he paused and looked around the room. Good. He understood that they were being watched then. He wouldn't make the mistake of saying Lou's name or share any information that perhaps he didn't want a man like Ricci to know. He licked his lips and said, "She's scoping out the situation before you go in. So you know what to expect."

Useful. Very helpful.

Konstantine loosed a breath he didn't realize he'd been holding. He wasn't sure if he should be. "Right. Let's begin with whatever you did before."

"I used old passwords to access the servers. Sometimes I was able to guess the new ones."

"That's called social engineering," Konstantine said. "A SQL injection from a logless VPN would be better."

King only blinked at him.

"You know how to create dummy IP addresses, I assume."

"Yes. But they still knew it was me."

"That's because you can't truly be anonymous even if you are hiding behind someone else's IP. They will trace it back to you eventually. Instead I would use a paid, logless VPN. I can recommend a few, if you like?"

King said that he did and Konstantine told him how to contact the service and set it up.

"Once you have your logless VPN, then you can use SQL injections from your browser to access the host database. Then all the data stored there will be yours for the taking. I would suggest you take *all* of it, indiscriminately, rather than search for specific items, say, *names*, or anything that could form a pattern. You don't want anyone to know what you are looking at exactly, now do you? So take it all and

go through it on a burner, offline, later."

King shook his head.

He handed the computer over to the man and let him try a few simple commands. He wasn't a complete luddite. Konstantine saw the knowledge and skills. But it was clear that the technology was advancing faster than perhaps this man had trained for. And maybe he didn't have the passion for the machines, like Konstantine did.

A young woman with a tray appeared heaped with chicken and pork covered in sauces, wontons and dumplings steamed, crab legs, a heaping plate of rice and noodles. It was enough for a large family *and* the two men who sat there. Leaving plates, napkins, silverware, soda, and water, she departed the moment Konstantine thanked her.

King only stared at the feast. He looked like he would rather vomit on the food than put it in his mouth. "Will he be offended if—"

"Not at all," Konstantine interjected.

King drank deep of the soda on the table, but he left the food untouched.

He returned his attention to the computer, working to recreate what Konstantine had demonstrated with ease. He was getting a little faster with each pass. His face relaxed and eyes focused at
least.

Konstantine ate a little bit of everything, hoping that it pleased his host that he did so. When King looked as though he was tired for now, Konstantine spared him.

"You know that none of this is necessary?" Konstantine said at last, as the man's practice was well underway.

King looked up, face pinched. He reached for the water pitcher and poured himself a full glass. Drank it down and filled it again, all while Konstantine continued on.

"I monitor all the intelligence databases. CIA, FBI, DEA, USSS, FPS, even the Coast Guard." He laughed. "And not just here. But Italian Interpol, most of the agencies in Europe and Russia too. China."

King's surprise couldn't be more evident. His mouth hung open.

Konstantine capitalized on the silence. "It would be nothing to protect the anonymity of our friend. I will continue to do so. Should something come up, I will handle it."

Then he seemed to recover himself at last, putting down his water glass, and scratched at his scruffy face with a yellowed thumb nail. "In your line of work, you must have business connections in every corner of the planet."

Konstantine said nothing, laying his fork against his demolished plate and taking another helping of the steamed dumplings.

"And you want to know who knows your business in each of those corners," King added. "Especially if business is going well."

"If business is going well," Konstantine countered, pointing with his fork. "There is no mention of me at all."

"Agostino changed that when he announced your name to every agency in the known world."

Konstantine smiled. "Perhaps. But my point is that it is no longer only my name that I keep an eye-out for."

King nodded, showing that he understood. "Then it doesn't matter if I can do any of this, does it?"

"If things go wrong tonight, perhaps very wrong, you will have to do the job."

"Hey, Mr. Konstantine, you get enough to eat?" Ricci stood in the doorway, his thumbs in his belt loops, pudgy belly hanging over the denim band.

"It was wonderful. You've been very hospitable,
my friend," Konstantine said. "I will treat you even better the next time you come see me in Florence."

Ricci was pleased with this answer. "Good, good. I'm glad to hear it. If you're ready, we should head down to the airfield now. Buddy says we've got the hangar to ourselves and no prying eyes for the next 45 minutes."

Ricci looked at the man powering down and closing the laptop. Konstantine also considered him for a moment.

King caught the exchange and said, "She wanted me to stay with you."

"Come on then," Konstantine said. "We wouldn't want to disappoint her, would we?"

Ricci didn't ask who *she* might be and Konstantine knew he wouldn't. Ricci had lived to be the ripe old age of 68 for a reason. He was damn good at keeping his mouth shut and his eyes and ears open.

"I don't have my passport," King said, pushing back his chair. "Not on me."

Ricci laughed.

Konstantine smiled and slapped the man on the shoulder while coming around the table, leaving his half-demolished feast behind. "The way we are traveling, mio amico, you will not need it."

# 29

L ou stood in her apartment, taking in afternoon light. She wanted a moment to clear her head before she went to Florence. Something about Konstantine and King together, the marriage of those two parts of her life—it had unnerved her. Don't overthink it, she warned herself. For all she knew Konstantine would die tonight, fighting in Padre Leo's church, the hallowed ground of the Ravengers.

Santi Augusti al Monte.

While so much about Paolo Konstantine confused and infuriated her, this she understood. Padre had been like a father to him. And he left this empire to his adopted son with the expectation that he would protect all that he'd built. Surely he felt some obligation to protect that legacy.

Her father had died too soon to leave her an empire, except of course the multi-million dollar life insurance policy meant to carry her through life.

What he'd left her was intangible. The drive. The thirst. He'd given his life for hers. If that was his
gift, she'd been too careless.

*Your life is your own to live*, Jack said. Good answer.

The Mississippi River shimmered and the white seagulls dove and bobbed from above.

She checked her five guns and the corresponding clips again. Double-checked that she had enough ammo to fight her way out, should something go wrong. Two knives stuffed into sewn slips at each forearm and one more at her right thigh. And at last, her father's bullet proof vest snug over her chest.

This first glimpse was only to get a sense of what they were walking into. The layout of the church, how many men Nico had, his plan for attack. She'd gather the intel she could, sticking to the unobtrusive shadows. Then she'd get King, take him back to New Orleans before he had a chance to get hurt.

Konstantine could do what he wanted with the information that she found. It wouldn't alter her plans in the slightest.

Lou stepped into the closet, welcoming the familiar darkness. The compass whirled inside, lining up those two invisible slots in the machine that would move heaven and earth. When the darkness softened and Lou herself stepped through, she felt the shift. Another floor in another country rose up to

meet her. Her hand finding not the opposite closet

wall, but a cool stone pillar.

The church came into focus around her. The orderly pews and clean stone gave no impression of the firefight that had taken place here a few days before. She knew her own bullets had chipped away at these ancient facades.

It was so quiet. Too quiet.

She slipped through the shadows, taking in the church from different angles. Men were stationed, waiting in the wings for Konstantine no doubt. But there was no sign of the men that Lou recognized. Those who were in Konstantine's closest entourage. Had Nico killed them outright?

Nico was nowhere to be seen.

Two men standing near the image of the weeping Christ spoke in hushed, whispered Italian. But she understood what happened next.

One man lifted the purple cloth to reveal a mess of wires and jugs of fluorescent fluid.

A bomb.

Nico was going to blow up the church—no doubt when Konstantine was inside. It made perfect sense. If Nico harbored as much hate for his father's betrayal as Konstantine said, why wouldn't he want to bring down his father's empire, brick by literal brick?

And take out the clever golden boy while he was at it?

No doubt he would make a big show of it. Station enough men here to oppose Konstantine, to make him believe that Nico was hidden in the bowels of the church, a prize to be had if only Konstantine could fight his way through.

But if Nico wasn't here, where was he?

Lou pressed her back into the shadows of the stone pillar and let her compass shift and whirl. It clicked into place and she stepped through.

A padded floor rose up to meet her. She wobbled on her feet, her body caught off guard by the unsteady nature of the flooring. She dropped into a crouch to steady herself and gain a better understanding of her surroundings. Pitch black. Not an ounce of light from anywhere. She couldn't even see her hand in front of her face.

And this strange floor… it felt like linen. A thick material with something stuffed inside it, billowing it into as stiff pillow-shape beneath her hands.

Then the lights turned on. Lights from every conceivable direction blared down on her like the light from a thousand suns. She moved to jump into the shadow, only to find there was no shadow. No seam, no crevice, no crack. So much light that she couldn't see any more than she could have seen in the darkness. She pulled her gun and shot wildly. The bullet connected with something, pinged off in an unseen direction.

Then she thought to shoot the lights. She would have to shoot out the lights. She raised her gun and aimed it at the sky.

An electrical current shot through her body. Her convulsing hand emptied the clip into the wall, not the ceiling. She crumpled onto the floor, unsure if she still held her gun or not.

*It's in the floor,* she thought. *There's a current in the floor.*

And then she thought nothing at all.

# 30

Every time King closed his eyes, he saw Lucy. He saw her sitting in a Café du Monde bistro chair, sucking praline chocolate off her thumb. He saw her walking beside him down Royal Street, her red sundress sliding across tan thighs. Her saw the sunlight sparking in her eyes.

The way she'd cupped his cheek and said, *I do.* The firelight dancing across her cheekbones.

He pinched the bridge of his nose and exhaled a ragged breath.

"Can I get you anything?"

King turned and saw a young man, maybe twenty, leaning toward his airplane seat, his face open and neutral.

"A coke," King said. "And some aspirin if you've got it."

The kid wandered away and King caught Konstantine's eye. The man sat opposite him, in an adjacent airplane seat.

King only vaguely noted his presence. He kept replaying the moments of Lucy's life on the screen of his mind. His only reprieve was his last conversation, when Naomi of the cancer center finally called to inform him of her passing. As if he didn't know.

There was no mention of the body's strange condition. No doubt Lucy was still covered in sand and her clothing reeked of campfire smoke. But why would they tell him that? Grieving family members were unpredictable. Explaining the strange discovery was an admission of guilt. They could face a lawsuit for wrongful conduct.

King was certain that whatever strange thoughts the attending physicians must've had over what they found in her room, they planned to keep those thoughts to themselves.

Nurse Naomi only said what all cancer center nurses were required to say. *She passed this morning. It was peaceful. We are sorry for your loss.*

"I'm sorry for your loss," Konstantine said, and the words echoed his own thoughts so closely that it jolted King from his mind and back into the airplane seat.

The small private jet held Konstantine and himself, a pilot, a bodyguard that Ricci had given to Konstantine for this trip, and the boy who waited on them all. Another plane full of muscle, the loaned army, would meet them on the Italian airfield. He'd heard the men agree that the muscle and the weapons should travel separate, should either be seized.

"Thank you," King croaked. His throat felt abnormally tight and it burned. Speech seemed impossible.

Konstantine turned away, looking out the window.

"It seems very strange," he began, in his accented English. His hands were loosely clasped over his crossed knee. "After traveling as she does, to be moving so...slowly."

Konstantine looked at the silver watch on his wrist and frowned. "It's been six hours."

That explained the darkness outside the plane window and the fact that the plane carried them forward in time.

King leaned over the armrest and peered out into the impenetrable darkness, one red bulb flashing on the end of the wing, and found the suggestion of gray clouds. He knew the ocean must lay below them, but he didn't care. He didn't care about anything.

"Something may have happened. She has no other reason to leave you in my company so long. Not that I don't enjoy it," Konstantine added diplomatically.

"Perhaps she can't…" King realized what he was about to say. "Maybe she has a hard time catching flights."

Konstantine smiled. "She met Donatello Martinelli on a red eye. New York to Rome."

King hadn't known this. He knew about her careful destruction of Konstantine's family—a family by blood, not bond—but didn't know the particulars of each kill. One was taken from prison, thought to have escaped. That he remembered because it had been all over the front page of every paper and nighttime news story.

"Do you think she ran into trouble?" King asked. At last the world was coming into focus around him. It was still raw with his grief.

The sounds were too bright. The light of the cabin was too bright. His own pain was too bright.

But he was here. He longed for the part that would come after. The hollowed-out numbness that would rise from the wake of the initial shock. The days he would lie in his bed and feel nothing but emptiness.

It would be a blessed release.

Konstantine smiled. "She's very capable."

"What do we do if we land and she still hasn't come back?"

It was easy sticking to the job, focusing on what needed to be done here and now. He had other thoughts about this man. About his connection to Lou. But in his limited mind all he could think of now was Lucy. The meteor of her death had left a crater-shaped hole where his heart should be.

Konstantine turned toward the window and considered the night. King watched the red light flash on and off on his face.

"You will stay with me as she asked," Konstantine said finally. "I assume you know how to use a gun."

"Of course." *The real trick will be not using it on myself.*

## 31

Nico knelt over the unconscious woman. The pure rubber in his boots—that which would protect him from the current in the floor should it come on again—found the padding springy, nearly pitching him off his feet and on top of her.

Not that it would have been an entirely unpleasant experience to land on top of that body.

"Strip her," he commanded. And the two men flanking him did as they were told. He didn't trust himself to do the task. Taking off her clothes seemed too intimate a gesture.

They made quick work of it, removing her guns, her armor, and the knives one by one from her slim body until only naked flesh remained.

"Her panties too?" one man asked.

"No," Nico said, perhaps too quickly. That thin swath of cotton was all that was holding his temptation back.

He knew it was in his power to take what he wanted of her. He'd seen the guards in the work camp do it any number of times to the women and the men. Women for pleasure, men for humiliation. Or perhaps pleasure as well. But the sight of the guards' pale, naked asses thrusting, muscles clenching while their pants sagged about the ankles—the way they carried on without regard for who was watching—it sickened Nico. He wouldn't have the men see him in such a way.

"Put the jacket on."

They rolled the woman onto her side. Her beautiful breasts lay on top of one another, her nipples the color of cinnamon. Thankfully the men maneuvered each of her arms into the canvas sleeves and then hid them from his sight.

"Should we bind her legs?"

"There's no need." Without her guns and weaponry, without her power to move like a ghost through this world, she was no threat to him. Under her flesh, under the bones, she was only a woman after all.

Nico dismissed them.

He sank onto his knees beside her aware of the risk. One of the men could turn traitorous. Flip the current on and knock him unconscious too.

They didn't dare.

He watched her chest rise and fall, her black

lashes long against her freckled cheeks. Her pale lips
were parted, offering the smallest hint of teeth.

He reached forward and brushed the hair back from her face.

Silky smooth.

How long had it been since he'd touched a woman? He couldn't remember. And it wasn't something he'd prioritized upon his return to Italy. He'd had only one ambition once he reached this city. He would see his father's legacy destroyed, his heir ruined. And all of that was going so well.

The world hunted Konstantine. His one advantage, this creature at Nico's feet, couldn't save him. And the surprise lying in wait for Konstantine…

It would rid him of his rival and what remained of his father's house.

Yes, it was all coming together just as he'd planned for all those, long, desperate years.

Despite the terror he'd known in that place, perhaps he should be grateful. For it had allowed him to plan with such painstaking detail, the perfect execution needed to win.

And now…all that remained was to decide what to do with his spoils.

His prisoner of war.

He could keep her in this room always. Visit her. Take from her all that he desired. Put a bullet between her eyes if at last her care became tedious. But that seemed such a waste of her talents.

No. He would win her over.

If such a man as Konstantine had been able to gain her loyalty—why couldn't he?

He was a thousand times the man Konstantine was. She would see that.

*You will serve me.* He stared at those soft, parted lips. He reached out and stroked her cold cheek. *You will give me the world.*

It was only a matter of time.

# 32

It was only twenty minutes from the jetway to Santi Augusti al monte. But this was enough time for Konstantine to consider Louie's absence with growing dread. He kept remembering her naked, wet body, the way it had looked when she'd stepped from the linen closet into his line of sight, while he cowered in her bath.

She'd been bloody, her scars from every battle shining on her skin.

And when his mind didn't torture him with that glorious vision, he thought of her on the deck of Ryanson's boat, bleeding herself unconscious as King and her aunt tried to fend off death.

These weren't only memories. They were sharp reminders.

She was powerful, yes. The most capable creature he knew, certainly.

But she was not immortal.

His heart hammered at the thought. *Mama*, he thought. *Proteggila.*

It was not the first time he'd prayed to his mother. And he knew it wouldn't be the last.

The armored transport van rolled to a stop outside of the church. From this quiet view of the piazza, all looked well. The pigeons bobbed along the cobblestones, pecking at the stones with curious beaks. Somewhere a dog barked and the distant sound of a Vespa cut through narrow alleys, no doubt traffic from the main road several blocks over.

At least the area was vacated. If it hadn't been, Konstantine was sure that the sight of twelve armored trucks rolling up outside the church would have been enough to encourage anyone to head home.

But as it was, it was nearly six in the morning. Traffic was minimal.

In his earpiece, the plan was rehearsed again with Konstantine breaking in only to confirm this or that detail. His ears were busy, but his eyes remained focused on the American in the seat across from him.

He watched the large man suit up. The driver was offering him a loaded Benelli and a vest. King was trying to shrug himself out of his black duster and roll up the sleeves of his collared shirt.

"You must stay in the van," Konstantine said without his thumb on the intercom, so that his voice would remain in this van only.

King didn't protest. Konstantine suspected that had this been anyone else, he would have faced a negotiation. But this man was here in the country illegally and running with a notorious gang. Perhaps he thought that this once, it was best to follow someone else's lead.

Yet Konstantine felt the need to reassure him. "The truck is armored. You will be safe inside it. I will come back as soon it's done."

"Sure."

Konstantine gave the order and black doors opened up and down the street. Men of every shape and color exiting the armored vans, guns drawn.

Then it was only the two of them. Konstantine hesitated.

"If she returns before I'm back," he began, but he wasn't sure how to finish.

"I think we both know she'll be jumping right into the fray," King said with a humorless laugh. "She has no interest sitting in the van with the old guy."

Konstantine nodded, but this was not what he had meant to say.

He meant if she appeared, wounded or in need, King should call him. King should come into the firefight and get Konstantine as if the mouth of Hell itself had opened.

Konstantine only nodded and stepped away from the van, his own gun warming between his cupped palms. It was cool in the early Florentine morning. Moisture hung in the air and chilled his face and neck. He took a deep breath, gathering his focus and will.

The objective was to kill only Nico and Nico's armed guard, sparing as many of the Ravengers as possible.

But the guns were going off even before Konstantine walked up the stone steps and entered the church through its stone archway. In the slender nave, the temperature shift was ten degrees at least, and it took a moment for his eyes to adjust from the early dawn of the piazza to the candlelit walkways inside the church.

Three men moving in formation ahead of Konstantine were doing a good job of sweeping the area. Too good.

In the upper level, masked men stood guard, their guns pointed down at Konstantine and his men as they entered. Their Harlequin masks and black clothing made them vengeful gods.

They shot everything that moved, without assessing who was truly a foe. Konstantine wove through the pews, seeking protection behind the stone pillars from the flying bullets. But something was not right.

The bullets missed him by wide margins. None of the men who had entered with Konstantine had been shot yet, though gunfire was constant and more than one man stood in the eaves above, with pistols aimed down at them.

A man from the upper landing was shot, and stiff armed, tumbled over the stone bannister and crashed to the floor below. Konstantine went to the man to confirm his suspicion.

"Fuck." He knelt beside the broken body and saw the situation clearly for the first time.

The man was bound with duct tape only able to move enough to give the impression of being alive and in command of his own body. But the gun that Konstantine freed with a blade was not loaded.

Blood poured from the two bullet holes in the man's chest. He pulled back the masquerade mask and saw wide, fearful eyes. Fellini, one of his most loyal men. Konstantine used the tip of his blade to very carefully open the tape covering the man's mouth, the tape that bulged and concaved with each rapid breath.

*He's going to die. He's going to die before I even*
*get the tape off.*

"I'm so sorry," Konstantine breathed, as he worked to remove the tape as carefully from the man's lips as possible. "Fellini, forgive me." He ripped off the tape, tearing the skin surrounding the mouth.

Of course Nico used his own men to distract him. He would have been a fool to sacrifice his loyal few.

He wasn't the fool Konstantine remembered from his boyhood. He would pay for that mistake now. How high the price was yet to be seen.

Finally the tape was free.

Fellini's breath came out in panicked puffs. His chest heaved and fell in short, sharp exhalations. He was trying to speak.

"Don't," Konstantine begged. "Don't speak. I'll send for the medic."

Into his microphone Konstantine gave the commands. "Stop shooting. It's only my own men who are here. Don't kill them. They are bound and gagged. Gather them up and bring them into the piazza. Send me Romero. I'm between the pews on the right of the nave."

"B-b," Fellini tried again.

"Shhh." He tried to soothe Fellini. "The medic is coming."

But Fellini wouldn't listen, or he perhaps he didn't know Konstantine had spoken at all.

"Bah, bah." The words wouldn't come. Blood bubbled up between his lips, painting them crimson.

Konstantine tried to shush him.

"*Bomb*," he said. His wide desperate eyes fixing on Konstantine's. "*Bomb*."

Konstantine's heart sputtered in his chest. His skin iced as all the blood rushed from the surface, seeking shelter in deeper cells.

A bomb.

"Bomb," Fellini choked out and then the light left his eyes.

Konstantine stood, running for the entry as he shouted. "Bomb! There's a bomb! Everybody out—"

The explosion rocked the cathedral and Konstantine was thrown forward by the force of it.

# 33

The textured surface of the floor came into focus first. For a moment, all Lou could do was look at the fibers, listening to her breath roll in and out and her nostrils. Then the strange black boots. They looked like the boots worn by an electrical crew and she understood why.

She sat up and noted each sore muscle, no doubt from the current which had coursed through her. Her vest and weapons had been removed and this pissed her off more than the fact that her pants, socks and shoes had been taken too. She couldn't be sure about her shirt, since the stiff canvas of the straitjacket sat close to her skin, but the feel of the harsh fabric against her nipples made her suspect it had been confiscated also.

The old familiar rage bubbled up inside her and she welcomed it. She hadn't felt something quite so seductive, so warm and inviting since Angelo Martinelli was alive, and the idea of killing him had driven her through every morning and night.

She was going to kill this man too. And she was

going to enjoy it.

"Perchè stai sorridendo?" he asked. "Why do you smile?"

She didn't answer him. Instead she moved her arms slightly inside the jacket, feeling for weaknesses. It would have been easier to escape had she been awake when they'd laced it up. There was a trick to making one's arms and shoulders bigger in order to allow escape by mere compression of one's muscles. The same was true of handcuffs. But her arms had been relaxed when they wrapped her up. Unfortunately, this meant the fit was quite tight.

She looked into Nico's eyes. They were brown, muddy water, no doubt hiding vipers beneath. She saw where her bullet had grazed his face before, but otherwise he looked well. Damn.

"You must know that I'm Nico. But I don't know your name."

And she wasn't going to give it to him.

"I bet Konstantine knows your name."

A muscle in her face twitch involuntarily. He smiled.

"Cosa ti paga? If you protect him because he pays you, I can pay you more. Whatever the price, I will triple it."

Her tongue rolled over cracked lips. "He doesn't

pay me."

He grinned with obvious surprise. "You have a beautiful voice."

She kept measuring the weaknesses in the canvas. If she weren't pinned in this room by the relentless light beating down from above, it would be easy. How many vertical, whirling blades there were in the world. She only needed one small cut in the fabric and she'd be on her way. She knew of a butcher shop in Austin, which hung its meat on hooks. One good snag. That was it.

But there were no shadows. The lights must have been placed just so. And no wonder all of her items were removed. She could have tried to hide beneath a pile of clothing under a body.

But no shadows were cast on the wall. And she realized it was because light came from the walls too. Perhaps from every angle, now that she thought about it.

This room had been designed to contain her. This was what she got for not confirming her kill.

"If it isn't for the money," Nico said, bending down to her level. Here a small shadow did form between his squat legs and the floor, but it must've been no larger than a book, and the palest gray.

Until the lights went off, she was stuck here.

"Do you love him?" Nico asked. "Are you bound to him by...?" He seemed to search for a word. "Affection? Feelings?"

She said nothing.

"He's not even your friend," he said. "It was only a matter of time before he betrayed you. He built this room. Why would he build this room if he didn't plan to keep you in it? Cage you like some animal?"

She knew her face gave him nothing and she was glad for it. Because inside, her heart pounded. The blood throbbing in her temples seemed to be leaking into her vision.

Konstantine held her wrists in the dark, forcing her to have mercy on her abused knuckles. His hot breath in her hair, sliding along her ear. *Did you get to say goodbye?*

Konstantine in her bed, pinned beneath her. How still he'd lain while her desire and grief rolled her like an ocean wave. The feel of his hard chest pressed against her back.

But it was Nico speaking now. "But I don't want to cage you. Think of what we could do together. Don't look at me like that! You don't think Konstantine had the same plans for you? You were only a means to an end."

Her anger crystalized in her chest.

Nico's smile turned wicked, lecherous as he let his eyes rove over her legs. "And what would happen to you when you grew bored of him? When he couldn't satisfy you?"

He inched closer to her.

"You need someone who understands thirst. Hunger. Who knows you can't lay in your own bed at night peacefully because of the hunger inside you."

He placed a calloused hand on her leg.

"Konstantine has had everything given to him, every moment of his life. My father let him want for *nothing*. He could never appreciate you."

Lou met his eyes and saw the wildness in them. *He's a little crazy. More than a little crazy.*

"I would," he said, lowering his voice and looking at her through dark lashes. He placed a sweaty hand on her bare thigh. "I would be a man worthy…"

She brought her leg up swiftly. Her knee connected with his chin. He rocked back on his heels, arms going out to break his fall.

The moment his back hit the padded floor, she was already standing over him. She brought her foot down on his face, splitting the nose like fruit dashed on the floor. Blood erupted from the crushed features, running over the cheekbones like water from a faucet. His rolled onto his side, spitting blood onto the floor in desperate gasping. She kicked him onto his back and collapsed onto him.

She had her legs on either side of his head, squeezing. His face, what part of the skin that wasn't covered in blood, turning purple as he suffocated.

"Is this what you wanted?" she asked him, squeezing harder, aware of his hot breath through her panties. Blood from his busted nose spread slick across her thighs. "Is this how you'll satisfy me?"

A door squeaked open only a second before half a dozen hands seized her, hauling her up and away from Nico. But she wouldn't let go. She squeezed harder and it took two men, then two men more, wedging their fingers between her blood-slicked thighs and his throat before they could pry her legs apart.

No doubt she'd find finger-shaped bruises along her inner thigh later.

She didn't care. She got in one more kick, this one clipping Nico's ear, before they'd safely pulled him from her reach.

She was dropped without ceremony onto the padded floor and Nico was ushered from the room before she could get off the flat of her back.

The moment her back slammed into the padded floor, her compass whirled to life.

*Go, go, go.*

Konstantine. King. Something had happened.

*Go.*

"I can't!" she screamed in frustration, knowing that these words meant nothing to the men around her. She wanted to punch someone, scream out her fury. But she was alone in the room, her arms bound and too much light to find relief. She turned and saw Nico's face framed in the door's small window. His face was a bloody mess and his eyes were murderous.

She would have flipped him the bird had her hands been free. She settled with an implied curtsy cut short when fresh electricity surged through the floor.

# 34

King didn't want to be left alone now. He'd never been the kind of man that needed company. He'd known men like that. Brasso, his ex-partner had been one. He wanted to lunch with the guys, party until the early hours, always with a woman or two under his arm, especially after his wife left him.

But King had always enjoyed his solitude. Until now.

Now every quiet moment was an invitation for his anger and regret. For blame.

Anger that Lucy, of all the lousy fucks in the world, was the one who had to die. Why not any of worthless men on the planet? Murderers, pedophiles. Rapists.

Regret that he hadn't been in her life sooner, that he'd let twelve years slip by without so much as a fucking phone call. A phone call! How hard could a phone call have been? *Hey, how are you doing? How has life been treating you? I haven't fallen out of love with you. Let's get a coffee.*

He was only distantly aware of the gunfire in the church, the *rat-a-tat-tat* recognizable to anyone familiar with the sound.

King's mind was a million miles away. Back in his old St. Louis brownstone, four blocks from DEA headquarters where he used to walk to work each morning.

He'd already settled into his pajamas, a cold beer in hand and a Rams game on the tube, when Jack turned up on his doorstep in the rain, begging for his help.

He'd looked like a kicked puppy. *I need you to find my sister.*

He hadn't known about Lou's condition then, or even about Lucy herself. But the moment his eyes had fallen on her beautiful face as she stepped out of her Chicago apartment and threw her beautiful legs over the seat of a bicycle…

He should've never let go. *What a fucking fool I am.*

*Don't do this to yourself, Robert.* Lucy's voice was so bright and clear in his mind that his breath sputtered.

His face pinched and knew he would cry if he didn't pull himself back. Yet he was reaching

toward that voice, leaning into it. Anything, no matter how
painful, that promised a taste of Lucy Thorne.

The driver eying him in the rearview looked equally alarmed. Babysitting a weeping American man in an armored van wasn't what he'd signed up for.

An explosion rocketed through the church, vomiting stained glass and the wooden doors out onto the street. The van rocked up onto two tires, skidding along the street until it slammed into the adjacent building. The sound of crunching metal assailed King's ears.

It was compounded by the force of the blast.

Then the building was coming down. A slow motion free fall of the collapsing dome and pillars.

Car alarms went off. The dogs that had been merely barking earlier, now howled.

"Shit." King had his door open and was running across the street. The driver shouted Italian after him, but he didn't stop. He peered through the powder-white dust, trying to estimate where the entrance had been.

He supposed he should feel terrible, being delighted by the sudden tragedy. No doubt, someone had died in this blast.

But this was action. This was something to do with the mind that was slowly eating itself alive.

He shoved aside the rubble slowly, methodically. There was a way to do it, to make sure that it didn't collapse and crush any survivors beneath. He focused on the pieces light enough to move by hand. Those that would require a crane or machinery, he left in place.

King knew all about this strategy himself. Brasso had informed him in excruciating detail why it had taken them days to pull him from the destroyed building that'd nearly killed him.

But now he had a new, real fear. That Lou had been in this building. That Lou had been in the middle of the action, as she was wont to do, and had caught the bomb full on.

King couldn't bear it.

He couldn't let himself believe that less than one day after losing Lucy, he would lose Lou too. Lucy had given up years of her life, her home, her time and her heart trying to do right by that girl.

King wasn't going to let that sacrifice be in vain.

His large hands seized a piece of demolished stone and moved it carefully to the side, laying it on top of a more solid rock base.

He kept moving, painfully slow.

"Anyone under there?" he called. He shifted one stone. He was careful not to pull a stone that would compromise his own footing and send him sliding into the rubble himself. He knew firefighters suffo-cated under the ashen rubble when mistakes were made.

King caught sight of a hand. A bloody hand, with one of its fingers twisted backward, broken at the second knuckle.

He removed three more stones until a smoky white face appeared. The hair may have been dark once, but now it was coated in plaster dust and crumbled stone.

It was as if the man had been turned over in a mound of flour.

King didn't dare pull him from the rubble until only his feet remained hidden.

It wasn't Konstantine.

His eyes were glazed with shock and his limbs trembled.

"Was she in there?" King asked, seeing a thick trail of blood running down the man's head from his ear.

The man didn't answer. He continued to stand on top of the rubble, mumbling Italian to himself.

Others were beginning to emerge from the rubble. Not many. Perhaps only one percent of the men who had entered the building with Konstantine now had two limbs to stand on.

Another man was bleeding profusely from a wound in his throat.

One was coughing up dark blood onto a pile of stones. King would've bet a thousand dollars he was hemorrhaging internally, and if he didn't get to a hospital soon, he would die.

But King didn't care about any of them. He cared only about one person now.

"Did anybody see a woman in there?" he called out. "Uh, una femma?"

They didn't seem to understand him. He spoke louder, his voice strident with his growing panic. "Lots of guns? Shooting?" He pantomimed the movement. "Anybody?"

"Chi? Di chi parli?"

"English, goddamn it! Speak *English*."

"She's not here."

King turned toward the voice and found Konstantine pulling himself from the ashes. He beat the dust from his own clothes and turned to spit on the ground.

"She's not?" King asked. Relief washed over him. *There is still time. There is still time to make this right.*

"No." Konstantine beat the dust from his clothes. He looked like a ghost of his former self, a starving phantom. "But I know where he has her."

# 35

Nico stood outside the padded room and spit blood onto the concrete floor. His face hurt like hell. It wasn't only the broken nose that he'd been quick to reset, should it fuse crooked, it was his split lip. His swollen throat that hurt even to swallow. All of it.

He'd sent all his men away, told them that he wanted a minute alone with the bitch to teach her a lesson about respect. They'd hesitated, but only until he'd turned his hateful gaze on them. Then they seemed to have no problem leaving.

She'd come to consciousness much more quickly now.

And she sat in the middle of the room, regarding him with her unwavering eyes. She seemed like a snake, unblinking, unmoving, lying in wait for the perfect moment to strike.

Her unsettling gaze was only intensified by the blood smeared all over her thighs. The bottom of the straitjacket was also dyed bright crimson.

Nico's blood.

If only she had some on her mouth, then the look would be complete. A lunatic sitting in a padded cell, and waiting for her chance to escape.

He had tried to reason with her. Tried to appeal to the bloodthirst he saw so clearly in her eyes. But he knew that none of it mattered now.

She wouldn't serve him.

He was beginning to doubt that she had ever served Konstantine.

Perhaps their paths had simply crossed. Or perhaps they had been interested in the same end. It didn't matter. It didn't change the fact that Nico would have to kill her now.

He wouldn't make the mistake of getting close to her again. He needed only be bitten once, so to speak, to understand the danger.

She hadn't needed her weapons or her armor to kill him. She hadn't even needed the use of her arms.

No.

He wouldn't challenge her. He would electrocute her into unconsciousness, using this red push button beside the reinforced metal door. And when she was out, he would go in and slit her throat.

He would watch the blood pour from her onto the padded floor, running along the creases where the cushions meet, as red as a Biblical river.

*Such a waste*, he thought. But it was better than the alternative. That he let her live only to find his own throat slit in an alley hours, days, or weeks from now.

His index finger went to the red button, hovered over it as he looked into those brown, unmoving eyes.

She smiled at him. Smiled as if she knew what he was about to do.

And he understood now why the men were so frightened of her. Why they called her Konstantine's *strega*.

He mashed the red button. Her back arched, body twisting. She was flung back, rolling on the padded floor, every muscle in contraction.

"Agostino! Agostino!" the men called. Feet pounded down the concrete hallway, running toward him.

He hesitated, looking away from her long enough to see what the commotion was about.

"Someone is here," they said. The youngest, a man with a buzzed haircut and beady eyes put his hands on his knees as if to catch his breath. He jabbed one thumb over his shoulder. "Someone is coming up the driveway."

Nico gave the unconscious woman one more look before turning away from the door.

Slitting her throat would have to wait.

Reluctantly he followed the messengers through the winding corridors, up the stairs to the atrium of the reception area. This had once been the main villa of this winery, no doubt overrun with tourists or wine enthusiasts. But no one had been here in a long time.

They'd found over two thousand dusty wine bottles in the cellar and moth-eaten furniture covered in white sheets. The sheets themselves were splattered with bird shit and inches of dust.

Sunlight spilled through the windows onto the portico.

Nico stepped out of the villa and onto the stone walk, giving himself a full view of the driveway. A kilometer and a half, maybe two out, he saw what had frightened the guards.

A line of armored trucks came single-file down the driveway, their tires spitting debris. Clouds of dust swirled up into the sky.

So the bomb hadn't ended Konstantine at all.

He was likely too cowardly to go into the church himself. It was probably his men that were killed in the blast. Just as well. He would enjoy ending Konstantine himself.

With his own bare hands.

He was certain he might enjoy it even more than murdering the little lunatic downstairs.

"Tell everyone to suit up," he said to the silent guards. "Konstantine is coming."

# 36

The truck bumped along the country road, forcing the men to jostle back and forth on the opposite benches. Konstantine's eyes were trained on the passing countryside outside the truck's window. He kept opening and closing his fist, and then catching himself doing it, forced his hand motionless and flat against his leg.

*If Nico hurts her, so much as* bruises *her…*

His scanned the interior of the truck. Nine or ten men were in this van. Probably eighty in all, if he counted the entire 7-truck caravan. He couldn't be sure how many men Nico would have at his disposal, but he expected as many as a hundred. He would be a fool to have fewer than a hundred in the event that she was able to rise against him.

He would find one of three scenarios at the winery.

In the first scenario, all of the men are dead. He imagined bodies strewn in the portico, pools of blood beneath them. Maybe he would find them slumped on the stairways or sitting against the wall with their brains drying on the stucco.

If this was the situation, it meant Lou had saved herself. And no doubt, Konstantine would be dead before the sun reached high noon. She wouldn't wait for him to explain himself. She'd end him before the moon rose.

In the second scenario, he would fight his way through Nico and Nico's men and save her from the padded room where he was no doubt holding her. And he would have a chance to explain what he'd done and why he'd done it.

In the third and final scenario, King would succeed in severing the power to the building and the lights would be turned off. In that momentary blackness, she would free herself, join them in the fight, and no doubt slaughter them all. Hopefully she would see King, know that it was Konstantine who'd come to save her—and that might buy his life.

He didn't expect gratitude. In fact, he expected a knife to the gut. But at least he would have a chance to explain himself in the latter two scenarios.

A chance to explain was the very best he could hope for now.

He sighed and ran a hand through his hair. He surveyed the men sitting knee-to-knee on the benches. The men faced each other on opposing benches, bulletproof glass windows framing the passing world beyond. Those who met his eyes politely looked away. The American cop didn't. But he wasn't truly seeing Konstantine either.

He wore his grief like a mask. The eyes fathoms deep and full of shifting shadows.

"Are you sure you can do this?" Konstantine asked.

King's eyes focused, light sparking in them. "Another gun wouldn't hurt."

"Of course. And I will send some of the men with you." He quickly added, "For cover."

He didn't want to insult the cop with words like for *your protection* or *in case you fuck up*.

He suspected the American wasn't fooled. He seemed to understand the implication clearly.

"My entrance will be the diversion you need. Stick to the plan and you should be fine."

"You don't think he will have someone guarding the box?" King asked, the purple bags under his eyes pronounced.

Konstantine forced a patient smile. "That's what the gun is for."

He hoped his façade of control remained intact. In reality, his nerves jumped and twitched beneath his skin. Sweat collected on the back of his neck. The interior of this truck was too hot. Too crowded. He wanted to open the back door and throw himself on the dirt road.

He remained in his seat, reviewing his plan for the thousandth time.

No doubt the power box providing electricity to the main house was guarded. And if Nico was aware of it, the generator as well. He hoped the man was oblivious to its existence, but in reality, the fact that he was here at the winery at all was evidence enough that he knew—and understood—Konstantine's investment in the place.

The winery lurched into view. A sprawling compound amongst the orchard rows. The green hills framed the ancient home beautifully. Sunlight shone on its sienna roof. He counted fourteen vehicles in the circle drive outside the exterior wall. Craning his neck, he looked out over the field to a structure in the distance.

"Once I get out, the truck will carry you out to the...work house," he said. He hesitated with the word *work house*, unsure if that was the best translation for the distant structure where the equipment and the generator were kept. The cop seemed to understand.

To his own men, the few they'd saved from the rubble of Padre Leo's desecrated church, he spoke Italian. "Tenetelo in vita se viene ucciso, dovete finire il lavoro. Tagliate il corrente."

He didn't expect the men to give their lives for some American they didn't know. But he wanted them to at least try to help him fulfill their mission. Though he wasn't sure any of these men knew how to disable the electricity.

The tires ground to a stop and the back doors to the truck swung open. They waited for open gunfire, for some retaliation. But they were only met with eerie silence. No bird song. No wind through the grass. It was the silence before the tempestuous storm tore off the roof. Dirt shifted as the other trucks pulled up beside them, mixing with those already parked.

All the men filed from the truck with the exception of the driver, King and the two men that would accompany him. Konstantine's boots hit the road and he turned back to the cop one more time. For now the open doors shielded him from any incoming fire, should they try to eliminate him before he even entered the portico.

"Remember you must disable the generator first," Konstantine said, unsure if he was saving, or damning his life with these instructions. *She will listen. She will understand. Mio dio,* he hoped so.

King only nodded and the doors to the van closed between them. Konstantine hesitated, watching the van circle around the parked cars before pulling out of his sight, leaving a trail of dust in its wake, the only sign it had been there at all.

Konstantine adjusted the body armor, checking the fit across his chest.

*I must look like Lou*, he thought. His head to toe black clothing. Protective plating over his thighs and outer arms. The chest and groin protected as well. The six guns within arm's reach and a belt's worth of ammo.

He saw men on the upper terrace then. Guns pointed at him from all directions.

But calmly they crossed beneath the archway and through the courtyard. They moved through the portico.

Nico didn't let them get far.

He stepped from the shadows and out into the early morning light.

"Konstantine," he said. His grin was wolfish, his eyes. "You didn't get my message, did you?"

Several of the men, more and more of them emerging from the shadows, laughed at their master's
teasing tone.

Konstantine saw he was outnumbered perhaps three to one. But Ricci's men were good at what they did. As well as those who'd remained loyal to Konstantine himself. He would have to hope it was enough. Or that they would get lucky.

Nico's grin was malicious. Hungry. "You aren't wanted, my friend. How embarrassing that you keep trying to take something that doesn't belong to you."

Konstantine noted his swollen nose, the purple-black bruise spreading across his face. The way his eyes were nearly swollen shut.

He smiled despite the rage wrenching his insides. He gestured toward Nico's nose. "Looks like I'm not the only one trying to take something that doesn't belong to me."

Several of Ricci's men laughed and Nico's eyes caught fire.

Konstantine saw the shirt hanging from Nico's pocket and the world stopped on a dime. It was the shirt he'd last seen on Lou that morning. It was bloody and torn.

Nico followed his gaze and grinned when he realized what Konstantine was looking at.

He pulled the shirt from his back pocket and lifted it up to his face as if to smell it. It was for show.

That busted nose wasn't smelling a damn thing. It enraged Konstantine all the same.

"What did you really come for, Konstantine?" Nico asked, eyes ablaze over the bloody, ravaged cotton. "The gang? The woman? Or your pride?"

Konstantine pulled his gun in a single movement and before he'd even exhaled the air from his lungs, he fired.

# 37

A gunshot made King's head snap up. He pivoted on the bench, craning his neck so that he could see out the armored van's window. He saw nothing but a smattering of cars collected in the circle drive beside the villa. It was the sort of villa he'd expected to find in the Tuscan hills. Though he couldn't be sure they were in Tuscany at all. They'd been in Florence that morning, but in what direction they'd driven after the church had been brought down, he couldn't be sure.

Thinking of the van rocking on its heels in the blast, the sight of that stone façade crumbling—not out, as one might think—but in on itself. It had triggered him. It gave him sweaty palms, a shallow pant and knocking heart.

King could forget about his claustrophobia on most days, so it was always surprising when it reared up unexpectedly and seized him again. And here he was amongst all these unfamiliar faces…it wasn't the time to fall apart. No matter how much his fear rolled him, or his grief.

*Lucy.*

He saw her beautiful smile. The way she'd looked when she'd slipped her arms around his neck and came up onto her toes to kiss him. First his nose, then each cheek, before impatiently, he seized her mouth with his own.

That life seemed so far away. Like a vivid dream he'd had years ago, but could still remember with shocking detail. It shone in its strange way. And Lou...

*Where the hell are you?*

He didn't believe she was dead. Couldn't believe it. That she would leave this world at all was like seeing the sun gone from the sky. The Louie Thorne he knew wouldn't miss this firefight for anything in the world. She was hurt or detained somehow.

Had to be.

The truck bounced to a stop outside a large shed. The back door opened and King slid from the bench into the open air.

He saw the villa in the distance.

Something whistled past his head and slammed into the armored door.

A second bullet followed. It bit the metal five or six inches from his face.

"Shit!" He ducked and took cover on its other side while the men around him burst into action.

More bullets flew as King hurried toward the shed, his hands over his head as if that would stop a bullet.

When he reached the wooden door of the shed, he found it locked with a large chain and padlock. King pressed the eye of his gun against the chain and pulled the trigger. Part of the metal was blasted away but he still had the slow task of getting it unhooked from the chain and unfastening the door.

The firefight continued around him and he couldn't be sure from which direction the men were coming. Only that they must be on the other side of the van. Something heavy slammed into metal. There was a distinct *thump - POP* and King suspected it was a body hitting the armored plating.

*If I don't get inside, I'm going to be next.*

The last of the chain fell away and he pried open the door.

The dark was nearly complete, with only thin beams of light filtering through cracks in the dilapidated roof above. King kept moving, heading toward the back of the shed where Konstantine had been sure the generator waited.

King found it, a bulky black box in a corner, with only dirt beneath it and rough wooden walls on either side. He bent down, his fingers rushing to inspect the surface for a plug to pull or wire to disconnect—any hint at how it might be disabled.

He found a thick cable running from the back of the machine to the wall. Then the cable continued up the wall, disappearing behind the landing above.

He pulled the cable, trying to wiggle it from its socket.

Nothing.

Placing his boots on either side of the box, he pulled again, throwing all his weight into it.

The cord popped free with a spark.

The shed door bounced open and three men clambered inside. They weren't Konstantine's men.

Before they realized where he was and what he was doing, he began to climb. He used a wooden ladder to follow the wiring up the side of the shed's wall. He climbed quickly, pausing only when a bullet punched a hole beside his head, offering a bright pinhole of sunlight. Then he climbed even faster.

He didn't understand Italian and had no idea what they shouted. But with every bullet hole and new pinprick of light, the message was clear.

Then he was shot.

A bullet bit into the meat of his lower left side. Something in his back spasmed and he almost fell off the ladder. One hand released completely and for a moment he hung there, unsure if he would crash to the dirt below. Then more gunfire erupted and the shouts commenced. But they didn't seem to be directed at him any longer. Someone else had entered the fray and was drawing the fire away from him.

He resumed his climb and with much effort hauled himself onto the wooden platform above.

His back burned. The fire in his lower back spread in all directions, sucking the air from his lungs.

But he crawled forward, still following the electrical lines, hoping to find the place where they met some sort of circuit box. His shaking hands caught on the rough wooden floor. The dirt and grit dusted his palms. His chest constricted and he coughed.

His hands grasped blindly in the darkness until his fingers found cool metal and then a switch. He flipped it, or he thought he did.

His vision swam. His limbs were so heavy that he felt as if he were underwater, trying to swim toward a surface he would never reach.

*Just as well,* he thought. *It wasn't worth it without you.*

# 38

Nico saw the gun jump in Konstantine's hand. Then the bullet slammed into the vest hugging his chest. He stumbled back a step, but didn't fall. The sting was nothing compared to the joy he felt in seeing the hatred on Konstantine's face.

So calm, so collected. Padre's perfect bright boy.

A pleasant boy who made friends effortlessly with his easy manners. He was never rattled, never overcome by emotion. Nico had always known better. He might wear a mask for the men around him, but the woman was the key.

She would be his destruction. The gap in his armor where Nico could drive the blade home.

Both sides pulled their firearms and the shooting began.

Gunfire erupted in the courtyard. Nico had time to dive behind a partial wall for cover. Konstantine's eyes never left him. He dodged the crossfire and raging men to make his way closer.

Nico followed his movements behind the lattice work, but it wasn't

possible to get a clear shot from here.

He peeked around the corner, gun up. Konstantine fired at him immediately. His bullet bit into the stucco beyond his head, blasting a quarter-sized chunk of wall away. Nico fell back, rounded a corner and took off down the hallway. He would come around the other side, through the adjacent door and snare him from behind.

Nico turned a corner, expecting to find another hallway. Instead he caught a fist to the face.

He rocked back on his heels, his shoulder clipping the wall. A door behind him snapped open and they crashed into a kitchen. He staggered past the counter and stools. Nico tumbled, taking a stool down to the floor with him in a clatter.

He opened his eyes the second before his nose was seized. Pain exploded through his face and he screamed. Two fingers squeezing the wounded bridge forced water from his eyes.

"Mio fratello," Konstantine climbed onto the man's chest. The light behind Konstantine's head burned like a halo, wrapping his face in shadow. It could be anyone delivering this vengeance. His own father. God.

Nico brought his knee up, felt it connect with its
mark and Konstantine stiffened.

Nico gained the upper hand. He rolled on top of the other man, pinning him down with his own weight. His head bounced off the floor. Now Konstantine was on the flat of his back, his face spotlighted by the overhead bulb.

The gunfire and men shouting continued, but this was better.

He could take his time in here. Enjoy this revenge that was always owed to him.

How should he begin? In what ways could he hurt Konstantine the most, wring the most pleasure from this moment?

"I don't want you to worry about your woman." Nico laughed, pulling his blade. "She's cold now but any horse can be broken, if ridden hard enough."

Konstantine tried to buck him, his fury clear in his eyes. But Nico knew how to keep the other man down.

"Since your gang is mine now, and your woman…" He pressed his blade against Konstantine's face. "What is there left to take, Konstantine? Your pretty face? Your life?"

He drew the blade across Konstantine's cheek, splitting the flesh. He started at the chin and moved upward, toward the eye. Like unzipping a woman's dress.

Konstantine screamed.

Maybe Nico would take it. The eye. Keep it in a jar on his bedside, even after he disposed of this corpse. Something pleasant to look at, to assure him of his power, before he drifted off to sleep each night. The tip of the blade had just reached the cheekbone when the light overhead clicked off.

For a moment, Nico sat in the shadows, his blade hovering above Konstantine's eye.

Gunfire faltered and the house was filled with the sound of men running.

The light overhead clicked back on.

Konstantine laughed as blood welled from his cut face and painted half his face and ear red. "You lost power. Do you know what that means, mio amico?"

The cut opened and spread as he spoke, blood pouring into the eye and over the cheek.

Nico launched himself off Konstantine. He was down the corridor without looking back. Ko

nstantine's cruel laughter trailed after him, but he barely noticed. He hooked a right, another left and reached the cellar stairs. He took the stone steps three and four at a time, his hands pressed against the cool wall for balance. Then he launched down the lit corridor. The lights flickered. The hallway darkened and then it came on again.

Something was wrong with the generator. That was why the overhead lights sputtered to life only to darken again. The flickering unnerved him. He expected the light to come on and reveal her there in the narrow hallway, standing before him as if from nowhere, a momentary phantom before she put a bullet between his eyes.

Or maybe she was still unconscious. Maybe she hadn't noticed the light had cut off at all and the generator would hold. He ran toward the door at the end of the hallway.

He had to know.

He had to confirm it with his own eyes. When he almost reached the metal door with its one viewing window, he slowed, his steps now cautious.

The lights stayed on.

He took a breath and cranked the large handle. The chamber door creaked loudly as it swung open to reveal the padded room.

Shattered glass sparkled like glitter on the floor, the ripped and bloody straitjacket lay in the center.

# 39

She was so angry, it took her three tries to get her pants buttoned. Her trembling hands missed the buttonhole with each furious swipe. But as soon as Lou had a black t-shirt over her head, she descended the stairs into her armory. It wasn't until she surveyed the shelves, counting gun after gun, that the calm finally began to return.

She chose each weapon with Nico Agostino's face blazing in the forefront of her mind.

Grenades went into her pockets.

She eyed the flamethrower lovingly, but had to be honest. It would limit her mobility. And with so many men crawling about that villa, she couldn't be hampered. So she stuck to what worked. Kevlar sleeves and a vest—though not her father's. And this loss only made her hatred burn hotter. As she loaded a new twin pair of Berettas and slipped them into hip holsters, she ran a list through her mind of all the little tortures she'd like to inflict on Nico.

A belt sat around her hips. She filled it with the bullets to be pumped from her gun.

She took a deep breath in the place that smelled of gunmetal and sawdust and the muscles in her back released. With more guns than hands, she felt like herself again.

*Let him go*, she warned herself. *Let him go for now.*

Her mind growled the way a dog would over a bone.

But if she thought too much about Nico, about his momentary seizure of her power, the rage would overtake her. It would claim the reins of her mind and set fire to all the control she'd carefully built there.

So she turned off her skittering thoughts. She gave her mind over to the dark, and shifted her compass to the foreground. It would be only instinct now. Instinct to carry her through the maze of this firefight and nothing more.

It had never failed her before.

Her armory dematerialized and in its place, a barn was built up around her. Or maybe this was a shed. The floor was dirt, the corners cluttered with unused machinery. At one end, twenty or thirty feet on her right, men clambered up a wooden ladder.

Lou didn't know what was so damned important on the landing above, what they were desperate to reach. She shot them anyway. The first, the one highest on the ladder, took a bullet to the back of his head and the force of it slammed his face forward into the rungs. The faceplant was followed by a loosening of every muscle. When he fell, he took the two men from the lower rungs with him. He was dead before they hit the ground.

One man lay on top of the other, like turtles stacked on their backs, arms paddling air.

She shot the second man, who was trapped beneath the dead weight of the first, in his face. The gore exploded out the back of his head, and painted the face of the third. A crimson mask with wide, unblinking eyes.

Lou shot him too. Then a second, third and fourth bullet were pumped into their faces as if it mattered. The trigger clipped empty.

Reload. She never took her eyes off the dead trio, waiting for even the smallest twitch.

She was done fucking around. If only she'd emptied her gun into Nico's face, she wouldn't have been locked inside that wretched room.

Blood dripped onto her outstretched hand. The droplet ran from knuckle to thumb. For a heartbeat, she thought it was from her kill. But gravity didn't work that way. She looked up and saw blood pooled on the landing above. It had seeped through the space between boards and was collecting like condensa-tion.

The shadow where two shed walls met took her to the upper landing.

It reminded her of the fish house in Miami. And having learned a lesson there, she crept forward cautiously, wary of any loose planks.

King lay on his side, breath ragged. In one hand he held the end of a black cable. Lou understood now that it was King who'd freed her. When he cut the power, she'd been able to slip through the shadows to the butcher's shop in Austin. One rip in the canvas and she had the jacket off.

The smell of fresh air and dirt mixed with the scent of blood. An earthy, ancient scent.

"King." She knelt beside him. His skin was clammy and his pulse too quick. She pulled the cable from his weak grip. *He stayed with Konstantine like you told him to. And it saved your life.*

A surprising wave of affection washed over her. "King. I have some beignets for you."

He groaned.

She smirked. "Hang in there if you want those beignets."

A tarp hung over a wooden bannister. Lou slid it off the wooden post and threw it over King and herself. She pulled him through the dark beneath it, no doubt resembling a magician's disappearing trick.

*Now you see them, now you don't.*

They appeared outside a hospital somewhere in New Orleans—at least, that's what Lou had been aiming for.

It was raining. Fat droplets beat the parking lot stretching out before her, the sound of tires treading shallow streams.

"Excuse me," she said.

The man smoking beside the entrance jumped. "Holy shit!"

His violent trembling caused the cigarette between his fingers to jump and fall to the sidewalk. He wore a white lab coat over turquoise scrubs. *Dr. Jindal* the plastic tag said.

"He's been shot," she said. "Admit him."

"Where the hell—"

Lou pulled her Beretta and pointed it at the doctor. "Admit him. Now."

The doctor howled and disappeared through the automatic doors. Light spilled onto the paved walkway where Lou crouched, protected from the rain. The cool breeze wafting through the walkway pushed the hair back from her face and chilled her cheek. It had the first promise of winter in it, a hint of ice behind the clouds.

King's eyes seemed to rove the mulched beds and bushy plants lining the sidewalk. His breathing was too shallow. Lou slapped his cheek, hoping to bring focus to that distant gaze.

"I'll be back," she said.

She moved to stand, but his hand shot out and seized hers.

Now his eyes were perfectly clear. "Don't."

"I'm not done with Nico," she said, gently.

"Don't—"

"I'll be back," she promised. She reversed the grip easily and squeezed him hard, giving him something to feel beside the pain. "I'm not done with you either."

The sliding door opened and five personnel emerged. Two women in scrubs pushed a bed like the one Lucy spent the last weeks of her life in. A third held a long, plastic board that looked like a poorly designed sled. Neon orange with hand-holes lining each side. The fourth and fifth were the doctor who'd been smoking and an officer no doubt here to arrest Lou for pulling a gun.

A long plastic sled was laid onto the concrete beside King.

"1, 2, 3." They lifted him and placed him on the stretcher before transferring him to the white cot. Lou waited until he was pushed through the automated doors into the hospital, but she'd taken a step back toward the shadows.

The officer peered into the dark, trying to see the woman the doctor described.

A sharp flash of lightning illuminated the breezeway, defining the pillars and walkway, the east side of the hospital and its meticulous landscaping. A heartbeat later, thunder rolled.

But the officer didn't see anyone.

If there had been a woman, she was gone.

# 40

Lou stepped from the hospital breezeway, alive with cool, electric rain, into the heat of an Italian sunshine. She took a breath, adjusting to the shift, then put King behind her. She couldn't think of him now, not with an army of men to face and vengeance to be had.

A dusty room sheltered her. Forgotten furniture sat beneath white sheets. This part of the house was quiet. She slipped out into the hall, following the sound of gunfire. She moved the Beretta to the left hand and pulled the Browning with her right. Two hands, two guns. That was better.

She turned a corner and found two men beating the hell out of each other. They traded knee strikes to the guts, feral punches to the face. A tooth, knocked loose, sailed across the room and skidded to halt at her feet. She was almost sorry to interrupt the show.

Lou put a bullet in each before stepping over their dropped corpses.

Around the next corner—what a maze this compound was—she found men exchanging gunfire across balconies. They popped up and down over the railings like weasels, bullets spit back and forth over the heads of the men fighting in the portico below.

Lou shot two from behind and as the third was turning, put a bullet in his throat, severing his cry midstream. He slumped, glassy eyed against the bannister. Taking their place, Lou fired across and got two men on the opposite balcony right away. The third went down and stayed down. No matter. Lou stepped into the corner of one balcony and emerged from the corner of the other. She shot the hidden man from behind with ease.

It was very easy to shoot the other two remaining men. Their mouths came open in surprised *Os* as they turned to find her suddenly standing over them, guns in hand.

She surveyed the portico and counted no less than forty men exchanging fire. Bullets whistled through the air in all directions. Others relied on their fists or knives. More than one blade caught the sunlight and flashed it against the walls. One man had a lead pipe as long as his forearm, which he swung into the skull of another. That skull deflated like a basketball on impact.

But she didn't see Konstantine.

Someone darted out of an adjacent room and crossed the portico in a panicked stride. She recognized Nico by her handiwork. His busted nose had crusted over nicely with thick, black blood. She raised the gun but he'd already turned a corner and disappeared. Damn.

He hadn't seen her from her claimed balcony.

What would he think when he saw the ripped jacket on the floor? She'd thrown it there only to frighten him. A loud and clear, *I'm coming for you.*

She hoped it had scared the hell out of him.

Nico. He would be the dessert after the end of a good meal.

Sweeping the portico, checking one last time for Konstantine, she removed a grenade from her pocket and unpinned it. She tossed it into the densest cluster of men, bodies so entwined it was hard to tell which violent limb belonged to which body.

The grenade exploded. Throwing men, blood, and dust in all directions. One side of the villa gave way, cascading like a mudslide from roof to earth.

Lou stepped from the balcony down into the thick of it.

She moved through the dust cloud, using it as cover. As soon as a clear shape emerged from the chaos, she seized it. She put bullet through bone. Silenced screams with strikes to the throat. She had to reload twice, tossing aside empty magazines in a careless way she'd never dared to before.

On her fourth reload, the dust cleared and she met Konstantine's eyes.

He leaned against a doorway. A kitchen stood behind him, the barest hint of a gleaming work surface and white cabinets.

His face was destroyed, the meat of his cheek lay open, revealing muscle and bone beneath. Blood clung like a bandana over half his face, making his green eyes seem even brighter.

Fear reared up inside her, clogging her throat and nose, setting fire to her insides.

She raised her gun and aimed. A flicker of doubt flashed in Konstantine's eyes before she shifted her aim to the right and took out the two men coming at him.

Seeing him had stopped her, but she wasn't done. She remembered herself. Using the last of the dust to shield her, she moved methodically to shoot down the few men still struggling to escape the cloud. She gave herself over to the task, pulling the trigger whenever a target emerged. A vital organ. A skull. The side of an exposed throat—all the temptation she needed.

"Se seite con me!" Konstantine called out over the firefight. "Partite ora o lei vi toglierà la vita!"

Men ran in every direction. They scurried like rats through the portico, out into the sunlight. Car doors slammed shut. Tires spun in the dirt.

Lou found the second grenade in her pocket.

Some of the men had regrouped in the east corner of the portico, they were working their way toward Konstantine. They became her new target. She pulled the pin and threw.

1…2…3…4…*BOOM*.

Dirt and brick and bodies were thrown into the air like confetti. The water main burst spewing a geyser ten feet into the air. A severed forearm with a serial number tattoo splattered against the walkway three feet from Lou.

The men who hadn't run at Konstantine's first warning, ran now.

All gunfire ceased, the cacophonous choir replaced with screams.

The spraying water settled the dust from this second explosion more quickly. Lou stood in the rain shower and turned in a slow circle, guns up.

Corpses lay heaped in nearly every corner of the portico, thrown about as carelessly as a child's toys. The water from the busted main ran red, washing
away the spilled blood from the flagstones.

She was soaked from head to toe. But no one remained. Except Konstantine.

She turned her gun on him.

"Wait!" he said, lifting his hands in surrender.

Watching his deformed cheek flap with his efforts at speech disturbed her. But she didn't lower her gun. All that was left was the wreckage, the bodies and the unspoken words between them. She was too close to finishing this to quit now.

He licked blood from his lips. "You are angry about the room."

"A room without shadows that electrocutes me into compliance. What's there to be mad about?"

"I can explain."

She put a bullet into the wall beside his head.

He flinched. "My face hurts. Can we—"

She emptied the rest of the clip into the same wall. So much for saving bullets.

"I was afraid of you." He licked his lips and more blood smeared across his tongue. His teeth were red with it. "I want us to be allies. More than allies. But you are your father's daughter. Your father—"

She took a step toward him, jaw tight. The gun was trained on that piece of flesh sitting between his eyebrows.

Konstantine's eyes fluttered, but he kept his position. His voice was stronger now. His own anger rose up to meet hers. "Your father was a good man but he was a fool."

A cold fire burned through Lou's chest. The gun jumped at the end of her sight.

"The world isn't black and white. It isn't us and them. This side, that side. He was played by the system he served."

"And Padre Leo was the Pope. And your mother was a saint. "

He looked down at his feet. He took a slow breath, collecting himself before meeting her gaze again.

"We must be better. We can't see the world as they saw it."

"How is building a room like that *better*?"

"I never wanted to use it."

"It seems very functional for a room that was never supposed to be used. And that fucking straitjacket!"

"I never bought the jacket. That was Nico."

"Okay, just the padded room then. Got it."

Konstantine's breaths were ragged. "I began building the room when you tried to kill me in June. But it was only meant to keep you from hurting me. It was never designed to hurt you. The current in the floor was only if you refused to be reasoned with. If every attempt to speak was met with violence. If I'd wanted to hurt you, or kill you, I wouldn't have picked electricity and a padded room to do it."

"You built the room because you were afraid I wouldn't stop trying to kill you?"

Her rage rose and crested. Rose and crested and with each punishing wave her arm trembled. Her whole body shook.

"Yes. It may come as a surprise to you, but I don't *want* to be murdered."

Too bad. She wanted to kill him. She wanted to wrap her hands around his throat and squeeze the light out of those infuriating green eyes. And yet— and yet…

He could have killed her at any time. He could have killed her months ago on Ryanson's boat when she was nearly unconscious with blood loss. He could have killed her in her own damn apartment. There were a hundred opportunities over the last few days. And it wasn't like she didn't have enough guns lying around for him to manage it.

But he had never so much as pointed a gun at her. Could she say the same? No.

It was more than that.

Her father *had* been a fool. She'd thought so herself a thousand times. When she learned how Gus Johnson had sold him out. Chaz Brasso had ordered the hit. Both men from his own department. His so-called friends. He was a fool for not seeing how power hungry the men around him were.

And a fool about Lucy, the sister he abandoned until he needed her to save his own kid.

Thinking all of this felt like a betrayal. To love him, but to also see the fault in him…

It hurt.

Konstantine saw her struggle and lowered his voice, speaking gently. "I'd hoped to never use that room. That isn't what I want for us."

He straightened himself, pushing off the doorway that had held so much of his weight. He took a step toward her. "Whatever I may be to you—now, or later—I'm not your enemy."

Lou lowered her gun.

And a bullet slammed into her upper arm. The force of it knocked her to the ground, into the water. Fire ate through the meat of her arm into her shoulder joint. It set her whole left side ablaze.

Fucking bastard.

She was going to kill him.

She sat up, seeing the stream of blood pouring down her arm, mixing with the small flood still pooling from the ruptured water main.

But by the time she pulled her gun and trained it on the doorway where Konstantine had just stood, it was empty.

A gun went off again and a guttural scream full of animalistic rage rebounded through the portico.

Her eyes were drawn to a flurry of movement.

Konstantine and Nico were locked in battle. One, two, three rapid fire punches slammed into the side of Nico's face and he went to one knee. His gun fell from his hand and splashed in the water. And Konstantine was already lifting his foot to stomp him.

He rolled away and the boot came down in a puddle of water. Nico pulled a knife and slid it into the meat of Konstantine's calf.

He howled and pitched forward onto his hands and knees.

Right.

Konstantine couldn't have put a bullet in her arm from that angle. Nico must have emerged from the basement, spotted them talking and shot her. It's her own damn fault for letting Konstantine distract her, letting her anger get the best of her. If only she could've forgotten about the damned terror room for five minutes, she would've remembered the real threat.

No point in crying over fuckups. It was time to fix it.

Lou tore the belt off her pants and buckled it tight around her shoulder. It limited her movement, but it would also keep her from bleeding out.

Konstantine ripped the knife from his calf and buried it in Nico's shoulder. He used his good leg to kick Nico back into the adjacent wall. But he only rebounded, as if on a spring board.

Konstantine screamed. Nico had his thumb in one of Konstantine's old bullet wounds, probing deep. Fresh blood bubbled up around the thumb as Konstantine seized the wrist, trying to rip the hand away.

Arm secure, Lou was up and moving just as Nico twisted his grip and wrenched another scream from Konstantine's throat.

One hard kick to Nico's side sent him sprawling off of Konstantine. Lou had her hands around his neck, hauling him up before he'd fully landed.

Slipping to the balcony above, she kicked him once, twice. He coughed and spat blood onto the floor.

When he whipped the knife toward her own legs
she jumped up in time to feel it catch the bottom of her boot. She twisted the wrist, took the knife and tossed it over the railing.

Then she hurled him over the railing after it.

He didn't even have time to scream before his body hit the wet stones of the portico.

Something cracked on impact. Lou peered over the railing to see the leg bent. From the knee, it twisted off at an unnatural angle.

But Nico wasn't giving up that easy. He tried to drag himself to sitting, slapping at the water as if to find his gun. Lou had relieved him of it on the balcony and left it there as she traveled down to the main level through the shadows.

Her boots now uneven on the bottom, sent ripples through the water.

Nico found the knife in the water.

Lou kicked it away.

He spotted a gun dropped by someone two or three feet to the right. He clawed for it. Until Lou brought her boot down and crushed the hand. Something snapped.

She pulled her own gun and trained it on his face.

"Konstantine!" Nico screamed, his face red, veins popping in fury. "We were supposed to be brothers! *Nostro padre lo voleva*!"

Konstantine dragged himself across the portico.

"He gave you everything." Nico's teeth chattered. "Everything that was mine! You owe me! At the very least you owe me my life!"

Lou arched an eyebrow. "You can lock him in a padded room. Since that's what you like to do to people who try to kill you."

Konstantine's stood hunched, his pained body folded in on itself. "No."

He trained the pistol at Nico's face and fired four times. The first bullet punched a hole clean through the skull. The other three only widening the first.

The gunshots echoed through the portico before being swallowed up by the rushing water.

For a long time neither of them said anything. They only stood over Nico's body and watched his blood darken the water around him.

Nico's eyes remained open, seeing nothing.

"So we're not enemies?" she said at last. She lifted her mangled boot and scowled at the scarred sole. *Bastard.*

"No." Konstantine fingered his wounded cheek, hissing. "But if you still want to kill me, please

do it now. My face hurts. Unbearably."

"I'm not in the mood." She bent and seized Nico's collar, hefting his soaked body. He'd make a good meal for her six-legged friend. "Maybe next time."

# Epilogue

King stepped out from beneath the green awning and into Jackson Square. He sipped his coffee and watched a man paint a Bob-Ross worthy landscape to a stop-clock, while a popular rock song blared from the boombox beside him. The cluster of bystanders clustered around him clapped on enthusiastically.

*It's a beautiful day, Robert.*

"Yes, it is," he said to Lucy. A woman walking her French bulldog gave him a wide berth and long sideways glance.

Crazy or not, everything reminded him of Lucy. Standing in the square, watching the street performers charm the tourists. The sight of a red balloon, released, floating up into the blue sky. The smell of pralines or jambalaya. Sunlight filtered through trees dancing on the pavement.

He plucked a fresh beignet from the bag and shook the excess powdered sugar off before plopping it into his mouth. He spotted Piper across the square at her army-green card table. She was reading the palm of a teenage girl, maybe seventeen, eighteen years old. Her black hair was pulled up in a messy bun on the top of her head and she laughed and blushed at whatever Piper said.

Piper caught sight of King and waved. He waved back.

He took his time down the narrow streets, walking east toward Melandra's. His leg was giving him grief.

The bullet that hit his lower left side and lodged in the meat had been removed cleanly, but not without cost. The nerves were damaged and his left leg was left weak. He couldn't walk without a limp now and a tingling sensation that ran up and down his entire left side.

He stayed on top of his physical therapy though. Walking. Stairs. Stretches. Anything to keep him from having a permanent limp. The doctor said he'd have full use of it again in eight or nine weeks. King suspected that full use would be similar to his full use of his shoulder. It would hurt him from time to time, but he didn't need daily Vicodin for it. Yet.

Only time would tell.

King stepped inside Melandra's Fortune and Fixes, and breathed deep. It was Morningstar and patchouli incense today. The air hung thick with it as several candles flickered from their pedestals. It was so nice entering the shop and not hearing the banshee wail of the skeleton that Mel used to keep by the door.

The storeroom opened and there was Mel, wearing her dark blue jeans and a black tank top.

"You're out and about," she said, obviously pleased. "How's the leg?"

He downplayed the pins and needles and incessant burning. "On the mend."

Mel snorted. "You better drink that tea I gave you."

King cringed at the thought of it. He'd tried one sip and found it tasted like dirt and crushed earthworms.

"Don't make that face," she said, eyebrows raised. "Drink it unless you want to walk with a cane."

"Canes can be cool. I can get one with a skull on top. Black maybe."

She rolled her eyes.

"You still coming over for dinner?" he asked. "I've got everything for the lasagna."

"I'll be over at 7:00," she said. "You better have the drag race show on for me."

King tipped his imaginary hat and started the slow climb up the steps to his apartment. He held the metal handrail and took them one at a time. He was breathing hard, sweat standing out on his brow by the time he reached his door.

It was dark and quiet when he entered.

He hesitated, listening to the ringing silence, expecting to find her there.

She wasn't.

Lou had checked on him twice in the three weeks since he returned from the hospital. He'd offered to give her Lucy's ashes, even though Lucy specified in her will that they were to go to King. Lou refused to accept them. So Lucy's urn remained on his enormous coffee table during the day, and on his bedside table each night.

He'd also tried to get Lou to talk about what had happened that day at the winery, but she'd brushed him off. She didn't seem eager to talk about Lucy or Konstantine.

She had promised to come back though, once they'd both healed, and help him get his P.I. business off the ground. He hadn't had a chance to tell her that the P.I. business would be a front for something else he had in mind. Another, perhaps better, way to help people.

But that conversation would come. If time was on their side.

King placed the sack of beignets on the kitchen island and opened the fridge. He gathered everything he needed for the lasagna from its shelves. The meat and cheeses. The sauce and peppers. He removed a pan from the drawer beneath the stove and threw the meat, chopped garlic and red onion into it. He stirred it while it browned. Once it was cooked and the danger of poisoning was behind him, he would make the layers in a casserole dish and hold it in the fridge until it was time to bake. Then he would take a long nap before Mel came over.

The kitchen already smelled like heaven when the phone rang.

"King."

"Robbie," a man said. "I heard you got shot."

When he recovered from his surprise, King spit out, "Flesh wound."

"Mm hmm," Sampson replied. A chair creaked on the other end. "That's what you said about your shoulder and you were in Quantico for months."

King stirred in the meat in the pan. "You calling to check on me, Sammy? Or do we need to have another chat?"

"No," he said. "No, that's all panned out."

King's hand faltered in the stirring. "Oh yeah?"

"Turns out that it wasn't even you who did the digging."

"Is that right?"

"According the data our IT guys pulled," Sampson said. "I just wanted you to know so you weren't worried. The department formally apologizes for accusing you of any wrongdoing."

"I didn't realize I *was* formally accused."

"All the same. I thought you'd like to know."

Silence hung in the phone before King choked out a "thank you."

"Dare I ask how you got shot?"

"Mugger. Here in the Quarter. They're getting bolder these days."

"Must be the recession," Sampson added. "Money makes desperate men."

King had fabricated that story as soon as his eyes had opened in the hospital room. He wasn't about to explain to a doctor and his staff that the bullet had come from a shootout in the Tuscan hills. Or they might've wheeled his bed right on down to the psych ward.

"You be careful out there, Robbie. You're attracting a lot of trouble these days."

King laughed, dumping the sauce from the jar into the sautéed meat and pepper. "It sure does seem to find me, doesn't it?"

Konstantine knew she was there before he stepped out of his bathroom and into his bedroom. Something about the pressure in his apartment had changed. A sensation on the back of the neck, like being watched. Premonition or no, the sight of her body silhouetted in the big window, not three feet from his bed, squeezed the air from his chest.

Her lithe form was bathed in moonlight as she gazed out over the night river. So beautiful that he didn't want to turn on the light and ruin the magic of this moment.

She seemed transfixed by the shimmering waters, by starlight shining on buildings and cobblestone. A boat tread water noiselessly down the center of the Arno river, cutting waves.

He continued to towel his hair, aware he was bare from the chest up. He'd stepped from the shower and pulled on his sweatpants for sleep. Had he known she would be here to greet him, maybe he would have left them on the hook behind the door.

"They call you the Executioner," he said softly, as if speaking too loudly might scare her away. "Not only in the Ravengers. Ricci tells me it's true the world over. You've become their boogeyman."

"A rumor you encourage, I'm sure." She spoke without turning around, her arms still crossed over her chest. He didn't mind. He appreciated the view from behind.

But finally she did turn and meet his gaze.

"The world stopped looking for you," she said. "One minute every agency in the world was hunting you, the next they're apologizing, calling it a mistake. Running a bullshit story about how a poor Italian farmer was martyred and his family's vineyard burned."

Konstantine smiled. "I needed an excuse for the pile of ash and rubble we left behind."

She turned away from him. He looked at the pale stretch of her neck and longed to kiss it. Those sharp collar bones. He was only a step away from wrapping his hand around her waist, and biting that little notch of bone.

*Brick by brick, passerotto.*

"Do you own all the world agencies?" she asked. "Or just the right people in each?"

"Does it matter?" he asked. She had enough truth for now.

He could tell she was still trying to realign her compass. She hadn't completely given up her father's position on drugs and the drug trade. On men like himself. But she was starting to see it more clearly, the way good and evil were not so clearly aligned. Not in the world and not even within themselves.

He would never own her. Never tame her. And he didn't want to.

But he wanted her to understand. He would give her the time she needed.

"And here I thought you were just a rich boy."

He gazed at her slender neck again. The little space behind her ear that must be as soft as a flower petal. "I'm not without my weaknesses."

"Yeah, your scar is ugly," she said.

He laughed, surprised. "I was told that it needs to fully heal before any plastic surgery is done."

The doctors had accomplished what they could in spite of Nico's malice, but he'd cut the cheek deep. It had taken four surgeries already just to mend the muscles beneath and save Konstantine from a lop-sided expression. He'd gotten lucky. The surgeon had done a good job of restoring him to his former glory, leaving only a jagged line from the bottom of Konstantine's eye to his chin.

"Don't," she said.

"Don't?" He stared at the river, side by side with her. Their shoulders brushed.

He couldn't name one feature of the landscape before him. It was only the heat from her shoulder, the shift of her hips he was aware of.

"You were too pretty before," she said. "Now your men might actually respect you."

He laughed. "There's a compliment in there somewhere."

"Not that you need your face to get what you want," she said. She was watching him again. He didn't dare meet those beautiful eyes, not while his knees felt weak.

"I have something for you." He was certain she was still pissed about the room, but he was determined to make it up to her, prove to her that he meant her no harm. "Before we burned down the villa, I found this."

He threw the towel on the back of the chair and crossed to the closet. He pressed on the top two corners of the wall, then the bottom two to release the false wood panel.

Behind it, he pulled out the bulletproof vest and offered it to her. "I had it repaired. The Kevlar was as thin as paper on the right side, along the ribs. The right knife or bullet would've punched right through. It isn't the best protection anymore, you know. They've upgraded this model about six times since your father was on the force. But it holds value to you so I thought you'd want to keep it. For luck."

She took it from his hands and turned it over, inspecting the extra layers that had been sewn in.

"Mario is very good. He kept the thin profile but added all this extra Kevlar here," he assured her, expecting her to be furious that the vest had been altered.

But then she found the white tag in the inside and the black scrawled *Thorne* across it. "He tells me that when you put it on, you won't even notice the—"

A hand seized the back of his neck and pulled him into a kiss. A hot mouth overtook his, forcing the lips apart with her tongue. Their bodies collided and all Konstantine could feel was every inch of her supple form against his. Full frontal. Thigh to thigh. Hip to hip. Her nipples brushing his.

One of her hands slid up into his damp hair while the other clutched her vest.

When he put his hands on her, he realized she hadn't brought a gun. She'd come to his dark bedroom, unarmed and now she was kissing him.

Damn patience.

Konstantine's arms slid under her thighs and lifted her off her feet. For a moment, all her weight sat on the cradle of his hips. He only made it three steps—only needed three steps—before he hit the side of the bed and collapsed. They went down, hitting the mattress like stones, her body pinned beneath his.

His mouth moved to find hers again but brushed only cool cotton. Her hard body was gone. Her heat evaporated.

He was left with only moonlit sheets and pillows.

He collapsed onto the mattress and laughed. He rolled onto his back and groaned at the ceiling. "I suppose I deserved that."

Fine. Let her go.

She wasn't the only one who enjoyed a hunt.

**Did you enjoy this book?**

**You can make a BIG difference.**

I don't have the same power as big New York publishers who can buy full spread ads in magazines and you won't see my covers on the side of a bus anytime soon, but what I *do* have are wonderful readers like you.

And honest reviews from readers garner more attention for my books and help my career more than anything else I could possibly do—and I can't get a review without you!

So if you would be so kind, I'd be very grateful if you would post a review for this book. It only takes a minute or so of your time and yet you can't imagine how much it helps me.

It can be as short as you like, and whether positive or negative, I cherish *every. single. one.* So do the readers looking for their next favorite read.

If you would be so kind, **please find your preferred retailer and leave a review** for this book today.

Eternally grateful,


Kory M. Shrum

# Acknowledgments

It's always best to begin with the wife, Kim. Because really, she puts up with me more than anyone. And it's lucky for me that she happens to be such a great reader herself, and she is able to make wonderful suggestions every time. My books are better because of her, but more importantly, my life is worth living because she's in it.

My love goes to my sweet pug Josephine, who passed on while I was writing this book. This is the last book I will have written with her nestled beside me on my office couch. Her companionship will be sorely missed. And love to Charlemagne "Charley" the newest pug addition to the family, who kept my feet warm while I did the last read through.

Thank you to my critique group, The Four Horsemen of the Bookocalypse: Kathrine Pendleton, Angela Roquet, and Monica La Porta. You guys give every story the critical eye it deserves and because of that, you make the books better—and me a better writer. Let's ride!

Special shout out to Diana Hutchings, nurse extraordinaire, for patiently answering my questions about gunshot wounds. Monica La Porta and Alison

Carminke for their help with the Italian—giving Konstantine and Nico some authenticity. And the dozens of Street Team proofreaders who helped me catch those last minute errors. Any remaining mistakes are my own.

Thank you to my street team who are always eager to jump in line for ARCs. You guys are incredibly supportive and helpful about catching those last minute typos. If you're interested in joining my street team, and receiving advanced copies of my work, you can let me know at kory@korymshrum.com

Thank you to the incredibly talented Christian Bentulan for the beautiful cover.

Thank you to every person who took the time to say hello online. To everyone who took the time to write me a sweet, thoughtful email, Facebook or Twitter message, blog comment, or leave a review for this book. By doing so, you are letting me know that you enjoy my work and want it to continue.

And for me, that's a dream come true.

# About The Author

Kory M. Shrum is an award-winning and *USA TODAY* bestselling novelist and poet.

She's an active member of Science Fiction and Fantasy Writers of America, Horror Writers of America, and best of all, the Four Horsemen of the Bookocalypse, where she's known as Conquest.

She can usually be found surrounded by books and blankets, with a pot of tea at hand, consuming stories of all kinds. She lives in Michigan with her wife Kim, and their rescue pug, Charlemagne.

She'd love to hear from you on her website: www.korymshrum.com

# Also by Kory M. Shrum

**Dying for a Living series (Complete)**

Dying for a Living

Dying by the Hour

Dying for Her: A Companion Novel

Dying Light

Worth Dying For

Dying Breath

Dying Day


**Lou Thorne Thrillers (ongoing)**

Shadows in the Water

Under the Bones


**Design Your Destiny Castle Cove Series (ongoing)**

Welcome to Castle Cove


**Learn more about Kory's work at her website www.korymshrum.com**

Made in the USA
Columbia, SC
28 July 2018